The Idle Warriors

Kerry W. Thornley

IllumiNet Press
1991

Library of Congress Catalog Card Number: 89-081797

ISBN: 0-9626534-0-3

IllumiNet Press
P.O. Box 746
Avondale Estates, GA 30002

First Edition

10 9 8 7 6 5 4 3 2 1

Printed in the United States of America

Author's note: For this printing a small number of deletions and stylistic changes were made to enhance readability.

For Bud Simco
and
Gregory Hill

Contents

Introduction

by David S. Lifton
Author of *Best Evidence* (Macmillan, 1980)
January 14, 1991

Kerry Thornley's manuscript, *The Idle Warriors*, has a special meaning for me. First, it provides an accurate picture — through the vehicle of a novel — of what it was like to be a Marine in Oswald's unit, Marine Air Control Squadron One (MACS 1), at the height of the Cold War in 1959. Here we have Oswald, as the fictionalized Johnny Shellburn, portrayed as the kibitzing wise-cracking fellow that Kerry knew, just months before Oswald defected to the Soviet Union.

Oswald's defection was an important event in Thornley's life. Having decided to be an author, Kerry was looking for a topic. Upon reading a newspaper account about what Oswald had just done, Kerry in effect cried "eureka". What a great story, he thought — and he had actually known this guy! Thornley knew exactly what his first book would be about — a Marine who became sufficiently disillusioned with his country, as a result of peacetime service in Japan, and decided to defect to Russia. *The Idle Warriors* was born; and the manuscript, complete with its pre-assassination portrait of Lee Harvey Oswald, was finished well before the events of November 1963.

So much for background. The special and more important meaning Kerry's novel will always have for me is that it constitutes a slap at District Attorney Jim Garrison, and his inability to take Kerry's Warren Commission testimony and the book he wrote — a writer's first work — at face value, the honest portrayal of Oswald by an observor who knew him. Instead, Garrison reversed cause and effect. No, he reasoned, Kerry hadn't told the truth. Rather, Kerry had set out to paint a false picture of Oswald — all part of a plot. On February 21, 1968, a few weeks after calling Thornley before a New Orleans Grand Jury, Garrison charged him with perjury. In an eight page press release, Garrison explained his view of the role Kerry played in a conspiracy to frame Oswald: "It was necessary to have a major witness testify in great detail to create an early image [of Oswald] as a Marxist so that there would not be too much public curiosity about the reasons for Oswald's abrupt department from the Marine Corps to sail to Russia."

The result: the beginning of a totally unfair and unjust prosecution of Kerry Thornley, someone I had gotten to know quite well back in 1965, and who, as far I could tell, had done nothing wrong but reported the truth about an interesting Marine he had once known while serving at El Toro Marine Base in Southern California. As events unfolded, the media caught on to Garrison and his so called "investigation", which seemed less and less like something designed to ferret out truth; and more and more – particularly if you were on the receiving end of things, as was Thornley – like something out of Kafka.

Later, I berated myself about Kerry's predicament, because it was I who had urged Kerry to testify before the New Orleans Grand Jury. Looking backwards, I should have known better – but then, hindsight is always superior. In the Spring of 1967, I had spent the better part of a day with Mr. Garrison, alone, in Los Angeles, and came away quite alarmed at the character and capabilities of this man who had announced to the world just months before that he had "solved" the Kennedy assassination. I had taken him to task for his reasoning in some particular matter, and, somewhat exasperated, had the temerity to ask what he thought had actually happened, what the truth really was. Details of our discussion are less important than what he said next. Looking me straight in the eye, Garrison intoned: "After the fact there is no truth. There is only what the jury decides."

Oh really?

Reality is whatever a jury can be persuaded to believe?

This corrupt methodology would turn every lawyer into a salesman, selling his wares to a naive jury. In the hands of a prosecutor, it is a prescription for disaster. It was the sort of thinking that led to the false prosecutions by Garrison of people who the New Orleans jury subsequently acquitted – defendants who I believe had no more to do with the assassination than you, innocent reader, or I – or Kerry Thornley.

To this day, I am astounded that Garrison, with this philosophy, with those acquittals, with all the damage he did to the assassination research movement, is a Louisiana judge. To this day, efforts continue in some quarters to rewrite history, to transform a man who was regarded by sensible people as a demagogue, into some kind of folk hero—someone who found the truth but, alas, just wasn't able to prove it in court.

Reconstructing the truth—whether about a crime, or a historical event—can indeed be difficult. It all comes down to the evidence. And on the question of what Lee Harvey Oswald was like during the time he was in the Marines, Kerry provided just that: a valid eyewitness account. History is fortunate that someone who knew Oswald was intrigued enough to write a book about him—before November 1963.

There are three reasons, then, to read Kerry's book. First, it tells us what it was like in 1959 to be a 19 year old Marine in peacetime Japan. Second, it presents a portrait of Oswald written before November 1963. Finally, Kerry's novel provides an insight to Mr. Garrison and his 1967 pronouncements that he had "solved" the Kennedy assassination: you read it now; he read it then. Remember, when reading it, that Mr. Garrison couldn't see it for what it was, but instead concocted an elaborate conspiracy theory about the book's author.

Kerry wrote this novel with the best of intentions—it was a writer's first work. Although several years (and thousands of dollars of legal fees later) the perjury charges against Kerry were dropped, *The Idle Warriors* bears witness to the price he paid simply because he knew Lee Harvey Oswald and decided to write about him. It was a price extracted because a District Attorney who became an assassination buff believed that truth was whatever he could sell to a grand jury; and then got swept away in a paranoid fantasy, misused the powers of his office, and made Kerry's life grist for his mill.

Read it. Pretend you are a juror. You decide.

Preface

by Kerry W. Thornley

Hindsight generally furnishes the best view of complex historic events. An important purpose of *The Idle Warriors* was to explain why Oswald became disillusioned enough to attempt defection to Russia at the height of the Cold War. By now I realize I failed.

In 1959, when I read in *The Stars and Stripes* that Lee entered the Moscow U.S. Embassy and plopped down his passport, I knew I had a theme for my planned book. Not only had I known Lee Oswald just months before, disillusionment with the U.S. was even haunting my dreams. That night I dreamt that Lee and a bunch of friendly Russians were showing me around a Moscow that looked, in the odd manner of dreams, much like nearby Tokyo.

A year later, after my discharge, I began typing from my notes this first polished draft of *The Idle Warriors*. In about another year it was finished. But I'm afraid it says more about me than Oswald, about whose interior state I could only guess.

In another way I succeeded. A secondary goal of this novel was to convey exactly the mood and flavor of peacetime Marine duty in the Far East - the humor, the bitterness and the rebellion. You will find it all in these pages, in spite of some glaring literary flaws.

Unity, plot and consistent viewpoint were stuffy conventions I thought I could all but skip — influenced, as I was, by *The Ugly American* (of which *The Idle Warriors* was to be a poor man's version). Only snobs, it seemed to me, were afraid of cliches. Occasionally, my syntax was so ambiguous that I have made stylistic changes so the intended meaning will be clear. A few artistic touches were so embarrassingly sophomoric that I insisted on changing them, too. Such improvements are rare, however, for better or worse.

As for the macho attitudes that pervade these tales, they were universal among the Marines I knew and in 1959, 1960 and 1961 I saw nothing objectionable about them, either. For that insensitivity, I apologize.

Perhaps the way in which Johnny Shellburn least resembles Lee
Harvey Oswald is in Military Occupational Specialty. That difference
seemed unimportant to me at the time of writing. Oswald had been an
Aviation Electronics Operator and I made Johnny a Clerk Typist. I
served first as one, then as the other. A security agreement I signed in
the service kept me from going into detail about Aviation Electronics, so
I made Shellburn a "Remington Raider" instead of a "Scope Dope" -
leaving the operation of radar to minor characters.

Thus, in the last chapter, Johnny Shellburn is revealed to have no
access to classified information. As my Warren Commission testimony
indicates, I heard that Oswald once had a SECRET clearance. In view
of Lee's intelligence community connections unearthed since then by re-
searchers, his security clearance — whatever it was — probably had
more to do with his journey to Moscow than anything I stressed in this
novel.

If I am now in a better position to understand at least a little more
about Oswald, I am much indebted for that to David Lifton. In 1965 he
called me up, introduced himself, invited himself to my home and con-
vinced me — in a single evening — that the Warren Report ignored
significant evidence.

As for Lifton's perspective on Jim Garrison as expressed in the
foregoing introduction, mine is different. If Garrison read *The Idle Warriors* at all, he remained under the misconception — expressed in the
same release Lifton quotes — that it "found its way to a publisher."
About eight pages were excerpted in my book, *Oswald* (New Classics
House, 1965). Otherwise, this IllumiNet Press edition is the first printing
ever of *The Idle Warriors*.

As much as I agree with Lifton about Garrison's slipshod dishon-
esty, I think his case against me nevertheless brought up some disturbing
questions worthy of respect. Why was I introduced to Clay Shaw a week
or two before the assassination? Why — at about the same time but on a
separate occasion — did my friend Clint Bolton take me into the International Trade Mart, of which Shaw was director? Why was my landlord
at the time of the assassination also one of Clay Shaw's best friends?
Why, shortly after my 1961 arrival in New Orleans, was I introduced to

Guy Banister? And why was Banister so interested in the book I was writing?

On top of that, I have figured out since testifying to the contrary before Garrison's grand jury that I also once met David Ferrie, besides meeting David Chandler as well. Both were high on Garrison's suspect list.

More recently, I find reason to believe that Gordon Novel — another of Garrison's suspects — may have been one of my pledge brothers, known to me as Gordy, in Delta Sigma Phi at the University of Southern California. When Garrison first pointed out that Novel and I both attended USC in 1958, I said, "So did 73,000 other students," and thought no more about it.

Such nagging considerations finally helped me discover the horrifying truth about my own involvement in the assassination conspiracy, which I began unraveling in 1975 because of the Watergate revelations. All that is another story, described in my as-yet-unpublished book, *The Dreadlock Recollections*.

Contrary to Garrison's theories, I was not one of those who took part in directly framing Oswald. But Lifton's assumption that I was not involved at all is wider of the mark. From shortly after the Bay of Pigs invasion until two weeks before November 22, 1963, I engaged in a number of conversations with a self-proclaimed Nazi who said he was going to kill John Kennedy. My problem was disbelief. But our final discussion came to a disturbing conclusion. He said, "The only remaining question is who to frame for it. I figure some jailbird." After a brief exchange, I ended the discussion with, "Aw, why don't you frame some Communist?"

Perhaps the most remarkable coincidence of all, however — if you wish to call them coincidences — is also most related to *The Idle Warriors*. When I was stationed at Atsugi Naval Air Station undergoing much of the grist for this book, Edward Howard Hunt (the Watergate burglar) was also there, on CIA assignment. We did not meet, but I was an outspoken radical with a reputation for "stirring up shit" and so, perhaps, I came to his attention.

All such mysteries notwithstanding, *The Idle Warriors* provides to my knowledges no clues for their solutions. I found Japan a country with many exotic beaded curtains and fascinating sliding doors — with noth-ing whatsoever behind them. As if by contagion, loud fanfare for silence seemed the order of the day in the barracks and on maneuvers as well. *The Idle Warriors* became rather a monument to the same thing.

Chapter 1

The Drinking Song

Like most Marines, he liked to talk. But on that warm night of summer showers in Yokohama, Jack Robles had no listener. The Japanese bartender was busy, the bar girls were with other customers, and Henry Hamilton, who was to meet him there at the Bar Seven Gates, had not yet arrived.

Since he could not talk, he drank. He also drank when he could talk, but then without fully concentrating on the serious task.

Intent as he was, this night after payday, on drinking, he soon felt no need of a listener.

"I ever tell you about the time I won the Rapid Retreat Ribbon? You know, it's a Marine Corps green ribbon with a yellow streak down the middle. Yeah. I got if for," he sputtered rhythmically, "exceptionally enthusiastic and speedy withdrawal from the possibility of any situation leading to possible action with any possible enemy who is, perhaps, armed."

He was at that relaxed stage when everything he said came out clever. It almost bothered him that nobody was there to grin. The room was filled with four separate layers of cigarette smoke. They did not whirl or mix, except when his vision blurred. Latin American music, as always in a bar aimed toward the Japanese smart set more than the American bums-in-uniform, put the scene to rhythm and gave unity to all movements of all people. The high-checked, golden faces laughed in another language

"Hey, Boysan, one more drink - absanta."

He put the green absinthe to his lips. Before downing it, he inhaled its licorice aroma. It burned like fire in his throat. He chased it with water, but still felt it mark the core of his body with an emerald line of heat. This, it occurred to him, was his pivot, the center of himself. To feel that very center marked clearly, that was his purpose in using strong drink. Hell, that sounded like one of the best theories to justify drinking he'd every thought of. "Next time I'm sober I'll think it over. Oh, I'll remember." The assurance was a lie.

All at once he leaned forward on the bar. He gazed at the rows of bottles along the wall. The bottles were at attention, in ranks, and ready to hear his message. He spoke rather thickly, but they would understand; Jack was sure that bottles, of all people, understood him. Didn't they contain as much alcohol as he?

"Let me tell you stories of beggars and thieves and opium eaters; let me tell you about monks, and statues of the Buddha. You know, I knew that guy - Buddha. Yeah. Let me see, he was a sergeant in Motor Transport, Camp Pendleton. Let me tell you about the women of Tokyo, and the roofs of San Francisco - and the heroes of Yokohama, Japan. Yeah, first let me tell you, let me tell you about this town!"

He said the last furtively, under his breath, and grinned the ugly grin of Jack Robles that no man in his outfit could imitate. He then drew up and prepared some gossipy, awful truth about Yokohama in his chaotic imagination. Just as he was about to speak, he lost his train of thought. He reproved himself silently, then stared long and hard at the top of a V.O. bottle to exercise his powers of concentration. Satisfied, by means of this demonstration, that he was still in control of his wits and was not making a fool of himself in front of all those dignified bottles, he continued to speak:

"I came here to Yokohama - brawling seaport of the Far East. I know her bars. I've walked her streets in heat and cold. I've made love to scores of her daughters. I've seen her tragic scenes - half-clothed beggar kids in the streets. I've heard the bawling of ships from every port as they arrived at North and South Piers. Yes, I've walked by the U.S. Embassy and been dwarfed by the wealth in that area. I've spent a quiet morning in a bath-house. I've eaten rice till it was coming out of my gills. I've tramped up and down Isezaki Street enough to wear out the sidewalks. And I've drunk absinthe. I came here to Yokohama - brawling seaport of the Far East. And I'll come here again and again while I live. Yokohama!" It was a toast, and, finishing the absinthe, Robles swung around on the bar stool, landed on his feet with a slap, fumbled through his pockets, left a wad of yen there, and waltzed awkwardly out of the

Bar Seven Gates, forgetting about his promise to meet Henry Hamilton there. His driving desire now was to dissolve and touch every part of every place in the city.

"It's July, by Gawd, the month of the greatest Caesar!" And the Japanese people laughed nervously at the drunken barbarian who spouted great truths in a foreign tongue as he reeled along the sidewalks in front of the clean well-organized shops. It was hot and wet out. The streets were freshly rained upon. Taxi cabs honked and skidded over reflections of decorative, neon street lamps.

"July, month of the greatest Caesar! Stand unafraid and proud! No other month dare challenge your superiority ..."

Robles continued to talk, but not to think, and, in general, wandered down to the dark sections of town. As he stumbled down a canal side, he saw images fighting in the shadows just down the alley. He turned, walked up a side street - got lost.

Music! He heard music - high-pitched, reed pipe, above, over the stars. His shoe was gone, Where? He looked. Nowhere, just gone. Evil and dark spirits were at work.

Japan is a superstitious nation. And Jack began to feel the reason: Ghosts were really howling along dark alleys at night. He heard the screams of spirits, some rattles, and the soft persistent whine of a night wind. It started raining.

Rats! Rats everywhere. He ran along the alley chasing rats as they scurried for shelter. He splashed among puddles and laughed, no one to see him now.

A flash of lightening turned creation blue. Thunder followed and windows rattled.. "ATOMIC ATTACK!" he yelled, "ATOMIC AT-TACK! RUN FOR COVER!" He ran several yards down the alley and plunged headlong into a refuse heap. "BONZAI!" He put a wet newspaper over his head and came to his feet. He forgot what he'd been yelling about; it was something important, he was sure of that much. Oh, that was it! "TO ARMS! TO ARMS! THE REDCOATS ARE COMING."

It began to rain harder. Swiftly, water flushed along the gutter. He got sick. After that he was dizzy and subdued. He got depressed and he got sick again.

He kept walking. He kept forcing one foot to the front. He knew he was now to spend eternity walking into the rain. He decided he was dead and this was the just punishment for his numerous sins. Somewhere in the storm Henry Hamilton was calling him - the last man he ever expected to see in Hell

Jack turned around and saw the big, husky Negro coming toward him.

"Lawd! The weather may be low tonight, but, Robles, you are under it."

"Are you insituatin' that I'm under the afluence of incohol?"

"Jack, you need some coffee."

Robles grinned, stupidly, out from under the wet hair over his eyes.

"Where on earth is your shoe?"

"It's not."

"What?"

"It's not on earth. Evil spirits took it." Jack looked serious when he said this; the silly grin was gone

"Man, you drank the only evil spirits around here. Come on now, we'll see if we can get you sobered up, then we'll get on back to the base."

The two warriors found a coffee shop. And in the coffee shop Robles began to feel better. Of course, when Robles felt well he always talked a lot.

"Hamilton, did I ever tell you about the drinking song I wrote the last time I stood the watch? No? Wanna hear it? No? Just for that, my friend, you're gonna."

The Japanese waitress, very pretty with lots of wild hair stacked on top of her head, plus an understanding smile, though she didn't understand a word of Robles' talk, refilled their cups.

Jack held his cup in the air, as if proposing another toast. He opened his mouth to speak, then hesitated. At last he put the cup down.

"Say, Henry, seeing as how this is a drinking song, how about me having just one little, tiny dri— Okay. Okay. Don't got sore!"

He raised his cup again, spilling about half of the coffee down his sleeve. Then he recited his song:

I'll drink to each fair maid I've met
That I have never laid, as yet.
I'll drink to every volume fine
Of which I've never read a line.
I'll drink to each bright dream anew
That I didn't ever make come true.
I'll drink to each adventure grand
In which I've never had a hand.
I'll drink a cup, before I die,
Of life for every drop gone by.

That night, back at the barracks, those who were not yet asleep, but in their bunks listening to the rain on the roof, heard a sound that was like the rain, but louder. It was Jack Robles, in rubber shower shoes, running down the center of the barracks. The sound continued for about thirty seconds, then there was a noise like a cheap gong. Jack ran into a tin wall locker and passed out. Hamilton, big enough to do the work of two men, put him in his bunk.

Jack slept deeply for many hours. Then formations of bottles appeared in a dream, and, once more, Jack Robles started talking.

Chapter 2

The Killer

Big Willy Cecil was a hollyhock of a man with absurd piano keys where his teeth should have been. No wonder they laughed at the lanky, grinning idiot when he shrugged into the Atsugi barracks, for the first time, dragging a sea bag behind him. Willy's arms were too long for his uniform and, whenever he didn't have a handful of gear, his hands were deeply pocketed. This was, of course, sloppy and un-Marine-like as hell.

Willy Cecil was everything a good, high-charging, up-standing United States Marine is not: sloppy, relaxed, harmless and detached. Willy did not give two hoots to a dang-damn about thing one; he never even let loose with a growled reproach of the chow. All this considered, it seemed rather strange that he should get nicknamed "The Killer".

Strange or not, within a week after he walked down the Yokohama gang plank - and rode through the lush greenery and bright silk rainbow of the Japanese countryside in summer - Willy Cecil was The Killer.

The draft that Willy was in, direct from the States, included men like Abe Diamond and Johnny Shellburn; it was a group that would raise some real hell in the Orient before long. Nevertheless, Willy started things off quietly. On his day of arrival, the Fourth of July, the only thing he did was drink beer, eat steaks, and get himself voted honorary member of Motor Transport for fearless participation in a slaughterball game.

The only other thing he did all that week that even approached violence was almost duke it out with Jack Robles. The way that little fiasco came up is a story in itself. The only times Jack Robles was ever in a good mood was when asleep or drunk. In Japan, of course, this was most of the time. Willy Cecil made the mistake of tangling with Robles just after he woke up one night and before he could get his hands on his hidden hootch bottle.

Shellburn, Diamond, Hamilton and Willy Cecil all met at the gate that night, coming in off liberty. Willy was in from wandering the muddy streets of Yamato, with an Akadama wine bottle in his fist, raising the economic level of the local street creeps and harassing the tolerant MP's.

The others were also returning from private celebrations, and they were feeling pretty good as, arm-in-arm, they march-stumbled into the barracks singing "The Marines' Hymn". The Duty NCO silenced their choral activities, so they set about another project.

Shellburn, who was the drunkest, thought it would be an excellent idea to hoist Robles' bunk on their shoulders and carry it outside and dump Jack in the sump. Diamond, who was sensitive, altered this crude suggestion by proposing they put Jack's rack in the sheltered base bus stop instead of the sump, a refinement for sure. Just think. At six a.m., the first bus would come, Robles would roll over, and there he'd be, looking up at a smiling driver and a bus load of people. Ha! The whole idea was such a big joke that Willy Cecil had to laugh before they got the rack half outside

Robles woke up just in time to see the ceiling slide away and expose the starry night. Naturally, the thought that his bunk was floating out of the barracks door made him unhappy. He let out a whoop of innocent outrage.

Upon Jack's whoop, Diamond and Hamilton sat their end down and ran. Shellburn passed out. Willy Cecil just stood there like some kind of sentry with no orders. Jack Robles cussed like a trooper and sprang out of the rack. "You stupid, drunk, sonovabichen jerk! Help me carry this rack back in the barracks or I'll stuff you down the cracks in the deck."

Willy Cecil was tall and scrawny, but he was also like wire, as those who played slaughterball at the Fourth of July beer bust were aware. Among other things, Willy was a lumberjack on the outside; so if it came to somebody getting stuffed somewhere, it wouldn't probably be Willy, drunk as he was. But, no, you couldn't get ol' Willy's goat that easy. He grinned his usual, stupid grin and picked up one end of the bunk.

It took a man of no lesser rank than captain to finally rile ol' Willy a little. One day, Captain Sims had all the new arrivals fall out for a surprise personal inspection.

Well, Willy's shoes were a mess, he needed a haircut, and his sleeves were about three inches too short for his arms. Besides, he could not answer the questions on general training subjects the captain fired his way. Captain Sims chewed Willy out, got real red in the face and, in general, acted pretty much like all captains.

When Sims dismissed them, Willy Cecil shrugged off toward the slop chute with his hands in his pockets.

The captain yelled after him, "Cecil, didn't they teach you anything in boot camp?"

"Yes, sir!"

"What?"

"To be a professional killer, sir."

The captain got redder this time. "Cecil, until further notice, you are restricted to the base."

Now that made Willy's jaws a little tight. But that's how he got his nickname. And shucks, when you think about it, maybe it was well worth staying on base a couple of weeks. Hell, who else has such a fine nickname? That's what The Killer wanted to know.

Chapter 3

At Kamakura

The wall locker was about six feet high, and Lance Corporal Shellburn's head nearly touched the barracks ceiling as he sat up there during his daily candle watching. Since the old Atsugi MACS squadron was full of nothing but screwballs anyway, no one payed a lot of attention to this standard-issue crackpot, Johnny Shellburn, who was so new in Japan he thought dozo, the Japanese word for "please", was his nickname. It was only guys like Willy Cecil, who'd known Johnny in the States, who were surprised by the sudden about-face in Johnny's whole personality.

"Shellburn, what's happened to you? You gone nuts?" Willy stretched out on an upper bunk near the wall locker.

Johnny Shellburn didn't answer; he just sat there on the locker, legs crossed, and blue eyes watery from not blinking, and stared at the candle.

"Well, ain't that a batch of bull," Willy muttered, closing his eyes. "I sit around here on base because the captain fell in love with my damned liberty card, and you, who could go out and have a blast, sit around here playing Buddha. Shellburn how did you get so goddamned mixed up in only twenty-two years?"

Shellburn didn't reply, of course, and Willy listened to the quiet of the barracks for several minutes. It was late afternoon, and everybody was either on liberty or at chow. "Shellburn? Hey, Johnny, no bull, knock it off a minute. I want to ask a question. Awe, come on Johnny, really. No bull, Shellburn, are you going to chow? Hey, Johnny - Johnny, let's go to chow."

Shellburn kept still.

"Awe hell!" Willy sat up in the bunk and rubbed his eyes, then rotated his finger in his ear for a full minute; he was thinking. When he finished thinking, he took his finger out of his ear, then leaned over and blew out Shellburn's candle.

"You intolerable dolt!"

"I don't know what you said but, by God, now you're talking, anyway! Let's go to chow."

"Give me a match," Johnny said coldly.

"Awe, come off it, Shellburn. Don't light that damned candle again. Ten more minutes and they close the mess hall, and I'm hungry."

"Look, Killer, do I hold your hand when you go to the head? Go to chow if you're hungry, but lay off. Okay? I'm trying to concentrate."

"That talkin' doctor over at sick bay will start concentrating on you if you don't watch out, Johnny."

"That's my worry. Now make it." Johnny relit the candle and tossed Willy's match box back to him.

Willy flipped the matches up on the locker. "Keep 'em," he said. He jumped down from the rack and went to chow alone.

"This meat looks like old combat boots," Willy said to Abe Diamond as he put his tray down on the table.

"Two weeks he's been here and finally he notices the chow is lousy!" Abe winked. "You know, Killer, that's the first time I ever heard you yell about the benefits. What would the Commandant say if he heard you talk that way about Marine Corps chow?"

"I could care less about the Commandant."

Stick Wicker, across the table from Willy, piped up, "What would he say if he heard you talk that way about Marine Corps combat boots, Willy?"

There was always a lot of good-natured fun at Willy's expense. His don't-give-a-damn attitude invited it and made it harmless. Willy shoved a big slice of gravy-covered meat into his mouth to avoid answering; it took too much thought, and Willy was thinking of something else.

The question was: When did it all start? The day they arrived at the new base, Johnny Shellburn was just good old Johnny. A couple of nights later he was still normal: a little drunk, but not weird, like with this candle bit. The Killer kept thinking and chewing on the gravy-covered combat boot.

Saturday. What happened Saturday? He and Johnny went over to the Enlisted Club and played bingo and drank beer. Yep, Johnny was okay Saturday. Saturday night he went to Yokohama on liberty. He said he was going up to see his girl, Yoko. Check Saturday off. Willy washed the combat boot down with coffee that tasted like dirty socks.

"Kee-o-rist! This chow is really bad tonight. I mean it usually isn't good, but tonight it's not just no good, it's bad!"

"Willy, welcome to the club," Diamond said, grinning at Wicker. "You're becoming a real gourmet."

"Yeah, Abe, it must be worse than I thought," Wicker said, "He didn't say a word about those eggs last Monday that tasted like aluminum foil. Remember?"

Monday morning at chow. That was it. The Killer chucked another hunk of boot leather into his mouth. Shellburn started acting like some kind of nut then. He kept talking about how everything depended on nothing. And he said that there was nothing but nothing, and not much of that. Some physics theory he heard in college, or some place. The moment came back to Willy very clearly:

"Hell yes, Willy, it's really very logical if you think about it in the right way. Take an atom, the smallest thing there is. Right?"

"Right, I guess."

"Okay, break it apart and what have you got?"

"An atomic explosion?"

"No. No. You have electrons and neutrons. But you know what happens? They disintegrate. And, get this, they turn into light waves. Now, what is light? Is light matter? Hell no, it ain't! So everything is made out of nothing."

"So?"

"So the Oriental thinkers and philosophers have been right on the nose for centuries and, just now, modern science is catching up with them."

That was how Shellburn was talking Monday at breakfast. At noon chow he just sat there looking at the salt shaker. That night he had duty section, and when Willy tried to get him to check out and go to the East Camp movie, he said he'd rather lay around the barracks and read. Ever since then he'd been real weird - staring at candles, reading, and telling his oldest buddies to get lost. Something must have happened to him

Sunday. Willy swallowed the last pieces of the boot and poured another cup of dirty socks.

"Anybody know where Shelburn pulled liberty last Sunday?" Willy asked as he, Diamond, and Wicker dumped their trays and headed back for the barracks.

"Where's Shellburn been lately?" Wicker wondered, "I haven't seen him out in town all week."

"At Kamakura," said Abe.

"What's Kamakura?" Willy wanted to know.

"That's where they got that big Buddha, you know."

"The Amida Buddha," Stick Wicker added. Wicker had been in the Far East many months, so he knew all those nickle and dime details.

Shellburn was not up on the wall locker any longer and the candle was out.

"Well, Buddha boy, you should've gone to chow. Sure was good. Best meat I ever tasted."

"Shut up. Can't you see I'm reading?"

"Lock me up!" said Willy, an expression meaning, "If I gave a damn I'd cry." Then he added, "I was a teenage nincompoop," and shrugged off toward the head wondering if he'd insulted Shellburn or himself.

When Willy returned, it was the candle bit on the locker again. Oh well. Willy picked up the book Johnny was reading: *Selected Works of Rudyard Kipling*. "Kee-o-rist! Rudyard!" That was worse than his own name - Wilfred. There was a bookmark; Willy opened to the page and looked in silence.

> Oh ye who tread the Narrow Way
> By Tophet flare to Judgement Day.
> Be gentle when the heathen pray
> To Buddha at Kamakura!
>
> For whoso will, from Pride released,
> Contemning neither man nor beast,
> May feel the Soul of all the East
> About him at Kamakura.

Yea, voice of every Soul that clung
To Life that strove from rung to rung
When Devadatta's rule was young
The warm wind brings Kamakura.

"I'll be damned!" Willy's mouth fell open. "Screwballs who write books!" Willy looked up at Johnny. "It must be catching." He put the book down and wiped his hand on his trouser leg.

Johnny Shellburn was blotting out all thoughts but those of the flame. And standing there before the great Amida Buddha, ancient one that sat serenely still as temples fell and emperors changed the old Japan, a feeling deep with warm respect enclosed on Shellburn's mind. He knelt beside the others praying there.

"Do you believe in Buddha, too?" asked Yoko, after Johnny stood, his prayer complete.

"I don't even believe in the Marines." He grinned at the wide-eyed expression on her face. "Let's go have some chow, girl."

Proceeding then, they walked along a way that led across the town to the Shinto Shrine of Hachiman, who, once the God of War, has been, since 1945, the God of Agriculture.

They stopped along the way to eat breakfast in a modern little restaurant. Yoko ordered rice omelets, but Johnny barely ate; he was too excited thinking how he, for years, had read of Kamakura. Now he was there!

Philosophy 1b: a brief survey on the Oriental philosophies. When discharged, back to school. He'd take that class over, and nod with wisdom while sitting in the aisle, his legs crossed. When the professor faltered he, Johnny Shellburn, would correct the man, speaking with authority, a pilgrim who has traveled wide, and fasted there at Kamakura!

"Now, we go to Hachiman Shrine," Yoko said after breakfast.

It was still early, that Sunday at Kamakura, and the morning mist clung to the trees and all but obscured the shrine at the far end of the long walkway. Before ascending the steps, they washed their hands in the ceremonial fount, and Yoko tied a paper fortune to the branch of a sacred tree.

At the shrine he gazed at the exact opposite of what he'd seen in the Buddha. Here was a god filled with holy rage. His face was contorted in anger, his eyes burned with hot-blooded insanity. He seemed to be cursing heaven and earth alike.

Yoko bowed her head and clapped her hands to summon the attention of a god who resided in Japan since creation. As with many Japanese, Yoko believed in both Buddhism and Shinto. Such a duelism was not difficult to understand. In the face of the Kami, Johnny saw all the wrath of Moses and the Golden Calf, in the face of Buddha, the serenity of the Nazarene at the Last Supper.

Yoko clapped her hands in conclusion of prayer. The two of them went walking, side-by-side, away, down the time-worn steps. Above, the leaves in the sacred tree rustled, and they felt the first puff of a warm wind.

"Damn you Willy! The next time you blow out that candle I'll strangle you."

"Let's go to the flick, Shellburn. I've seen this one and there is this dame in it and, I swear, she has ...." Willy stopped. Shellburn was lighting the candle again. The Killer shrugged off toward the slop chute; he decided to get drunk.

The flame was a bright jewel; it didn't waver, but glowed steadily.

"I am tired, Johnnysan, we walk-walk all over Kamakura today, no?"

"Me too, Yoko." Johnny unlocked the sliding door on Yoko's little house in Yokohama.

They removed their shoes.

"I will make some tea, no?"

"Sounds real good. I think I'll stretch out on the cushions in the living room. Where shall we go next week?"

"You are strange boy, Johnnysan." She rattled some teacups and a tray.

"Why's that?" Johnny lined the cushions up in a row.

"All other boyfriends I have, before, they never want to go every place. Just want stay home and make love. You, every place, always go look. I think you maybe tak'san smart."

It is the tradition, Johnny reflected, of the Oriental woman to flatter without necessarily having ulterior motives.

"Smart?" Johnny laughed. "Everyone always think I'm smart." Not many enlisted men had a year of college, but Johnny didn't feel that made him any wiser than the next guy. "I think Japanese woman is smart."

"Why?" Yoko brought a tray with two cups of green tea to Johnny's side.

"Well," Johnny paused to sip the tea, "Japanese woman always shy, yet she is very bold. Stateside woman all the time talk-talk, make too much noise."

"I think so too," Yoko knew she had no competition from the States. If Johnny had a girl back home, Yoko would make him forget. Yoko knew how to do this. She blushed, and sat beside him.

He studied her gentle face, and kissed her lightly; she smiled so simply, so exactly happy with life at that moment. Johnny quoted, half to himself, "Be gentle when the heathen pray ..."

The fire of victory was in his blood that night as he and Yoko walked along the street of Yokohama's Chinatown. The lights were bright, and the racket of the Pochinko pinball machines filled the air.

"Let's go in here and have dinner, babe."

"Diajobi," Yoko agreed.

It was a nice, air-conditioned Chinese restaurant. They sat in a booth, secluded by a mysterious beaded curtain.

"Let's have Chinese noodle soup, and fried rice, and fortune cookies and chop suey..." Oh, it was a glorious night! "...and next weekend let's go to Tokyo, okay?"

"Diajobi, Johnnysan."

"And we'll invite Stick Wicker and Abe Diamond along too. And I'd also like you to meet my friend, Willy; we call him 'The Killer', but Willy's on restriction. He got salty with a captain..." Johnny was a regular talking machine tonight.

"Let's go to the bathhouse," Yoko suggested when they got home.

Johnny found the Japanese bathhouse quite a new experience. You go there with a wash pan and soap and a towel under your arm. You pay the lady a hundred yen, about twenty-eight cents, and then a couple of pretty, young girls help you undress! Then you sit by a hot water faucet, fill up your wash pan, and pour it out over your head. Next you scrub yourself down with soap and rinse off in the same way. After that you climb into a real hot bath and soak. When he got out, one of the girls handed Johnny his towel.

"Boy, a place like that would be something in Boston!" he told Yoko on the way back to the house.

Stick Wicker was on his fourth gin fizz and Willy Cecil was on his second beer; it amounted to the same thing. Willy was just loosening up and trying to talk louder than the combo in the Enlisted Club could play. "So I make like Shell Scott and try to figure this bit out. Shellburn was normal Saturday. He was nuttier than a loon Monday morning. Therefore, I figure, something happens to this kid Sunday. Maybe he fell on his head, I don't know, but whatever it was - it must've happened Sunday, you see."

"At Kamakura?" asked Stick.

"You better Hong Kong believe it was at Kamakura! You should see this nutty book he's been readin' - no murder, no sex, no nothing - just a bunch of poems and junk about limey doggies and stuff."

"What's the name of this book?"

"The Complete Works of Rutledge Kipsing, or some damn thing. Anyway, there is this one poem in there about this here Kamakura where Johnny fell on his head. That place must be a bigger hangout for crackpots than Southern California!"

"So you really think he fell on his head," Wicker laughed quietly and smugly.

"What else?"

"Killer, when you've been in the Far East as long as I have, you'll stop worrying every time one of your buddies goes psycho. It happens to everybody sooner or later. No, this ain't bull; I've seen it. I don't know why, but a guy gets stationed over here and zowie! He goes bugs."

"Aw, come off it, Stick, this is serious."

"No bull, Willy. I know, easy duty, lax outfit, good liberty, and everything else a guy could want. Just the same, everybody starts crackin' up."

"How so?"

"Oh, hell, every way in the book: fighting, breaking windows, biting hunks out of beer glasses, throwing each other in the sump, arm wrestling with burning cigarettes between their arms, stealing the OD's jeep, decorating the barracks with shaving cream..."

"Yeah, but that ain't like watching candles. All them things you mentioned is fun, and a guy has to let himself go once in awhile, but Shellburn just sits there and watches this candle. And, damn it, Stick, the candle isn't gonna do nothing. What's so blasted interesting about a candle? You'd think it was a television set or something?"

"Well, Willy, I gotta admit Shellburn's case is unusual, but just look around you sometime. Look over at that table by the stage. See that guy?"

"You mean Jack Robles?"

"Yeah, you know Jack. He's been in this outfit longer than any other man. He keeps getting put in the brig, and he never has been up for pfc. Now you know how Jack gets his kicks? He gets drunk and sits there and talks about the great Universal Truth. Pure gibberish!"

They paused to order another round of drinks.

Stick Wicker continued, "All these guys over here change. It happens to everybody. I think maybe it's because the duty is too good. You know how Marines like to gripe. Well, you run out of things to gripe about. Yeah, there are the little things like chow, Captain Sims, and civilian dependents."

"Little things? I could write up a speech on that Captain Sims alone. That's the jerk that secured my liberty card."

"Yeah, but don't you see? All officers are like that in the States. Here, the only s.o.b. is Sims; the rest are good guys. Look at Lieutenant Valingsworth. He laughs if you salute him!"

"Well, whatever it is, and whether it happens to everybody or not, I'd give my left eyeball to know what happened to Shellburn at Kamakura." Willy rotated his finger in his left ear passively, as Stick Wicker poured half the contents of a salt shaker into his gin fizz.

"Shellburn will get normal again; everybody always does."

Monday morning Johnny sat on the train, pleasantly exhausted from the weekend and Sunday night, ready to start the rail-guided dash back to Atsugi. On his lap were the things he'd taken with him to Yokohama: his shaving kit, a change of clothes, a Japanese-English dictionary, a Petri camera, a bamboo fan and a book of Kipling.

He turned to the poem on Kamakura. It had long been his favorite. Suddenly, the realization struck him again. He, Johnny Shellburn, had been to Kamakura! The weight of that idea seemed to break something inside his body. He felt a flood of emotional turmoil; he felt what his Zen Buddhist buddy in Southern California called satori, enlightenment. Or was it enlightenment? All Johnny knew was that he was in love with someone, or something, or both.

He read aloud: "For whoso will, from Pride released..."

Chapter 4

The Little Mutiny

"On Sunday, 12 July, Corporal Hamilton assumes duties of Duty NCO. I have read and understand orders concerning duties. Relieve Sergeant McCall at this time. Respectfully submitted, John H. Hamilton, Corporal (E-4) USMC." Henry Hamilton returned the pen to its holder, blotted the entry and closed the log book.

His uniform was sharply pressed; his shoes were like glass; the big Negro corporal relaxed for the first time that morning and grinned as another Marine approached his desk.

"Hi, Jack."

"What say, Henry?"

"Where you headed at this hour of the morning?"

"Sick bay. I'm going to see if I can get something for this hangover: pills, sympathy, a Purple Heart, anything." Jack wrote his name, and other appropriate information, on the check-out sheet.

"Good luck. Dickenson is the Duty Corpsman today."

"Oh, that alcoholic fellow?"

"Look who's talking." Henry's white teeth flashed.

"Not anymore. Not me. No, sir! I'm on the wagon from now on." Jack Robles looked so serious, like some ancient Greek discussing the ethics of mankind, Hamilton had to laugh.

"Well, I'll see you after I go have a talk with the pill popper."

Henry watched Robles disappear out the door for the Duty Room and wondered how his best buddy managed to hold together. Nowhere in Japan was there a man who drank as much as Jack; he had all the love of an Irishman for strong drink and all the intellectual bent of a Greek for justifying his drinking with reason. Quite a guy.

No sooner did Jack leave, than Henry saw trouble coming down the barracks toward the Duty Room. Little Sergeant Phillips had been in the outfit just two weeks, and during that time, had put twelve men on report. Such things were not to be done in the First Marine Air Wing, not without consequences.

"Corporal Hamilton, I want to put a man on report. That freckle-faced punk with the red hair, he went and broke a window, so put his name in the book. Understand?"

"Perfectly, Sergeant Phillips, but what is this man's name?"

"I don't know. I don't got no time to run around this here barracks all day memorizing names. He was that freckle-faced kid."

Hamilton knew Phillips meant Pfc Walters but he didn't like Phillips, and he didn't feel like doing more than duty required in this mess. "I see, and that's what you want me to put in the book: 'At 0930 Sergeant Phillips reported the breaking of a window by this here freckled-face kid, whose name and number he did not bother to find out, but whose nickname might be Red.'"

"Why you smart alec-" A quick look from Hamilton kept the little sergeant from saying something he might have regretted. "Er-a-a. W-well, I'll get his name. He ran when he saw me coming, but I'll find out where he is." The sergeant turned on heel and left the room. "I'll get his name, by God."

Hamilton got up and tacked back the upper left-hand corner of a recruiting poster that had come loose on the wall behind the desk. The full-color poster showed a U.S. Marine on guard. Inscribed below was a single word: "DUTY".

The sergeant was back. "Listen up here! Them there men in the barracks are all covering up for him. Now I want that man wrote up in the book, and I want them friends of his listed there too. Understand?"

"Well," Henry said slowly, "let's go have a look at the situation."

The little blond sergeant and the big Negro corporal walked down the center of the barracks in step.

"There," he pointed, "that there's the window he broke. See?" Pfc Walters, of course, was nowhere in sight.

"Why, Sarg, that's only a ten inch square of glass. We could have the man pay for it and let the houseboys install a new one. Shouldn't cost more than a few hundred yen."

"Corporal Hamilton, I am a Sergeant in the United States Marine Corps, and I want that man wrote up! Understand?"

The troops began to gather around in a silent, ominous circle.

"Sarg," acting as spokesman, Stick Wicker said, "I suppose you don't know we got an unwritten rule in this squadron; when a man steps out of line we take care of it among ourselves. That way discipline is kept without the man losing a stripe."

"Discipline? What do you air wing poges know about discipline? When I was in the infantry, we had discipline."

"Did you have blanket parties in the infantry, Sarg?"

"Is that a threat? Corporal Hamilton, that there man threatened me; write him up."

The circle started closing in on the tiny sergeant.

"Stop!" The men stopped. It was Henry Hamilton's voice, deep and firm. "I don't want you men giving Sergeant Phillips here a blanket party, because I'd have to make an entry about it in the book and, well, I just don't know how to spell his name. How about it, Sarg? Which is it? Just the plain word itself? Or Sergeant Bastard?"

There was laughter among the troops, strained, nervous laughter. Tension was beginning to evaporate. Hamilton was sensitive to such things, the danger of mob violence was passing.

"Hamilton, I'm going to hold you responsible for them words, and you're going to find out what a pure bastard I can be."

"Go ahead! Slug 'im, Hank! We won't see a thing. Right, boys?"

"Another threat! Another threat!"

"Look, Sarg, just you calm down." Henry was wearing thin. "You're going to get yourself in trouble with these gentlemen. Now let's just everybody go back and tend to his own business. Come on, break up the crowd. We'll just forget anything happened this morning, and if that makes your jaws tight, Sarg, suppose you take your troubles to the Chaplain."

Sergeant Phillips looked pale and confused. This was not his Marine Corps. You didn't handle things like this in his Marine Corps. Suddenly, it came out: "You damned nigger!"

Henry's temper flared. There was a bit of scuffling and he had Phillips by the ankles. He was bouncing the man's head on the deck. "One word you left out, Sergeant. I'm a damned BIG nigger!" He threw Phillips, who was more scared than hurt, into an undignified heap on the floor and returned to the Duty Room.

He opened the log and wondered how to record the disorder. He was willing to take responsibility for his own actions. But he wanted to spare Pfc Walters, if possible, and let the troops take care of the broken window. He lifted the pen.

There was a strange noise. Somebody was trying to sing. "Oh, I'm a squared-away Marine, I never drink at all, 'cept a little tomato juice and sickbay alcohol. Hyp! 2-3-4." Private Jack Robles marched into the Duty Room, halted - hiccupped - and saluted. "Private Robles, Commander-in-Chief of the First Provisional Underground Mess Kit Repair Battalion, reporting in, sir."

"Good Lawd, man, what have you been drinking now?"

"Hangover medishun, shir, I mean shur. Took three bottles, but it cured my hangover."

"Lawd, I never saw a man get drunk so fast!"

"I ain't drunk; I'm cured." Robles grinned proudly.

"Man, you're cured and pickled both. Go in there and sleep it off before the OD comes by and sees you like that."

"Yes, sir! About face! Forward hic!"

Hamilton put the pen to paper and muttered, "Hell, who'd believe it?" He wrote: "1000 - All secure, nothing to report."

Chapter 5

Ginza Street Blues

They stood in Nishi Ginza, a Japanese girl and three U.S. Marines. People were passing in droves, the busiest corner on earth, the biggest city in the world.

Acting Corporal Wicker led the way, they saw the Imperial Hotel and they saw the great Emperor's Palace. They rode trains and subways. They dined at the Shirokaba - six stories high. Wherever they journeyed, remarks by Abe Diamond kept them laughing - happy.

The night was still fresh. They went to night clubs: New Yorker, Albian, and the Volga Russian Restaurant.

Around the town by taxi, more like a roller coaster, they sped to Tokyo Tower to see the town at night, below them, shining warmly. They saw fire flys in the July sky.

And, after midnight, they sat and listened to a juke box play Japanese jazz and Elvis Presley records in some little place off Ginza Street. Four exhausted people. Yoko placed her head on Johnny Shellburn's shoulder and fell asleep.

"Well, boys, it won't be long before I sail across the sea to the land of the big PX." Stick Wicker, small and skinny, looked rather pathetic, tired and sad. "Before I leave, I could tell you guys a couple of things but," he yawned, "you'll find out for yourselves. You've got fourteen months ahead of you."

"Don't remind us," Abe said.

"It'll go by fast. And when the time comes for you to go back, you'll wish to heaven you were some lucky, stupid boot just getting in from the States."

"That's not the way I hear it," Shellburn pulled out a deck of colorful Japanese playing cards.

"Oh, we old salts just put on a big act about being anxious to leave. It makes you boots look up to us."

Shellburn laid the cards out on the table. He just learned to play the game the other night, and now he was going to teach Abe.

Stick sauntered over the juke box. He decided not to waste his money and, instead, went out walking along the empty streets of dawn. He checked his watch: 2:00 a.m. - Tokyo was quiet now.

"A little over a month left," he said aloud to himself, "you are getting short, Mister Stick, very short."

He thought back over the year and remembered the first time he'd ever ridden on a Japanese train - clean, streamlined electric cars. It was spring then; people carried bamboo and paper fans as they were doing again this summer, have done every summer past, and will do during every summer to come.

"Someday you'll come back here, Stick."

Stick Wicker stood on a corner. The great city belonged to him alone. The reed pipe of a fish peddler warbled many blocks away.

He thought of manuevers on Taiwan: the hot-shot Nationalist pilots, itching to shoot down a stray MIG, the little kids standing by the road giving the thumbs up and shouting, "Ding how! Ding how!" Okay! Okay! He suddenly thought of the coy, little Taiwanese girl, with a tear on her cheek, who said she loved him and made him promise to write. She never answered the letter he finally got around to sending.

Suddenly a light drizzle began; it was almost a mist. He inhaled deeply and smiled. This was his private sayonara party. Watery confetti filled the air with shaving lotion tingles, with Oriental jingles, cryptic and secretive bells of night.

"Toyko, pain butcher of the Orient! Why doesn't Sandburg come here," he wondered, "and write about a real city?" My gosh! He never thought it would hurt so to have to leave a place.

He walked by a newspaper building with locomotive presses ticketing out the morning express. Presses printing newspapers in Japanese - papers that, if he remembered the date, he could find in a library someday and read. So what.

He arrived in the Nishi Ginza again. There was one other person on the world's busiest corner: a young blue-suited Japanese patriot who kept spitting. He looked at Stick and said, without accent, "Are you in Japan with the service?"

"Yes, I'm with the Marine Corps at Atsugi. Where did you learn to speak English so well?"

The youth answered, mouthing each word carefully, in a superior fashion, "I was born in the States." Wicker once heard the same tones of defiant pride from a Mexican exchange student at Columbia University who, between puffs on his pipe, once informed him: "In Mexico, today, to be young is to be a Communist."

Stick supressed any look of surprise, which he knew would be so entirely satisfying to this blue-suited one who kept spitting because he didn't have a pipe to puff on. "From which part of the States do you come?"

"Dayton, Ohio." He spit again.

Stick never enjoyed talking to people like this - silent answer men who expect you to pry information out of them. Oh well, there was nothing else to do, except go back and watch Shellburn and Diamond play cards.

"What circumstances brought you to Japan?"

"The war."

"You were deported?"

"Yes. My father is pure American, my mother is Japanese. We were living in the U.S. when the war broke out; then, in 1943, we were sent back to Japan - I don't know why." He was talking more now, and spitting less. It was a strange story, the life of this man. "I spoke only English. I had to go to Japanese school. They used to hate me." What bitterness!

"Do you remember the States."

"Dimly, but they are the only happy memories of my life."

"You don't like Japan?"

"I hate these people and everything about them." The patriot was turning out unpatriotic.

"Soon I return to the States. I am to report for active duty with the United States Army."

"You joined the Army?"

"I was drafted."

"How ironic!"

"Suppose I serve in the Army for a few months and decide I don't like it. Can I get out?"

Now it was Stick's turn to be superior. "I'm afraid not."

"Suppose that, after serving my two years, I live in the States for the required time and get full citizenship rights. Will I be able to return to Japan and visit?"

"Whenever your heart desires, if you have the money, you may go anywhere except Red China."

"Thank you. You have been most helpful."

"The pleasure was mine."

"Please excuse me, but that taxi pulling up is for me. I must go now."

"Good luck in the Army."

Stick headed back for the little place with the juke box, and he turned a new wonder over and over in his mind: the Japanese kid who was born in Dayton, raised in wartime Japan, wished only to return to Dayton, had been drafted, and would - doubtlessly - be stationed in Japan. "That is what I call getting the short end of the rod. What a fucked-up place this world is."

Abe, Johnny, and Yoko were asleep on each others' shoulders.

"Let's hit the deck, people, it's time we caught a taxi for home."

Yoko opened her eyes and smiled with them while Johnny yawned and rubbed his; Abe jumped to his feet and stretched.

"Where'd you disappear to, Stick?"

"Anything up?"

"Just a couple of misplaced persons."

"What?"

"Never mind; I'm too tired to make much sense." He felt sure he'd never sleep again.

Chapter 6

The Atheist Chaplain

"Who built the ark?"

Response: "NOAH!"

"Who built the ark?"

Response: "NOAH!"

Using the opening lines from a Harry Belefonte record as his point of departure, Bob Kidd launched into his sermon.

"Brothers?"

"YEAH!" The lusty response was sung by the spectators, twelve United States Marines in working uniform.

"Verily I say unto you -"

"Hallelujah!" yelled Private Robles.

"No shit!" shouted Corporal Wicker.

"Verily I say unto the drinkers among you -"

"Sweet Jesus!"

"There shall come a day of retribution!"

"Praise God!"

"And the fires of Hell will destroy the sinners!"

"Glory be!"

"Brothers?"

"YEAH!"

"The Judgement Day is at hand!"

"Praise the Lord!"

"And JC's gettin' ready to come down out of Heaven! And when JC comes down out of Heaven, the whole wide world's gonna rock!"

Wicker grabbed an empty nail keg and jumped up on a crate.

"It's gonna roll!" Wicker was pounding out a basic rhythm.

Kidd began to chant, "We're gonna rock around the cross tonight. We're gonna rock, rock, rock until broad daylight! We're gonna rock a-a-round that o−o−ld, rugged cross tonight."

The congregation burst into ribald laughter.

"Brothers?"

"Glory be!"

"Hallelujah!"

"No shit!"

"Brothers? Sinners? Are you ready for Jesus H. Christ?"

"YEAH!"

"Is your house in order? Are you ready for Jesus H. Christ?"

"YEAH!"

"Then stand back, you apple-knockin' sinners, 'cause here I am!" Kidd threw out his arms in a cross-like fashion. The congregation went wild. They raised him on their shoulders and sang.

"Old JC's a jolly good fe-e-llow. JC's a jolly good fe-e-llow..."

"No! No!" shouted Wicker, "'Christian Soldiers.' You guys trying to be irreverent or something?"

"Onward, Christian so-o-ldiers, marching as to war."

"Turn the other cheek!"

"With the cross of Je-e-sus, going on before."

"Love thy neighbor!"

"Christ, the Ro-o-yal Ma-a-aster, leads against the foe."

"Love thine enemy!"

"Forward into ba-a-ttle see our banners go!"

"Peace on earth!"

The singing procession marched out of the working area and vanished toward the base bus stop.

Pat Hoolahan's face was livid. "Those sacrilegious bastards!"

"Take it easy, Pat. Calm down." Henry Hamilton smiled.

Pat Hoolahan - a little fighting Irishman with a turned-up nose - bit his lip.

"I've seen people do idiotic things, but this Bob Kidd is positively stupid."

"Just chalk it off to ignorance. Kidd thinks he's real smart now. In the Good Lord's time He'll straighten things out."

"I've a mind to give the Good Lord a helpin' hand." Mouse, as Pat was called, held up a battered, clenched fist.

"I don't think He needs your help, Mouse; He's done fine up till now without it. Come on, boy, the sun's going down. Let's go to chow."

That night, after taps in the Atsugi, Japan, barracks, there was a general bull session going on in Bob Kidd's cubicle.

"Bull shit! It ain't reasonable. Nobody's gonna tell me there's some old man on a cloud running the universe."

"That's a childish attitude, Bob."

"Christ on a crutch!" Robles came in on Bob Kidd's behalf, "You religious idiots talk about childish attitudes!"

"Hell," Johnny Shellburn became defensive, "I'm no religious idiot, I'm an agnostic. I'm just trying to see what makes you so sure there's NOT a God. How can you know one way or the other? Hell, as I see it, it takes just as much brainless faith to be sure there's not one."

"I have only one comment" Jack Robles said, "if there is a God, may He strike us all dead with lightning right now." Robles paused and looked up, "See! That proves it. There is no God."

In the next cubicle, Pat Hoolahan made the Sign of the Cross, and prayed silently: Dear God, please shut them up, and help me go to sleep.

"All I have to say is just what I've said all along." Henry Hamilton's deep voice repeated, "One of these days you'll get your answer. It might be too late, but you'll get it."

"Well, here's the way I see it," said Jimmy Brown. "Deep down I feel there is a God."

"You feel, but -"

"Just hear me out, Jack. Okay? Deep down I feel there is a God. Now I'm not saying that means there is one. I realize that. It's just a hunch I got. But since I don't know, I figure I'll play safe and believe. That way, if there isn't, I haven't lost anything - and if there is, well, I won't burn in Hell."

"Hell is a state of mind," added Hamilton.

"You know what I'd do if I was God, Brown?"

"No, Kidd, what would you do if you were God?"

"I'd reserve the lowest place in Hell for people like you, people who believe just to be on the safe side - the very lowest spot in Hell."

"Gee, thanks."

"Nothing personal."

"I understand, but I thought you didn't believe in God, Bob."

"Sweet Jesus Christ! There you go! Did I say I believed in God? No! I said IF, Jim, IF. Why do you Christians always insist on putting words into people's mouths?"

"Who's putting words? You said it, not me."

"Aw shit!"

"There's a good, concise, logical statement," Henry said.

"Hump you and the horse you rode in on, Henry."

"Hey," said Robles, "How can we have a constructive discussion if you guys just sit there and chop each other? Here's some food for thought: America is based on the principle of separation of Church and State. Right?"

"Right."

"Okay, then why do I, an atheist taxpayer, have to pay the salary of the Protestant and Catholic Chaplain? Huh? Explain that one."

"Hey, I never thought of that," Kidd said.

"Unconstitutional as all hell, ain't it? Let's write the Civil Liberties Union."

"Better yet," Shellburn spoke up, "march on the Senior Chaplain of MAG-11 and demand equal representation."

"You guys are nuts," Jimmy Brown laughed.

"That does it!" Pat Hoolahan got up, put on his shower shoes, and walked down the barracks to the Duty Room. Acting Corporal Wicker was at the desk.

"You on duty, Stick?"

"Yeah, what's up, Mouse?"

"It's your job to keep the barracks quiet, right?"

"That's what the Good Book says," Wicker pointed to the Duty NCO Log and grinned.

Aw hell, couldn't these bastards say anything without being sacrilegious? "Never mind. I just thought I'd see if it would be okay to play my radio."

"Shit, work out, man. You know I'm not chickenshit. Just keep it soft so guys can sleep."

"Yeah, sure."

Mouse lay back down and tuned his transistor radio in on the Far East Network and put it against his ear to drown out the neighboring conversation.

The next morning there was a sign up on Bob Kidd's locker: ATHEIST CHAPLAIN. GET SAVED CHEAP! CUT-RATE CONFESSIONS! BAPTISM EVERY FRIDAY, MIDNIGHT, AT THE SUMP! Below the lettering was an upsidedown cross; underneath it, also upsidedown, were the words, "Jesus Saves, 4 percent interest."

"Did you see what those stupid bastards did?" Mouse said to Hamilton at morning chow.

"Yeah, I saw."

"You know what that upside down cross means? Devil worship."

Several others at the table, friends of Hoolahan, joined in the discussion.

"That Robles is crazy. That's all there is to it," said Charley Fenwick, the Catholic Chaplain's Assistant.

"Well, Bob Kidd is worse," Mouse answered.

"Yeah," said another, "you know what those guys have been doing? Every night, when their crew gets off watch, they hold a big, mock revival meeting out in the area. Boy, I sure wouldn't want to be in their shoes when I die."

"I say we should talk to Father Brennan about this."

"Lot he'd do about it," Fenwick said.

"Well somebody ought to do something! Damnit!"

"Temper, Pat. Temper." Henry Hamilton was calm.

That night, Pat went on liberty in Yamato. He sat in the Flame Club and drank beer - alone. He clenched his beer glass and frowned. Why was everybody so damned mediocre? Hell, he didn't want to start a war, but what kind of man is it that won't stand up for his own beliefs? Hamilton just puts up with it; Brown is afraid to have an opinion; Shellburn is on their side; Fenwick, the one man who might be able to do something, won't even bring it to Father Brennan's attention; they are a big pack of cowards - one and all.

"Another beer," he slapped the coin down on the bar; it sounded like a rifle shot.

It would be okay if they'd just keep to themselves about it. But no, they have to publicly ridicule everything sacred. There's a recruiting poster, out in the operations classroom, with a picture of a Marine corporal, in prayer, beneath a stained-glass image of Christ. So what does that fool Kidd do? Pastes up a comic strip balloon that says: "Don't you believe in going through the chain of command, Corporal?" And do any of the officers do anything? Lieutenant Valingsworth looks at it and laughs!

Bang! "Another beer."

It was still early in the evening. Bob Kidd was stretched out on his bunk reading. Hamilton was on the next bunk shining his shoes. The lights were still on, but the barracks was quiet. Those who were not at the Enlisted Club or on liberty were busy getting ready for an inspection the CO was having.

Henry looked up. "Hi, Pat."

"Hi, Henry. Well, well - what have we here? How's the atheist?"

Kidd didn't notice the sarcasm. He hardly knew Hoolahan, and he was mildly surprised at the question. "Temporarily out of business -" he said absently, "inspection tomorrow."

"Well, I think somebody should put him out of business for good."

"Too many believers need saving."

Hamilton was first to detect the chip on Pat's shoulder. "Better lay off, Pat."

"Shut up, Henry. It's time somebody did something about our atheist bastard friend here."

"Well, well," Bob Kidd put down his book, "and just who is that somebody going to be, little man?"

"You think I can't lick you because I'm little?"

"I didn't say that."

"That's what you mean, though. Isn't it?"

Kidd returned to his book.

"What's the matter, atheist, cat got your tongue?"

"Mouse," Henry said again, "you better lay off."

"Who's side are you on, Hamilton?"

"I don't take sides."

"That's the trouble with this place, nobody takes sides. Nobody but me and the atheist bastard here."

"Look Hoolahan, if you want trouble, just say 'atheist bastard' one more time." Kidd threw down the book and sat up in the bunk.

"Atheist bastard!"

Kidd was up and swinging. He connected several punches with the left side of the Mouse's head. The Mouse went down on a nearby rack. Kidd stepped back. The Mouse lunged, grabbed Kidd in a headlock and brought him down on the bunk. Kidd rolled across the rack and they both came down on the barracks floor. Kidd slipped away and jumped to his feet. As the Mouse got up, Kidd let a rain of punches fall on him. Once on his feet, Mouse tore into Kidd with unbelievable fury. Bob Kidd fell back against a locker and slid to the deck then rolled over and struggled to his feet. Hoolahan launched another two-fisted attack. The Atheist Chaplain was ready for this one. Just then, Charley Fenwick grabbed the Mouse and pulled him away, and Jack Robles stepped between the fighters. Henry Hamilton sat on his bunk and watched passively.

"Le'me go!" yelled the Mouse.

"Robles, get out of the way!" Kidd hollered. "I said get out of the way, Jack, or - so help me - I'll kill you too!"

Wicker stepped in front of Bob Kidd. "Take it easy, Bob, it isn't worth it." These words seemed to calm him down.

Meanwhile, Fenwick soothed Hoolahan.

When the two men regained their tempers, the referees and spectators dispersed, leaving them alone.

Kidd, shaken, but not hurt, went back to his rack, picked up his book, and pretended to read.

Hoolahan was much calmer, but he felt a throbbing in his eye and upon touching his face, found a little blood. "Well, friend, I'll wake you up at five in the morning and we'll settle this thing out behind the barracks."

"If that's what you want."

"That's what I want," said Mouse, turning to leave.

"Just a minute, Mouse. Just what is your bitch, anyway?"

The Mouse sat on the bunk across from Kidd. Kidd put down the book.

"Well, it's this way, Kidd, you been putting down my Lord. I don't like it."

"You mean you're pissed just because I chop JC?"

"Right."

"So, a typical Christian, you decide to duke it out with me."

"Now wait a minute, boy, you swung first."

"After you left me no choice."

"Right."

"Why?"

"Like I said, I don't like your cracks about religion."

"Anybody ever tell you it is supposed to be a free country?"

"Great. But that doesn't mean I got to sit around twenty-four hours a day and hear you tear down what I believe in. Hell, it's not so much things like your little sign, and those idoitic sermons; it's all the damn bull shit after taps. You could at least let people sleep."

"For that I apologize. Really - I see your point. There'll be no more discussions in the night, but as for chopping old JC - I'll say whatever the hell I like."

"In that case, I'll belt you whenever the hell I like."

"Look, Hoolahan, don't you figure JC is big enough to take care of Himself?"

"That's pretty hypocritical talk for an atheist."

"Shit! I didn't say there is a JC - I said, 'Don't you think JC,' if there is such a thing, 'can look out for Himself?' Without your help, in other words."

"That's beside the point."

"Okay, Christian, have it your way. You might as well start swinging right now, because I'll keep on saying what I feel like saying. And I'll tell you something else."

"You do that."

"I'm going to turn the other cheek. Not because I believe in it, but just to show you that, even by your standards, I'm a better man than you are."

"Well, I'm not going to hit you right now for a number of reasons.

One of them is that I've had a few drinks tonight. Another is that you're a little shaky now, and I don't think it would be quite fair of me to take advantage of it."

"Look Mouse, I'm shaky because I'm mad and, believe me, Christian, that will not work to your advantage."

"I don't like the way you keep saying 'Christian'."

"Well, then, you better do something about it - Christian."

Mouse laughed as if a good joke had just been played on both of them. "Now who is leaving who no choice?"

"Well, regardless of who started this, I'm ready to see it through to the end. Now, I guarantee I'll keep chopping your Lord, not after taps, but any other time I feel like it. So you might as well get used to the idea."

"Stand up and get knocked down again, that's all there is to it."

"I'm sorry you feel that way." Kidd picked up his shaving kit, threw a towel over his shoulder, and headed for the showers.

The next time Pat Hoolahan saw Bob Kidd was the following afternoon in the squadron coffee mess. The Mouse was standing at the counter sipping a cup of hot chocolate. Kidd walked in and ordered a cup of coffee. He glanced at Hoolahan out of the corner of his eye. As he put cream and sugar in, and stirred, he sang softly: "Christianity hits the spot: twelve apostles, and that's a lot, Holy Ghost, and a Virgin, too - Christianity's the thing for you." The Mouse remained still, brooding over his hot chocolate. Kidd turned and walked out, cup in hand.

"Hey Bob," Mouse heard Wicker yell just outside the door, "You got a good sermon ready for tonight?"

"Nah, that shit gets old after awhile."

Just then, Jimmy Brown came in the door. "Hey, Mouse, the gunny wants you to drive a six-by over to the armory."

Pat dumped the last of the hot drink down his throat.

"Well, Mouse, I hear you put that atheist bastard in his place last night."

"If it's Kidd you're talking about, Brown, you can shut up." Hoolahan slammed his cup down and stomped out.

Bob Kidd happened to be waiting at the taxi stop that evening when Mouse was heading for town. "Hey Pat, I'll split a taxi fare with you."

"Sure, Bob."

When Henry Hamilton dropped in the Flame Club, some hours later, he was not surprised to see them drinking together. He just smiled his usual, calm smile and bought drinks for everybody.

Chapter 7

Our Motto

Long, tall Willy scrutinized his liberty card with open-mouthed wonder. It was a happy reunion, almost miraculous.

Before Willy had been in Japan one week, over a month ago, there had been the trouble with Captain Sims, the all-Marine s.o.b. who restricted Willy Cecil to the base for two weeks.

At the end of the two weeks Willy had the duty. After that he had time to pull liberty about twice, man of rare talents that he was, before he got put back on restriction.

His second restriction was the result of a whole series of evil coincidences. It all started when, one morning, he passed Lieutenant Shultz on the way to work. Willy was puffing on a big cigar, and the lieutenant didn't like being saluted from behind a cloud of foul smelling smoke. Still, this was only a starter.

That afternoon Willy stooped into the Operations Center. It was sunny out and not yet accustomed to the darkness of the room, he ran smack into the good lieutenant. Of course, without the cigar, it would have been okay; as it was, he practically burned Shultz's nose off.

"Good afternoon, sir," he said, rendering a snappy and proper salute, the following day.

"Good afternoon," the lieutenant returned. Then he stopped and checked his watch. "Good afternoon? It's eight in the morning, you idiot! Tuck in your shirt!"

That afternoon Willy was happy to note he was on a working party. It is not customary to render salutes on such affairs. If he could only keep his mouth shut, and cigarless, he thought he would be safe. He was helping erect a squad tent; he was inside, lacing up a corner, when Abe Diamond, who was outside, joked, "You're good at this Willy. Why don't you do the rest alone?"

There was a stock reply. He stuck his hand through the unlaced portion and made an obscene sign toward where he thought Abe stood. He got no answer; so he stuck his head out from under the tent flap. Abe was not there, but Lieutenant Shultz was.

Well, two more weeks on the base dragged by and finally Willy held his liberty card in his hand. He stuck it in his pocket and headed for the yen sales booth in the Enlisted Club. There he exchanged ten dollars for three thousand and six hundred yen. He was rich.

Willy loped along in his usual manner, shrugging with every step out the East Camp gate and down the rice paddy road to Yamato. What a night this would be!

He stopped in the Flame Club. Bob Kidd and Pat Hoolahan sat there arm wrestling and laughing.

"Hi ya, Willy? How's things?"

"Can't complain. Got my liberty card."

"Congratulations!" Kidd said, "That calls for a celebration. One beer for Killer Willy Cecil!"

"Wow," Willy said. A tall, well-built bar maid brought the beer. "What's your name, babe?"

"Tomiko."

"Put on a record, Tomikosan and let's dance. You boys'll excuse me a minute?"

"Sure, Willy."

She looked like a legendary Indian maiden with those high cheeks and that fire in her eyes.

"Listen, babe. I've got a buddy. See? And I'm gonna slip him my liberty card and let him turn it in for me. I can climb the fence in the morning. Now at eleven thirty, when this joint shuts down, you and me are going out on this town. Understand?"

Her answer was a smile.

After the music stopped Willy shrugged over to the arm-wrestling arena. Clearing his throat, he said, "Uh, say - Bob, my old, old buddy. Do me a big favor."

"Sure, Killer. You name it."

"Stick my liberty card in the box for me when you go back."

"Hey, boy, you get caught making it over that fence and you'll never see that thing again."

"I know what I'm doing." He handed Bob Kidd his liberty card.

"Okay, Willy, if you say so, but remember the boy that warned you."

"I'll see you later, Tomiko. About eleven. Okay?"

"Diajobi. Okay."

"You guys be good." Willy shrugged on down the main drag past Yamato Station, across the tracks, past the new department store, and turned into the Yamato ginza to check into the Bar Renown.

He was crystal gazing in his beer glass when a girl slipped up out of nowhere and kissed him on the cheek. A new age was here! His evil luck was changing tonight. Yep, tonight he'd go home with Tomiko and now, wonder of wonders, this new girl-female was caressing him and whispering, "You want to dance, handsome?"

Before he could answer - Willy was sometimes slow - the music stopped. The next record was undanceable. That decided, he turned to look at her. Nice. Small, soft, and curved properly. She brought his forehead down and kissed him there. Her smile danced. Wild Japan's bars must be full of diajobi dolls! What had he been missing? No more back talking to officers for this kid. She kissed him on the chin and on the cheek. Wow, babe, go slow! The night is young yet. They embraced and kissed.

A conflict was now in Willy's mind. Should he stay here and try to make it with this Oriental passion flower? Or, should he go back to the Flame Club and have a pow-wow with the Indian princess? Well, hell, he had to be fair. Tomiko was the first after all. This one would just have to wait her turn.

Willy hit a couple more bars after leaving the Renown. He didn't do so well in these. In fact he had the feeling that behind his back, people were laughing at him. Aw shucks, nobody laughs at Killer Willy Cecil.

Finally the time came for him to amble back by the new department store, across the tracks, past the station, and down the main drag to the Flame Club. Why were people giggling? He looked down to see if his fly was open. Nope.

Kidd and Hoolahan were gone. The bar was full of strangers.

Damnit! Every dumb stud in the place was laughing at him. All except Tomiko.

"What's so gawdawful funny?" he demanded.

"Go in the bathroom and look in the mirror," said the Mamasan behind the bar.

Before he got to the bathroom door, he knew what he'd find - a face all full of lipstick. He thought of exactly what kind of surprised bellow to let out when he reached the mirror. It was like a surprise party when you knew about it in advance. He would still pretend surprise when his ugly mug jumped out of the mirror and shouted: "Surprise! Surprise! Surprise nightmare, you idiot. You big, skinny fool."

"OH, NO!" he shouted pretending to laugh. He left the bathroom door open so they would hear him laughing at himself; so they would hear what a good sport he was, and so Tomiko would know it was a joke - a big, funny joke. He wanted to spit at the mirror.

He grabbed a paper towel and came back out of the bathroom rubbing his face vigorously. He sat at the bar. There was a frozen moment for him to survey the situation. The Mamasan was still behind the bar, laughing. Tomiko was behind the bar also. Her face was expressionless, true to the Indian tradition his thoughts gave her.

Some stud, a stranger, was sitting at the bar grinning at him. He grinned back, patiently, almost breaking his jaw. Some dame he'd never seen before sat with the stud. She smiled demurely then looked bored. He turned back toward Tomiko. Best to change the subject; explain later.

He reached into his pocket and brought out some hundred yen pieces. "Scotch on the rocks," he said to Tomiko. He slapped the coins down on the counter a little more loudly than he intended.

There was a long interval before she finally picked up the money. She said nothing, only smiled an unusual, forced smile. A small and empty conversation got under way and then died. He sipped his scotch.

At that point, Abe Diamond, the lean-faced curly headed buddy from the Lieutenant Shultz affair, entered the bar.

"Say, Abe?"

"Say, Killer?"

"Snew?"

"Notathing. You?"

Here was Willy's chance to clear the air. "You ever see that little slut over at the Bar Renown?"

"You mean Judy, the humorist?"

"Yeah, that's her. You know what that little bitch did tonight?"

"What?" Abe grinned.

"She came up and started talking to me and kissing me! I ignored her, of course."

"Of course."

"And when I came in here everybody laughed. And you know what?"

"What'd she do, put lipstick all over your face?"

"Yep."

"Yeah, she's rotten. She ruined a white shirt of mine the same way."

Thank goodness! Tomiko, who was standing near, heard every word. Now she knew he was not making love, just the innocent victim of circumstance, or a woman's mischievous whim; both amounted to the same thing in Willy's book.

Willy and Abe went on discussing the trials of life. Abe figured he might be catching a cold. Willy had a nervous twitch lately. Abe had better quit going to the Swan Bar; all the girls there were wise to his line. Abe hadn't made out in weeks. Some broad did actually offer him five hundred yen to go to bed with her, and Abe was as amazed as anyone. It turned out that she had the clap.

That deserved a big idiot's laugh from Willy.

Abe laughed too.

Tomiko put on some soft mood music. Willy looked at her with blue, filmy eyes. "You're a doll, babe," he said with his eyes.

She smiled warmly.

He looked down at his drink. Then he brought it up to his lips and sipped nervously.

She came out from behind the bar and sat in one of the booths nearby.

He kept his eyes on the scotch on the bar. He drank a little more.

An arm came around his shoulder and filled the glass.

They smiled at one another like kids. It all reminded Willy of his one and only high school love.

"Abernathy."

"Here."

"Ames."

"Here."

"Anderson."

"Here."

"Eeny."

"Here."

"Meeney."

"Here."

"Miney."

"Here."

"Moe."

"Here."

"Cecil. Cecil. Cecil. Where's Cecil?"

"Oh - er - here."

"Diamond..."

"At ease."

"Squadron, attenshun. Section leaders, report."

"Adminsectionallpresentoraccountedfor, sir!"

"Motortransportsectionallpresentoraccountedfor, sir!"

"Commsectionallpresentoraccountedfor, sir!"

"Operationsectionthreemenabsent, sir!"

The plan of the day sounds like so much gibberish to a man asleep on his feet: "Plan of the Day for Doomsday, 95 August 1775; Officer of the Day: Captain Queeq; Sergeant of the Guard: Acting Sergeant Lifer; Duty Section 1 has the duty.

"Attention all hands: It has been noted by General Congratulations that your fine work is in order on the excellent results of the last and everlasting dedication and sponsorship of proud fighting spirit and tradition of the men and officers of this wing. Signed by direction of Commanding General Floop."

"Squadron, tenshun!"

"Section leaders, dismiss your sections!"

"Section, fall out!"

Willy Cecil yawned and rubbed his eyes amid the scramble onto the big, cold trucks. The trucks wheezed and puffed along the road to the working area. A long day followed.

Love was like that. He would kiss her naked body. He would kiss her lips and the corners of her mouth. He'd kiss her chin, her neck, and her soft shoulders. He'd caress her breasts, wetly. Hard and passionate Indian Maiden in the Japanese teepee!

A block and a half separated the bus stop from the Flame Club. The worst part about it was the front; the windows were opaque, and you never knew what you'd find inside the leather-covered door. The door was heavy; it had been a hard day.

There were not many people that Willy didn't get along with, but one of them was Jack Robles, the dark, hawk-nosed drunkard. Jack Robles was sitting with Tomiko.

Willy let it pass. "A beer, dozo." He worked on it in short, angry swallows.

Then the original grinning stud of the lipstick fiasco entered. He sat in the corner, and Tomiko left Robles to talk to the stud. Willy saw Tomiko sitting in the stud's lap. The stud was whispering some hurried, important sentences. She was smiling, and she nodded. The grinning stud left.

Tomiko walked over, smiled and seated herself next to Willy. She filled his half-empty glass as she was hired to do. She made small talk with him, as she was hired to do.

"How are you, Willysan?"

"Fine," he hummed through his clenched teeth. He drained the glass and ordered another.

She poured it for him as she smiled; it was her job.

He looked in the other direction and pretended to be fascinated by the doorstep of the men's room. Finally, she got up and walked away.

Willy picked up his beer and moved over to a small booth. If she joined him, he would forgive her, he thought. She looked at him and smiled and he forced a weak return. The original stud of the lipstick foolery came back. Willy left his beer sitting there, half finished. He did not have to look far for a cab back to the base. If he hit the sack early, he wouldn't be sleepy during the morning muster again. Wasted dreams!

As the cab passed the Swan Bar, Willy decided it would be better to get good and drunk.

He found Abe in the Swan Bar. Abe was way ahead of him; an alcoholic stupor numbed his eyelids.

"Fuck 'em all, Killer - every frigin' money-lovin' whore in the world. Fuck 'em all!"

"Slow down. I'm gonna get every bit as tight as you are. We'll paint Yamato red!"

"Paint Yamato red! Do or die! That's our motto, Killer."

"No. Our motto is Yamato. Hey, chosan, a scotch on the rocks."

He looked around and smiled bitterly. "Yep. Sure am glad I didn't lose my liberty card again. I wouldn't miss this for the world."

Chapter 8

One Windy Night

On a cool night of winds, clear-eyed and bell-minded with possibility, he stood beneath nothing and kept watch on the rain. The dampness induced a melancholy.

Chanting, an echo called from the time of Solomon when blazes made mystic shadows on black and hollow temple walls guarded by warriors.

In the back hills of mindlessness, a monster prowled. The light of the Red Star put restless patterns in the storm.

At 0100, he kept up the log: "All secure." Johnny Shellburn was protected by the sentry booth, but all around the outside the storm spun wildly. It was late August and this, he heard, was only a tame sample of the typhoons due next month.

He tried again to tune the short wave set. No luck. No disappointment showed on his sharp-featured face. It was a face saved from cruelty by gray-blue eyes. The eyes were resigned and tired. He liked to tune in on Radio Peking and Radio Moscow while on post, and listen to the latest Red blat. It kept him awake. Oh well, perhaps the tubes were damp, or the storm interfered with reception. The booth shuddered in a fresh blast of wind.

The wind sounded like uncertain sirens, going high and dropping off and going high again. Shellburn said aloud, "No rest for the wicked!" He was unable to hear himself. There was a new blast from the west.

He sat down on the chair and pulled his field jacket up around his ears. Hell, there was no use standing up; you couldn't see ten yards. Can't go to sleep. Don't dare go to sleep. He'd have to find something to think on. Time would go faster. In three more hours he'd hit the hay.

He thought about home, so far from Japan and the Marine Corps. Town in California with green glory on its grey morning in the endless

La Puente Hills. The smell of pine, euycalyptus, citrus and cedar trees was drawn across his mind. Those morning walks in the hills!

The headlights of a jeep, blurring with the weather, came toward the sentry booth. It was the Officer of the Day coming to check post. The sound of the wind doubled when Johnny threw back the door to admit Lieutenant Valingsworth.

"Good morning, sir!"

"Good morning, Corporal. Everything all right?"

"Post number one all secure, sir."

"Yeah, fine." Valingsworth was not much for the military formalities. "Shut the door before we blow away."

"Yes, sir."

"Any Communist spies try to steal the plans to the coffee mess?"

"I don't think so, sir."

"You can drop the 'sir' crap, Corporal, it's too windy for that."

"Yes, sir - I mean yes, Lieutenant."

"Where're you from?"

"La Puente, California, sir."

The Lieutenant was fatigued; a sad-looking man. He was lonely and wet. Drops of rain hung from his shaggy eyebrows. "Not far from El Toro is it?"

"Not far at all."

"I used to have a girl in the next town, El Monte."

"Is that right, sir?" Habit made him keep saying "sir".

"Yeah. Got a Dear John from her last month."

"Sorry to hear that, sir."

"Well, it was my own fault."

"Why's that, sir?"

"I haven't exactly been a straight arrow over here; you know how it is. Well, some joker sent her a picture of me with my arm around one of the girls out in town."

"Good Lord!"

Valilngsworth laughed at himself. "Well, Corporal, I'm heading up for the tower snack bar. Can I bring you back some coffee?"

"If it's not too much trouble, I could use a cup - black."

"Okay, Shellburn, shoot any spies you happen to see."

"Will do, sir."

There went one hell of a good man. Few officers in the outfit pushed their rank, but there was no other to be found like Lieutenant Valingsworth. A damn good man. Now why would anybody play such a dirty trick with his girl? There's just no figuring people out.

As the wind died, the rain increased. Then, suddenly, the rain stopped. There was no sound but a low, steady wind. Lance Corporal Shellburn decided to check the area. All was quiet. Crates were blown over and a tent had collapsed. He'd report it in the book. No serious damage. The wind was cold.

"0200 - Checked post. Two radar crates overturned by wind. One squad tent down in Restricted Area. All else secure."

Lieutenant Valingsworth drove up with a box of two covered paper cups in his lap. Shellburn opened the door.

"You said, 'black'?"

"Right, Lieutenant."

"Here you go." The Lieutenant opened the second steaming cup for himself. "Well, the sky seems to be clearing a little."

"Yes it does. I sure hope we have good weather today."

"That's right. You have the day off, don't you?"

"Yes, sir, but first I'm going to sleep about four hours."

"I don't blame you. I should get some sleep myself." The Lieutenant's eyes were puffy and his whole, droopy face reminded Johnny of a cocker spaniel. "I drink as much coffee as I can hold. It keeps me going till I pass out."

"Yeah," Johnny said, "I'm a java fiend myself. Between coffee and cigarettes I stay sane."

"Keep up the good work, Johnny, and don't fall asleep. I'll see you Monday."

"Okay, sir. Here, I owe you ten cents for the coffee."

"Forget it. If anything comes up, I'll be at the BOQ."

"Thank you, sir!"

"Oh, by the way, go ahead and smoke if you want. I don't think the place will burn down."

"Thank you, sir!"

The jeep sputtered off.

Lance Corporal John R. Shellburn decided to check the post one extra time. Hell, it wouldn't hurt.

It started raining again; heck with the post. He lit up a cigarette. That Valingsworth sure was a good guy. It was too bad about his girl. How did a character like that end up as an officer in the first place? Poor, silly son of a gun.

On a cool night of winds, clear-eyed and bell-minded with possibility, he stood beneath nothing and kept watch on the rain.

Before his watch ended, there would be a red glow in the east. The rain was erasing the footprints Shellburn failed to notice around the radar crates and around the tent in the Restricted Area.

Chapter 9

Summer Festival

As he walked toward the chow hall, Abe took pleasure in the thought that it was Friday, his day off. His hangover was almost gone. All he needed was to get something in his stomach. He thought it would be a simple matter.

Johnny Shellburn ran into Abe Diamond at the mess hall door. Johnny was also in civilian clothes.

"So you got the day off," Abe said. "So do I."

"Yeah, but if you think you're going to noon chow I got news."

"What?"

"That old gunny in there just kicked me out. 'No civilian clothes in the chow hall during working hours.' Ain't that a bitch?"

"He wants dress blues?"

"This Marine Corps gets more chickenshit everyday. Let's go out to town and get a bowl of rice. Got your liberty card?"

"Sure. Say, how come you got the day off?"

"I had guard this week. You?"

"Watch stander's liberty."

"How'd you swing that?"

"Oh, I pulled a few strings, threatened a couple of guys, bribed a couple and blackmailed two others. Why?"

Abe and Johnny flashed their liberty cards at the gate. The Japanese bus happened to be passing and they climbed aboard.

"So where do we chow down? I'm famished. Besides, I got a hangover."

"There's a little place in Yamato Ginza, or we could eat in Yokohama. Where you headed, Abe?"

"No place."

"Good. You'll have to come to Yokohama with me."

"Say - maybe your girl, Yoko, has a nice looking friend!"

"Won't hurt to ask."

Abe was in deep thought as the bus rolled along the bumpy road to town. "I'll tell you what let's do: We'll get some cookies and a couple of those little pink balls of rice in Yamato - that'll hold us over till we get to Yokohama - then we'll have lunch. After that we'll go see what this chick of yours comes up with. Then, if all goes well, we'll blast Yokohama wide open."

"I read your last - loud and clear."

"What you need is a light marching pack." Abe surveyed Johnny's accumulation of gear as they sat down on the train for Yokohama. "What with that camera, the books, those clothes, and the cookies and rice balls - you look like some kind of peddler."

"I think I'll get me an AWOL bag one of these days. I take this same crap with me every weekend. I can leave most of it at Yoko's house."

"Yeah, damnit, I've got to get me a girl in Yokohama. Those Yamato women got no class." Diamond wondered what Jean would think if she could hear him now. How he had sworn to be true the last time he saw her! Oh well, what the hell? "You know something, Johnny, I've got to quit messing around like this. Hell, I'm engaged to a girl in the States."

"So you don't want Yoko to fix you up with a little girl from Ginzaland?"

"Oh, I'll mess around until next week. Sudden changes are bad for the constitution. Everybody knows that."

"Next week," Johnny repeated with a smile.

The electric engine buzzed, the conductor's whistle blew, a bell rang, the car doors slammed, and all three cars were smoothly off toward Yokohama. Riding the trains, buses, and streetcars of Japan was Abe's private happiness. Ah, the many Oriental faces! An old papasan was sitting, frowning a little, and pretending to be very important in his old-fashioned kimono. An old mamasan sat next to him. She was quiet and dressed in a drably speckled kimono. She was fanning papasan. On the other side sat a dirty, unshaven day laborer with khaki clothes and khaki teeth. Tied around his head was a rag, the eternal symbol of the Japanese working class.

Abe noticed that Johnny was asleep. He wondered why others didn't share his joy in life's little things.

Two cricket-sized kids, a boy and a girl, whispered and poked each other in the ribs. Their young mother and father, in Western clothes, sat nearby. The mother had a slumbering baby tied to her back by a long silk sash; the father was absorbed in a Japanese newspaper.

Five high school boys clowned around directly across the aisle. They were uniformed in black yachting caps, white shirts, and black trousers. They carried on an excited, clippity-cloppity conversation.

In the course of forty minutes the train pulled in and out of many villages. When they pulled into Nishi Yokohama, Abe awoke Shellburn. "Better start getting your stuff together."

Factories and large houses, almost stacked on top of one another, flew by the windows. They passed two great stockpiles of broken bottles and they went by a judo school. Finally, they rattled and rolled into an echoing grand central building known as Yokohama Station.

They caught another train for a one-stop ride to Sakuragicho Station, up near Isezaki Street.

As they walked along the streets between the station and Isezaki, it began to sprinkle.

"Hey! Looks like more rain." Abe noted the clouding sky. "Let's go eat, man."

"Okay. Where to?"

"There's a nice Stateside restaurant across from the Matsuya."

"Onward."

Drums of thunder sounded the charge; the two Marines headed for a taxi cab.

After lunch, they were off to the Bar Olympus where Yoko was working. "A couple of beers, Yoko. When do you get off work, babe?"

"Mo s'koshi. Maybe two, three minutes. Then change dress."

"What's new, anything?"

"Yes." She poured the beers. "Tonight I take you to a party."

"A party?"

"Honto."

"Well," Abe licked his lips, "things are getting bright. No doubt your party have tak'san pretty josans, ne?"

"No girls. This family party. Friends of mine live by shrine; have Shinto festival."

"Shinto festival! Shellburn, you get me into the damnedest things! I came here with you, lured by the idea of some swinging little lass, and your girl wants to take us to a pagan festival, and not even an orgy at that."

"Hold your perch, friend. I'll communicate with you in a minute." Shellburn was staring at the golden glass of a Nippon beer in a mystic manner.

"Oh, Gawd, not this Zen Buddhist kick again! Yoko, anybody ever tell you your boyfriend was nuts?"

"I'm not nuts. Besides, it was Amida Buddhism I was practicing, not Zen. Furthermore, I've been off that kick for over a week now."

When Yoko went to change her dress, Johnny turned to Abe and started talking excitedly. "I was just putting on that meditation bit to get you to shut your big mouth. I happen to know this family she was talking about and, get this, they have the wildest daughter you ever laid your lovin' green eyes on! Only trouble is she doesn't speak English; so you've got to have Yoko's help as a translator. You could have screwed everything by pushing that 'fix me up' bit."

"How's that? Slow down. I don't quite read you."

"Don't you see? When you meet this chick tonight, be sincere, like she's the first love of your life. But you'll still need Yoko's help so you've gotta sell her on the idea that you're a straight arrow, the clean-cut young man and all that crap. Yoko is this dame's friend and you know how women stick together."

"Yeah." Abe grinned in his beer. "Yeah, yeah." He toyed with Johnny's idea awhile. "How old is this chick?"

"About sixteen or so."

"Yeah, yeah, yeah..." His voice trailed off into soft mumblings and scheming meditations.

The late afternoon sky had cleared. Dragonflys darted about. There was a mysterious, singsong Oriental music echoing through the suburb.

"They are having a ceremony dance now. Pretty soon they bring presents to shrine," Yoko explained as they walked along the street.

"Swingin'!" Johnny was enthusiastic. "Real downright crazy! I hope I brought enough flash bulbs."

"It's all idol worship, Johnny. You've got to remember that," Abe intoned. He was in one of his briefly serious moods. "Graven images!"

"But, Abe, look how much more fun these people have. Shinto is the religion of life, of enjoyment."

"Eat, drink and be merry. Tomorrow they may take away your liberty card."

"Exactly!"

"This is Papasan's house," said Yoko. In the Japanese-English bastard language, the respected head of the family - or any other elderly gentlemen - is referred to as Papasan, or Honorable Papa.

They stepped into the porch and removed their shoes. They greeted the lady of the house, Mamasan, who bowed to the floor. "Kunichiwa," good day.

"Kunichiwa," they returned.

Abe looked around for the wild little chick. There were just a couple of young boys playing in the living room. If Shellburn was lying, a day of reckoning would come! Mamasan led them into the main living room. They drew up cushions, crossed their legs and sat, after much smiling and bowing, of course.

"Where is Papasan and, uh, the rest of the family, Yoko?"

"Papasan is at work. There is just one other: Babysan -"

Abe gave Johnny a hard look.

"-and she is a movie usherette. She will be home mo s'koshi."

Abe's look softened to comradely love. Good old Johnny. Now all that remained was to see this Babysan.

Papasan came home next. Since, aside from Abe and Johnny, no one but Yoko spoke English - and since Yoko was out in the kitchen - they had a clear field for plotting out loud.

"You've got to get in with the old man, Abe. That guy rules this house with an iron hand. You should see the way-" Yoko returned to the living room to make introductions.

"Kunichiwa, gozaimus," Abe said, bowing low. Good day, sir.

Papasan and all the family laughed.

"What's wrong?"

"Not say 'gozaimus' with kunichiwa. Is bad Japanese," Yoko pointed out.

"Why not? You say 'ohyo, gozaimus' for 'good morning, sir.'"

"Yes, but not 'kunichiwa, gozaimus'."

"Ain't that a bitch, Johnny. I screw up right at the start."

"The noble patriarch" - he said "noble patriarch" because he knew Yoko's English vocabulary did not include such rare, high-falutin' words - "does not seem particularly perturbed; as a matter of objective observation, I detect genial amusement."

"As I contemplate your observation more closely, I concur. Further, it is my opinion that we have resolved upon an excellent method of private communication in the company of your beloved."

"I fully agree."

"Henceforth, I propose we employ it whenever our malignant, warped thoughts justify such a means." Thus, two hard-talking Marines became ivory-tower intellectuals in their discourses.

Papasan was a fat little man with a small mustache and cruel features. He smiled, but perhaps his smile was more hostile than a frown. He spoke to them in Japanese.

Yoko translated: "Papasan is having evening prayer before the family shrine. You excuse please."

"Certainly."

Papasan knelt before the Buddhist alter at one end of the room. He prayed silently for about a minute.

"Papasan, he makes wash tubs for a living," Yoko informed them at random.

"He didn't clap his hands." Abe was disappointed when Papasan arose, "I thought all Japanese clapped their hands when they prayed."

"Only when they pray to the Shinto gods." Shellburn was getting to be a real expert on this stuff.

Papasan sat down on a cushion which Mamasan had anxiously provided. The rest of them followed his cue. Now that everyone was seated in a big circle, there was one of those moments, awkward only to Western minds, when the conversation lagged for many minutes.

Finally Abe put in, "Please tell Papasan we are very happy to be his guests, Yoko."

Yoko relayed the message. Papasan smiled his evil smile and spoke. "Papasan say maybe you like to look at family pictures."

Ah! The good old family album, international conversation piece yet. Abe relaxed. "Certainly." Now to make a hit with the old guy!

For several minutes Abe and Johnny admired picture after picture. It was really interesting, photos of Old Nippon, snaps of dedicated young men in uniform, Mamasan in her wedding kimono. Hey! The gal didn't look bad in those days. Would her daughter take after her? Or the old man? What a thought!

After the album, Papasan hauled out some Japanese pictorial histories dating from Admiral Perry upward. Soon there was a lively discussion on Japanese history, which probably lost in Yoko's translation.

By the time dinner was ready, they were breaching the delicate subject of World War II. All went well. Abe was amazed at Johnny's enthusiasm - especially when he started telling Papasan what the Japanese should have done right after Pearl Harbor to win the war. Papasan was enraptured. Abe was taken aback.

"Hey, man, whose side are you on?"

"Shut up. I'm establishing excellent international sentiments in order to facilitate your endeavor."

Some excuse! Abe wondered if old Johnnysan was turning into a blue-eyed Jap or something.

Dinner was spread out on the squat dining room table. Plates were full of all the foods the Japanese sukiaki houses are famous for, including sukiaki - or, in Yoko's pronunciation, s'kiaki - that delicious mixture of beef and vegetables. And, speaking of delicious, Babysan arrived.

Abe's mouth fell open. Hadn't Johnny said to expect the best? He'd figured that Johnny was exaggerating a little. No. There she was, framed in the door against the orange evening sky, slim - but filled well in the right spots - and what a pert little smile! Abe thought he saw Shinto devils dancing in her eyes.

"So this is Babysan."

Yoko introduced her by some Japanese name. She made a full bow, falling on her knees to the floor.

Abe almost did the same, involuntarily, when his knees buckled. She was real! She moved! Not a figurine in fine porcelain, but a real, living chick!

Abe tried to say good evening, which is kombanwa; it came out, "Komban wow!" He didn't notice. Oh man, she was smiling at him!

It took Abe fifteen minutes to get reoriented. By that time everyone was seated around the table talking and dipping into the chow. They'd offered the Americans forks; both Abe and Johnny refused; they were proud of their new ability to eat with chopsticks.

Sake was served with the meal. Two big bottles of it sat on the table, so everybody began feeling pretty happy. There is a Japanese custom where you pour the other guy's, or gal's, sake and they pour yours. As with all such nonsensical drinking customs, it's a hell of a lot of fun, though nobody has ever figured out why.

Johnny poured sake for Yoko; Yoko poured sake for Johnny. Abe poured sake for Mamasan; Mamasan poured sake for Abe.

Johnny filled Papasan's glass, and Papasan filled Johnny's glass.

Babysan poured sake for Abe, and Abe poured sake for Babysan, wondering vaguely if that sex store made anything, harmless in the physical sense, that you could put in sake. For shame! What a thought.

Even the kids were each allowed one glass of sake since it was a Shinto holiday.

They heard the beating of drums in front of the house. Mamasan slid back the big window-wall doors. They had a grandstand view of the shrine across the street.

The omatsuri, the summer festival, was under way.

Young boys were bearing a small shrine on their shoulders and jumping up and down, chanting. Somebody set off some fireworks. The drums throbbed and reed pipes played. Wheee!

Abe poured sake for Babysan, and Babysan poured sake for Abe. Wheeeee!

Some older boys came down the street with another shrine. Everyone was dressed in hapi coats or kimonos. Lanterns hung from the torii, the gate of the shrine. The smell of incense drifted into the dining room.

Papasan poured a glass for Mamasan and vice-versa.

While Abe was watching the festival, stuffing himself with sliced raw fish and cucumbers, and trying to make points with Babysan, Johnny was having an enthused discussion with Papasan. Sake and sign language made a translator unnecessary.

"Yes, yes," Johnny said, "and Tojo."

"Haasoo, Tojosan des'ka!" Papasan went over to the family shrine, the one he prayed to, and removed from under the statuette, a picture of Tojo. Papasan prayed to the spirit of Tojo as well as those of his ancestors!

A blast of fire crackers on a string interrupted the conversation. A group of men came jumping down the street with still a bigger shrine. The portable shrines were all sitting in front of the permanent shrine across the street, the ginja.

Papasan nicknamed Johnny, "Ginjasan" because of his enthusiasm and questions about Shinto. Liberally translated: Honorable Church.

There was music now that reminded Abe of a Hebrew song. He began to sway and chant.

Yoko, Mamasan, and Papasan all gathered around to exclaim over the pictures of Johnny's family that he pulled from his wallet. Abe poured sake for Babysan and so forth, chanting beautifully all the while. The chant helped ward off the heathen lure of the pagan festival. It relieved his sense of guilt at enjoying it so much.

Babysan looked on with undisguised admiration.

Honorable Church demonstrated his ability to assume the full-lotus position of legs crossed, palms of feet up. Papasan did likewise and they laughed as if they shared the secret of some lodge brothers' handshake.

Everybody for blocks around was full of sake.

That night Abe slept soundly on the soft cushions in Yoko's living room. Johnny and Yoko made passionate love in the bedroom. Yoko had offered to get Abe a girl, one of her bargirl friends for the night, but old Straight Arrow said, "No, Yoko, that wouldn't be fair." Abe could be an expert martyr. His green eyes were misty and his face was long and sensitive to begin with.

"What you speak about? Why 'not fair'?"

"Not fair to the one I love."

"Who, Abesan, you got girl in States?"

"No, Yoko. No girl in States."

"You love Yamato woman I think. No?"

"No."

"Who then?"

"Oh" - there was a long sigh - "just someone."

"Not Babysan you speak about!"

"Why, Yoko, how did you guess?"

"This dame dame, not good, Abesan."

"Why 'dame dame'?"

"Babysan nice girl; you keep away."

"Well!" Abe looked woeful. "What makes you think I'm not a nice boy?"

"Papasan old-fashioned Japanese. He no like this. Strict."

Abe rolled his eyes upward. "Yoko, me and Papasan are like that." He crossed his fingers. "I friend of Ginjasan over here. Right, Honorable Church?"

Johnny who had been watching passively, rolled his tongue around in his cheek thoughtfully and let fall his weighty conclusion: "Yep."

"But Babysan have Japanese boyfriend." Yoko was tossing in the kitchen sink for good measure.

"Babysan may have had a Japanese boyfriend. Did you see the way she was looking at me tonight?"

"That is the way of the Japanese girl. Just flatter."

"What do you think, Honorable Church?"

After the proper silence: "Nope."

"Any more questions?" Abe looked at Yoko.

"I tell you, Abesan, if you not leave Babysan alone - you get tak'san," very much, "trouble".

"Okay, Yoko, you win. I'll let unrequited love haunt my days. I'll keep away from Babysan."

Yoko looked skeptical.

"One question though: In which theater is she an usherette?"

Yoko didn't answer. She just repeated two words and, then, let it rest: "Tak'san trouble."

The street car rolled to a stop. Abe and Johnny climbed aboard.

Yoko was at work so, to kill time that Sunday morning, they rode the street cars, at random, around Yokohama.

"Well," Abe said, growing thoughtful, "there couldn't be too many movie houses in Yokohama, a couple of dozen maybe. Why don't we check them out one by one?"

"Hell, and see shows all day?"

"Why not?"

"In Japanese?"

"Why not?"

"I don't know, Abe; why not?"

"Next show we pass, we'll get off."

"Yeah, why not?" Johnny warmed up to the idea. "Why the hell not?"

She was not at the first place, but the movie wasn't bad. It was about a Japanese school teacher and his class, very much human interest.

The next show was a samurai picture, Japan's answer to the Western. Since after about half an hour they both started going to sleep, they left.

"Something tells me we're never gonna find her this way, Abe."

"Yeah. What time is it?"

"Twelve; noon on the dot." It was one of those overcast days that seemed like a perpetual morning.

"Let's go eat."

"Why not, Abe? Why not?"

They ate in a place at the corner of Isezaki and Saguragi with huge dragons across the front.

"After chow," Abe suggested, "let's try that big place up the other way on Isezaki Street."

"You're a determined cuss."

"Why not?" It was becoming a pretty silly joke, this "why not" business.

"That's what I always say, 'Why not?'"

"Yeah. I noticed you always say that."

"Why not?"

They were eating soba, Chinese noodle soup, which takes a lot of skill with chopsticks; so they quit talking and concentrated on the slippery noodles. Since it was Abe's crusade, he bought the tickets to the three-story theater on Isezaki Street.

He came to a halt so suddenly that Johnny almost ran into him from behind. There she was, not an usherette, a ticket taker for the American movie, *Al Capone*, with Japanese subtitles.

Abe walked up to her as if he was afraid she might break if he came too close and said, "Hello, Babysan."

She smiled her usual, admiring smile. Her cheeks were high, with just a light touch of make-up, and her eyes were gently fixed on Abe.

They just stood there, Abe feeling real sad because there was no way to talk to her. Johnny was right; you needed a translator in a deal like this, but how could you have a translator for a love affair?

Behind Babysan's tiny figure, beside the door for the Al Capone movie was a full-length mirror in which Abe could see himself looking back at himself over Babysan's shoulder. He was vaguely pleased to see that he was so handsome, a fact he never quite adjusted too. He also looked forlorn. He noted his long, thin face and dark, curly hair. Of average height, he looked taller because of his long face, and also because of his hair. His eyes, he noticed, were unreasonably tired and big.

What could he say?

He didn't have to say anything, and besides, he couldn't. Maybe he should let it drop. "Tak'san trouble," he murmured as he lowered his eyes. "I'll see you later, kid."

"Well," Abe said, back out on the street, "we found out where she works."

"Very useful information," was Johnny's sarcastic reply.

They went back to the Bar Olympus. It was time for Yoko to get off work. As soon as they got there, Johnny and Yoko got into a private quarrel about something. Abe never found out what it was about. Anyway, it turned out with Johnny muttering, "Come on, Abe, let's get outta here." It was the last time Johnny and Yoko ever saw each other.

"What happened?"

"Nothing."

Abe decided to stay out of it; Johnny's jaws were tight.

"Where we going now?" asked Abe.

"Babysan's house."

"Why?"

"Christ, Abe, do you want to make that chick or not?"

"What's that got to do with it?"

"She gets off work in an hour. We're just going to happen to be dropping in for a visit."

"What about Yoko?"

"To hell with Yoko."

Johnny suddenly seemed very anxious to have Abe make it with Babysan.

The family was around the dining table when they arrived. They saw Abe and Johnny approach.

Papasan waved his hand at them in a peculiar manner; Abe thought he was motioning them away; so he turned to go.

"Come on, silly," said Johnny, "that's Japanese sign language for 'come in!'"

"I'll be damned. They do everything back asswards over here."

They removed their shoes and entered.

Papasan smiled. It was not his cruel smile. It was plain that he'd come to like these young barbarians, especially Honorable Church, so well informed on the tactical considerations of Pearl Harbor.

As usual, there was much bowing.

Babysan was not home. Abe noted that.

Papasan offered them tea. The family was seated for tea, and, as polite guests, the Marines did not refuse.

Looking out the window, Abe noticed all traces of the previous night's festival were swept away. The shrine across the street looked forsaken and colorless.

"Kombanwa, Abesan." It was Babysan standing in the door. Tonight the sky behind her was grey.

The minutes were spent in a family discussion of signs, mutually understood words, and tak'san laughter.

It was not long before Papasan and Johnny were reshaping the Solomon Islands campaign. They'd worked out an elaborate symbolism by now. Conversing on war was not a problem.

The two young boys had a net on the end of a long pole. They went out to snatch dragonflys from the evening air.

Mamasan disappeared into the kitchen.

Babysan took Abe by the hand and led him to the door. She put on her shoes and motioned for him to do the same.

Abe congratulated himself. Now he was getting somewhere.

They strolled down the street together.

A teacup was an island; a saucer was a fleet, and Johnny's hand was a flying squadron. While Johnny made the engine noises, Papasan supplied the guns and bombs. Never before had a war produced such good feelings between two people.

Abe wanted to stop and watch the sun go down. There was a clear sky on the western horizon. But she was taking him somewhere. They walked up to the door of a house; she knocked.

A young man of about twenty answered; they entered.

Babysan introduced them to one another. "Abesan - Komurosan."

Komurosan bowed and smiled. He was young, muscular and handsome.

Babysan looked at Abe, nodded in the direction of Komurosan, and said one well-rehearsed English phrase: "Boyfriend."

Abe bowed low; he could not smile.

Abe and Johnny left their host early that night. They were very polite. They bowed many times.

They did not speak to each other as they walked down the street toward Yoko's house. There was no need.

Johnny reached in his pocket, pulled out the key he always carried, and opened Yoko's door. Yoko was not home. Johnny gathered his camera, shaving gear, clothing and books under one arm. Before stepping outside, he threw the key in on the bed.

The two Marines walked toward Yokohama Station.

It was Sunday morning. The chow was pretty good for a change.

Johnny worked on a plate of scrambled eggs. Abe sipped a cup of coffee and stared at the mess hall's blank wall.

"I got a letter from Jean," Abe said dryly.

"Oh?" Johnny wasn't much interested.

"She said my last letter was really well written."

Johnny slurped his coffee loudly.

"You know, Johnny, I think I'll write a book."

"Oh?" Johnny was really not at all interested.

"It's going to start out, 'I have loved across the sea.' That's going to be my first line."

"Why not? Say, let's go to Tokyo this afternoon."

Abe saw that Johnny couldn't care less; so he finished his coffee and looked at the empty wall.

The summer festival was over.

Chapter 10

The Idle Warriors

On a train to Tokyo Johnny thought of war. He saw the little children in the car and thought of how such as they went up in hot light at Hiroshima and Nagasaki. He gave vague questions to his benumbed mind and waited for the answers.

Next to Johnny sat Abe Diamond, probably thinking about the book he decided to write that morning, the one about how he'd loved across the sea.

Both Marines were thinkers; both thinkers were lovers; both lovers were disillusioned. Japan was a great place to learn about life in the world outside Disneyland, U.S.A. Both were learning fast.

The whys and wherefores of senseless war took second place in Johnny's mind when Abe said, "Here we are, Shimbashi Station."

Johnny picked up his camera and followed Abe through the stampede.

When they emerged from the exit onto the cluttered Shimbashi Ginza, Johnny said, "Well, Abe, now that we're here, what next?"

"Well, we could take in a show."

"Listen, this show business has to cease. My eyes are beginning to hurt from too many movies. Besides, it's against my principles."

Abe laughed. "You got principles yet!"

"Yes, as a matter of fact, I believe in certain things about travelling."

"Like for instance?"

"Well hell, Abe, we've been stationed over here for two months already. What have we done worth doing in that time? I can think of one thing: the day I went to Kamakura."

"Hold up! Don't start preaching Buddhism again. I've had enough of that for awhile, thanks."

"I'm not. I'm preaching reality. You can't spend your life in a movie. Let's walk around Tokyo and live."

"Hell," Abe was half angry and half entertained, "I'm alive." He offered his pulse as proof.

"Forget it."

A panel truck with loud-speakers on it made further conversation impossible for a few seconds. Some excited Japanese slogans poured out over the paper image of a white dove. The truck moved on down the narrow street.

"Japanese pacifists," Abe remarked.

"Yeah. Quite the thing, that pacifism, once you lose a war."

"I'll tell you what, Johnny, let's compromise. You can soak up culture all you want. We'll go to the Kabuki Theater."

"But I don't know anything about Kabuki."

"So what?"

"I'd like to read up on it first so I'd know what was going on."

"What's to know? A bunch of Japs put on a play."

"Abe, you just don't learn about a country that way."

"Don't tell me how to learn about a country; I've been a hell of a lot more places that you have: Mexico, Canada, Jamaica."

"Never mind, Abe. All I'm trying to say is—"

"I know what you're trying to say. Let's don't go into that again. I'm right, you're wrong; let's don't talk about it."

"Well, go to your goddamned Kabuki Theater. Maybe I'll see you around some fine day. So-long!" Johnny walked off in long, swift strides.

"Yeah. Have a blast, stud."

Johnny decided to follow the peace truck, but it was already out of sight. He walked toward Hibiya Park wondering exactly how to spend the bright afternoon. As he crossed the street, a little taxi cab came swerving around the corner and he jumped back.

"God damn! I'll meet my death crossing a Tokyo street yet." He didn't like Tokyo. Abe was a Tokyo man. He was a Yokohama man. Most Atsugi-stationed Marines were Yatmato men; they preferred the Americanish little bar town to the Westernized cities. "There must be something about Yokohama that reminds me of Los Angeles. Abe is from New York; it figures that he should like Tokyo."

His plan for the afternoon was formed. When he reached Hibiya Park he sat on the grass under a tree to meditate.

In his shirt pocket was a folded-up sheet of government bond typing paper. He took it out, pressed it against his knee and wrote.

"Dear Sonia:

"Have I ever told you how much I enjoy knowing at least one girl who thinks about the serious side of life? It's true.

"Have you been in to L.A. lately? To the First Unitarian Church? How is their ban-the-bomb campaign progressing? Good people working together can do much!

"When I think of why I am over here, a fighting man in a foreign land, I'm often happy to realize that there is nothing for me to do here. We are warriors, but idle warriors, nothing more.

"There are those who say war is inevitable. My sitting here under a tree, as the Lord Buddha did in India centuries ago, throws doubt on their words. I think the Cold War will end soon.

"A friend of mine, Abe Diamond says..." He paused. He struck out the words. Abe was no longer a friend.

The sound of the peace truck's loudspeaker reached his ears. It was going by the park. This time, lines of students followed it. Some of them were waving red flags. One of them saw him and yelled, "YANKEE GO HOME!" which made him uneasy. He drew out a cigarette. It was a Japanese brand he smoked, Peace Cigarettes. Before he had time to light up, he saw a fight break out in the mob following the white dove. The truck turned the corner and the mob followed it. Soon all was quiet again - and peaceful.

He reread his letter many times in the next hour. Sitting beneath that ancient tree of Buddha, half-listening to the buzzing summer crickets, he waited for a closing line to form among his thoughts. In vain he waited. "This letter is obsolete," he remarked. He tore it up.

From his shirt pocket he drew an envelope. He crossed off Sonia's address which he wrote earlier. In bold letters he scrawled, "Do not open until August of 1965." On a scrap of torn letter he wrote, "The idle warriors will not be idle long. Johnny Shellburn - Tokyo - 1959." He sealed the envelope, folded it, and put it between his ID card and his Yokohama Turkish Bath card. He put them in his wallet, got up and strolled toward the Imperial Palace, and on to take pictures of the Yasukuni Shrine on Kudan Hill, dedicated to the Japanese war dead.

Chapter 11

The Feud II

Sergeant Wooly, a rotund little soul with thick glasses, ran up and down the barracks waving his arms. "Reveille! Reveille! Everybody up! Six hundred hours! Reveille!"

"Aw, can it!" Johnny muttered softly. Climbing out of the rack, he launched into an automatic string of swear words.

"Why do mornings always taste like stale beer?" somebody groaned.

"Reveille! Reveille! Anybody not up in five minutes goes on report."

"La-tee-friggin-da. Lock me up, you googy butterball nco."

"What?"

"Nothing, Sarg." Johnny reached into his locker and pulled out a stack of wrinkled papers.

"What you got there, Johnny?" asked Willy Cecil.

"Notes for a lecture. I think I'll enter this Techique of Instruction Contest. Who knows? I might win myself a trip back to the States."

"What's your subject?"

"Conduct on Liberty in the Far East. It's a little peptalk on Japanese-American relations."

"Other than sexual?"

"Exactly. The squadron-level competition is today. I don't think anybody else in entering in the sergeants-and-below group." Johnny eyed the pages one by one.

"Let's go to chow."

"Okay. Let me make a couple of changes first." He crossed out a sentence and rewrote it. "There."

It didn't seem right at morning chow without Stick Wicker. Stick was sent back to the States yesterday.

"God damn. I didn't even get a chance to say goodbye to Stick."

"Me neither," Willy said, "so don't feel like the Lone Ranger."

That lucky son, Stick. Almost a damn civilian by now. It was time they got to muster.

"Jesus, what a day!" Johnny said. It was late afternoon and the hot showers felt real good.

"How'd you make out in the contest?" Willy asked.

"Seeing as I was the only man in it, I won. The major was real impressed with the speech. Says he thinks I might get through on the MAG level if I practice up on it."

"Good deal."

"Win that and then go to Iwa Kuni for the First Marine Air Wing Finals; win that and my trip to the States is in the bag."

"I suppose you'll want to stay in the barracks tonight and rehearse the damned thing."

"Nope. I've got some irons in the fire out in town. Tonight I go out and sin." Johnny washed the smell of the base from his body. "Besides, the MAG contest ain't till next week."

Johnny thought about Tachiko, his girl from the Royal Coffee Shop, and Mariko, his girl from the Swan Bar, and the Innocent Drunkard, a new girl in the Flame Club. Her real name was Hanako, but he called her the Innocent Drunkard because of her amazing split personality. One night she would be like a sweet, fresh college girl. The next night she'd be bombed out of her mind. He never knew how he'd find her.

"Say, Willy?"

"Yep."

"Who's got that conga drum that used to be Stick's?"

"Let's see. Stick sold it to Robles; Robles lost it in a poker game to Sergeant McCall; he hocked it and sold the ticket to Hoolahan; Hoolahan took it out of hock and sold it to Bob Kidd. Bob Kidd has it. Why?"

"Oh I think I'll borrow it. I bet it would be just the thing to interest my latest interest."

He went to town with his crumpled lecture notes in hand. In the Royal Coffee Shop he flirted with Tachiko and mumbled about Japanese-American relations, other than sexual.

"The Communists are trying to sell you short. The purpose of their propaganda is to make you, the average American, look like a product of a decayed system, a slob in the eyes of the Japanese people. If you fail to set a good example; if you are not discreet; if you are not open minded; if you fail to be courteous to your hosts in this nation, then you are providing the enemies of democracy with weapons, weapons of evidence necessary in winning allies in the Cold War.

"Would any man in this classroom sign a phony Communist confession? Well, to behave in an unMarine-like manner while on liberty is to do the same thing — endorse Soviet propaganda."

He still needed a good conclusion. "Tachiko, honey, be a real doll and get me another cup of coffee.

"I will feel that I have achieved the objective of this lecture if you men remember just one thing and make it your general order in the Far East: Refuse to endorse Soviet propaganda!"

Good. It was to the point. He folded the notes and crammed them in his pocket. He'd win that trip to the States yet.

"Thank you, Tach." Johnny put one arm around Tachiko. With his free hand he stirred the coffee. With his mind he divided the evening between his three girl friends. He wondered where he could find Bob Kidd.

Kidd was in the Flame Club and so was the Innocent Drunkard. First things first. The Innocent Drunkard was innocent tonight.

"You want a beer?"

"Diajobi, Johnnysan."

"One for me, too."

She sipped the beer and ate crackers. She was damned cute. She wore a ponytail and she had a turned-up nose. Every inch of her was alive and young.

"You like drums?"

Her eyes flashed. "Lub drums!"

"Fine. I'll tell you what..." He told her he had a conga drum back at the base; he would go get it and they would go to the Song Bar and work out. She was all for it.

Johnny went over to where Kidd was sitting. He bought Kidd a beer. He talked to him about old times and the great fun they'd enjoyed way back in July. It was August now. He congratulated him on his nice-looking girl in the Bar Renown. He mentioned Bob Kidd's sharp mind and quick wit. He laughed for three full minutes at Kidd's latest joke.

"Tell me something, Bob." Johnny bit his lower lip and wrinkled his brow.

"Sure, Johnny."

"How would you like to sell your conga drum?"

"Who to?"

"Me."

"How much?"

"Twenty bucks."

"Nope," Bob said without smiling, "I couldn't charge you that much. It's pretty banged up so you can have it for ten."

Good old Bob! "Where is it now, back in your locker?"

"Yeah. You know my combination if you want it tonight."

"Thanks. I'll go get it."

"Work out." Bob motioned in the direction of the base. It was understood that the monetary part of the exchange would be settled on some future payday.

The rhythms of the record filled the Song Bar. Johnny worked a skillful frame of sounds around them. Then he mastered the record. He started swinging and blowing the core of sound and the record became as nothing. In moments like this he did his best thinking. He thought of the change that Japan had forced on him in the last couple of months.

In Toyko, a week ago, there'd been the argument with Abe Diamond. He came away from that feud with a general feeling that, along with people and freedom, war was linked with destiny. He gave that fight a name, for it had changed his thinking. He called that little argument over nothing, "Feud I." From now on, each such feud he got into, or saw, would be numbered. He was a firm disciple of Private Jack Robles who once said, "Organize things mentally and you shall find the great Universal Truth," and then got drunk. The rhythms got faster.

The song of the drum would carry him to success this night. The Innocent Drunkard would be his. He waited and drummed. She was to meet him there after work and the time was near. A girl entered the Song Bar.

"Hi, Johnny." It was Mariko, his girl from the Swan Bar.

Johnny's hands grew stiff. There was only the sound of the record. "Hi, Mariko." Two words echoed in his head: think fast, think fast, think fast...

A friend came in on Mariko's heels, Tachiko. Oh, my gods! He didn't know that they were friends. It was clear that they were planning to destroy him. No hope. The girls, he noticed, were both high.

The bartender came out of the back room and the girls ordered mixed drinks.

"I'll have a rum and Coke. Hi, Tachiko. Make that a straight rum."

"Hi, Johnny."

"Sure, Johnny, rum."

For a sickening minute it all seemed like one of those movies where a Joe Palooka named Johnny is the most popular boy in town. All the girls, overjoyed at his return say, "Hi, Johnny!" The soda jerk and his buddy, say, "Hi, Johnny. Sure, Johnny." The mailman and the gas station attendant say, "Hi, Johnny." The milk truck driver and the cop and the mayor say, "Hi, Johnny." The telephone repairman, the village idiot and the town drunkard all say, "Hi, Johnny." And Johnny goes back to war and gloriously gets wiped out after writing post cards home and winning the Congressional, etc. In the end, we see Johnny's face in the clouds and the band plays "When Johnny Comes Marching Home," and the men, women and kids all cry in their popcorn.

The war ends, the movie goes on TV. In the cold light of the electronic appliance, years later, it is just another world War II propaganda movie and nobody cries anymore.

"Hi, Johnny." It was the Innocent Drunkard, more drunk and less innocent than before. With her was some broad he'd never seen before and didn't ever care to see again, haggard and whorish as could be. He had seen enough junkies to know a mainliner when he saw one. Her arms were marked with lines of needle scars. The Innocent Drunkard was not much better looking than her new friend. What a change a few drinks brought about in that chick. Yipes! She was a drunken slut with messy hair.

"Hi, Johnny!" repeated the village idiot, the jerk at the fountain, and the old maid. Somebody change the channel! He drank deeply of his rum.

The Innocent Drunkard ordered a beer. Her companion ordered nothing. Tachiko and the Innocent Drunkard exchanged a few Japanese pleasantries and then Tachiko threw a drink in the Innocent Drunkard's face. There were quick and choppy sentences between them. Soon they were out in the street in front of the bar fighting. A huge mob gathered around. The two girls were rolling in the mud.

"Good God," muttered Shellburn standing in the doorway, "Good God Almighty." He said the words cooly.

Later that night, when the MP's found him half-asleep and totally drunk in a rice paddy, he kept muttering the same senseless sentence over and over. "Somebody change the channel. Please, somebody change the channel."

Chapter 12

The Orators

The sky over Iwa Kuni, Japan, was turquoise. There was nothing but sky that day. There was no land and no sea. Even the clouds in the sky below were blue.

Gunny Baxter touched him on the shoulder. "Fasten your safety belt and put on your life jacket," the gunny yelled. His voice was far away sounding against the loud drone.

To Johnny, all was a dream. He obeyed as the troop plane circled for a landing.

As they awaited their baggage in the flight terminal, Johnny said to the gunny, "It just doesn't fit. I've been thinking about if for the last hour and, so help me, it doesn't make any sense at all."

"What doesn't?"

"This whole deal. Things like this never happen to Johnny Shellburn. And even if they did, they don't happen in the Marine Corps."

"Corporal Shellburn, it's really not my place to say this, after all, I've only been with this outfit fourteen years, but I think you'll find the Corps isn't the piss-poor organization you seem to think it is." It was a typical statement for Gunny Baxter. To him the Corps was God, Mother, Country, National Anthem, Great Protector, Loving Provider, Truth, Virtue, Wisdom and the American Way of Life wrapped up in one neat, military package.

"Well, comes the end of this month and I'll be exactly eleven years behind you as far as time in the Corps goes. But Christ, the three years I've put in seems like thirty."

"That's because you're young."

"Maybe so. Anyway, this is the first decent thing to happen to me since I left boot camp."

"And what was so decent about boot camp?"

"Leaving it."

"I see." The gunny grinned like a wise man with hidden knowledge. Johnny felt himself getting bitter as Marine Corps coffee the last few months.

He and the gunny got a taxi to the administration area, a group of tin huts aptly called "The Pentagon." Soon they were going through the standard hurry-up-and-wait game. Hurry up and check in your orders; wait around to get them stamped. Hurry up and apply for a liberty card; wait around to get it signed. Hurry up and load your gear on a truck; wait around while they find a driver. Hurry into the transit billet; wait around while they decide which bunk you're to have. Hurry over to check out your linen; wait, wait, wait while they look for the jerk with the keys to the locker. Aw shit! After such a day, a man wants to get drunk.

Johnny hurried over to the Enlisted Club; he waited while they decided whether or not temporary personnel were entitled to enter.

Once inside that sacred domain (he was eligible under Marine Air Facility Order mumble fuss, sub paragraph et cetera point infinity) he made a forced march to the bar.

"One rum and Coke, please."

"Johnny Shellburn!"

He turned to see himself sitting on the stool next to him or, rather, to see his double.

"Mike Cervata!" His boot camp squad leader, the best friend he ever had and the finest Marine he ever knew! "How many ages has it been?"

"Many, many ages."

They shook hands. People always mistook them for brothers. They were both five ten and a half. They both weighed one fifty. They both had thin faces, high cheeks and sharp features. Johnny had light hair and blue eyes; Mike had dark hair and bright, black eyes, but they looked and acted like brothers.

"When did you get stationed here?" Mike asked.

"I'm just down here for a couple of days on the Technique of Instruction Competition. I'm stationed up at Atsugi."

"No shit? I'll be competing against you."

"Well damn my salty hide! And up till now I thought I would win the trip to Washington."

They both laughed. It no longer mattered who won.

"Hell, Johnny, I know better than to think you'll give up that easy. After all, who was it that pulled me through that ninth-week inspection?"

"And who dragged me across that obstacle course that day?"

"Hell, weren't me. Must have been some other guy."

"It must have been two other guys if it weren't you."

"I'll tell you what: There are about a dozen other men in this contest; if one of us happens to win first place, the other one buys the beer tomorrow night."

"It's a deal."

After taps Johnny had a dream about boot camp. He, Mike and the rest of the platoon ran along the great grinder. Sergeant Hendrick, the Drill Instructor, shouted the cadence. It was just like old times.

"Sound off!" shouted the DI.

"ONE - TWO - THREE - FOUR!"

"Louder, girls!"

"ONE! TWO! THREE! FOUR!"

Somebody in the ranks muttered, "One, two, three, four, I hate the Marine Corps."

"Knock it off!

"Run! Run! Run! Run!"

One day, Sergeant Hendrick had called him and Mike from the ranks and had them stand at attention in front of the others. "When the rest of you people look as much like one another as these two men, and can march as well, my job will be done."

But it was not that way in the dream. In the dream it was Mike and Sergeant Hendrick who looked alike.

"Run, you bastards, run!"

The dream faded.

The next morning a great number of sleepy Marines were herded into the station theater at top speed; then they waited.

In a ready-room behind the stage, a boy lieutenant scooped the contestants in on a lot of unnecessary details. "As you men know, this is the Fifth Annual Technique of Instruction Competition."

Well hell! How could they help but know?

"As you also know, this is the First Marine Aircraft Wing Finalist Competition."

No shit, Little Beaver!

"There will be two winners: one from the staff nco category, and one from the sergeants-and-below. The winners will go to Washington and will compete in the Marine Corps finals at Marine Headquarters as representatives of the First Wing.

Big deal - representatives of the First Wing.

"Each of you men has a twenty-minute lecture prepared."

Tell me more, thought Johnny.

"After you deliver the prepared lectures, you will each give a five minute impromptu on a subject you'll be assigned thirty minutes ahead of time."

We know the rules, idiot. We've only been through this on two other levels.

"Are there any questions?"

Just one. How did a stupid bastard like you ever get through college?

"Okay. The first speaker will go on in fifteen minutes. May the best man win."

Hey! Somebody write that down!

The staff nco's spoke first. Johnny and Mike paced the deck and drank coffee. They cased their competition in the sergeants-and-below group. There was a little buck sergeant with Coke-bottle glasses, a seventeen-year-old pfc, a grey haired private, a corporal with red hair, and a couple of nondescript studs. They all sat together in the ready room. They smoked, gave each other advice and told jokes, drank coffee, mumbled to themselves and tried not to act unnerved.

Johnny and Mike kept aloof. Standing outside the room, they discussed the old days.

Mike went on first. Johnny watched him from the wings. Mike's subject was guard duty. It was a neat, military lecture. The timing was good. There were no gimmicks. The training aids were simple.

Next was the buck sergeant. His subject was marksmanship. It was a good lecture, but the little man made one mistake. He stood behind the lectern and the troops could see only the top of his head.

The seventeen-year-old pfc spoke on traditions and history, a good subject, but he lacked confidence.

The grey-haired private talked about field sanitation. His lecture was titled: "Maneuvers Can Be Hell". It was well presented.

The red-headed corporal was next. His speech ran five minutes over the time limit.

Lance Corporal Johnny Shellburn walked out on the stage. He moved the lectern out of view, a move calculated to impress the judges that he didn't need such superficial junk, and also a move to point out the buck sergeant's error. He began in a voice filled with confidence.

"I'm Lance Corporal Shellburn, gentlemen. I'm here to talk about liberty - your liberty."

The sleepy private in the third row began to wake up. One of the lieutenants on the judges' panel made a quick note. The faces of hundreds of Marines were turned upward, toward Johnny Shellburn.

"The subject of this twenty-minute class is conduct on liberty; it concerns you directly. It's about the liberty you will pull in the town of Iwa Kuni on this very date. It's also about another kind of liberty: the liberty that thousands of people are ready to die to defend - or to destroy."

The private in the third row rubbed his eyes and straightened his posture. On one side of the stage was Johnny's training aid, a large, yellow board with strips of paper tacked over it. Johnny ripped away the top strip. Beneath it were black letters forming the word "ALLIES".

"Allies are nations which are friendly to one another. If we wish to preserve our freedom, we must have allies."

Johnny went on to explain that allies are necessary in winning the Cold War. He tore away the next strip. The word "NECESSARY" stood out against the yellow background.

He next stated that each man's conduct on liberty was evidence necessary in winning and keeping allies. The next word on the yellow board was "EVIDENCE". He explained that evidence was a weapon in the Cold War. The next word was "WEAPONS".

"What are these weapons? Courtesy, openmindedness, and discretion. They make up the example you set."

After fifteen minutes of the lecture had passed, the board looked like a word list: ALLIES, NECESSARY, EVIDENCE, WEAPONS, COURTESY, OPEN MIND, DISCRETION, EXAMPLE.

Johnny placed a large picture in front of the yellow board. It was a picture of a note, a germ-warfare confession, thrust through prison bars on the end of a bayonet. The hand of a prisoner was using a fountain pen to stab and tear the note. "This man is refusing to sign a germ warfare confession. This man refused to endorse Soviet propaganda."

Johnny paused. The private in the third row was leaning forward for the next words.

Johnny's eyes swept the theater. They came to rest on an old gunnery sergeant with a chest of ribbons and medals.

"Gunny, may I ask you a question?"

"Yes." The gunny stood up.

"Have you ever signed a phony Communist confession?"

The effect was startling. There were shocked expressions on the judges' panel; the auditorium was filled with whispers and unrest.

"I most have certainly have not!"

"Thank you. I'm sure no self-respecting Marine ever would."

"Now let each man ask himself this question: 'Have I ever endorsed Communist propaganda by my actions?' Actions, gentlemen, speak much louder than words. What about your conduct on liberty?"

Johnny had them. They were with him now, all of them: the old gunny; the private in the third row; the hundreds of faces; and the lieutenant on the judges panel. They approved.

He pushed the picture over to the right enough to reveal the first letter of each word on the yellow board. Reading top to bottom, they made the phrase: A NEW CODE.

"Today I'm going to give you a new code. I'm going to ask you to remember a simple sentence for the rest of your Far East tour. Gentlemen, please, refuse to endorse Soviet propaganda!"

He summarized and held a question period. When he left the stage he checked his watch. The class ran twenty minutes to the second.

That afternoon the same speakers gave five-minute impromptu classes. Johnny's subject was traditions and history. He talked about Wake Island. "And there is a story told," concluded Shellburn, "that when radio contact was made with Wake Island after that invasion, Major Devereux had just one request: Send us more Japs!"

Suddenly, bombs were falling on the station theater. They must have been bombs, because Marines never applaud basic training lectures.

That evening Johnny and Mike walked out of the gate to pull liberty in Iwa Kuni. The night was warm, clear and quiet. Johnny thought about what a peaceful village this was.

"That speech was so damned good, that rather than buy the beer, I'm going to take you out to the house for a party."

"From a military standpoint, you know, your speech was superior to mine."

"From a military standpoint that salty, old private with the speech on field sanitation had us both whipped, Johnny. But this ain't the military; it's the First Marine Air Wing and you won and it makes me damned happy."

"Mike Cervata blasts the Marine Corps! I never thought the day would come."

Mike stopped in his tracks, threw his head back and laughed. It was that wild laughter of the young warrior in love with life. Johnny remembered it well.

"Mike, remember what Sergeant Hendrick used to yell when the platoon got out of step?"

"'You're marching like a bunch of common people!'"

Their laughter mingled and they turned down a dusty path along the river near the bridge.

"Wait till you see this pad of mine," Mike said, "and the girl I keep there."

"I can't wait."

"You don't have to; it's just beyond this next house."

They laughed again. There was something funny in what they'd just said - neither could have explained what.

Her name was Suzie, a nickname derived from her last name, Suzuki. The thing that impressed Johnny most was her hair. It was black and glossy from the top of her head to her waist. She was tiny, and the hair made her look like a flower painted in black ink on rice paper. She smiled and bowed slightly as they stepped out of their shoes.

"Why this little pad of yours is a palace, Mike."

"A palace with a princess." Mike smiled proudly. "Pull up a pillow and sit down. Suzie, bring Johnny a cold beer."

"A cold beer! You mean you've even got a refrigerator in this place?"

"There's bottled proof."

"Hey! This is Stateside beer. What's up? You strike oil or something?"

"More or less."

Suzie put a record on the hi-fi. Johnny and Mike relaxed to speak again of old times.

"Well, Mike, I wish I was in the MP's like you. That candy-ass radar outfit up at Atsugi has no spirit. Until I started making out in this contest I was hell bent on becoming a drunken bum. You should have seen me the night I fell asleep in the rice paddy. Man, was I ever out of it!"

"We both had the disadvantage of having a good DI. It don't pay to get trained for the infantry and end up in the air wing; it's too much of a let down."

"Very true. Since I came in this Marine Corps I've known only two Marines worth the title, Sergeant Hendrick and Mike Cervata."

Mike smiled. "I ought to slug you for that. Have another beer."

Time went by too fast that night. Mike had to be back on base at midnight and before they knew it, it was eleven thirty.

"They gave me a liberty card with no time restrictions on it. I don't know if it was on purpose or not, but I decided it would be kind of silly to ask." Johnny checked his card once more to make sure. "Yep. 'Hours: Unrestricted.'"

"Hell man, you can stay out all night."

"Well I'll walk back to the gate with you and you can point out all the good places to get drunk in after midnight."

"Before we leave, Johnny, I want to show you something. Come in the other room here."

Johnny followed Mike into a small room adjacent to the main room. "I'll be a sonofabitch."

"You asked if I'd struck oil. Now you know."

Johnny's first impulse was to believe all his preconceived notions were wrong about the black market being evil. Mike Cervata would not have cartons of cigarettes stacked to the ceiling, PX cameras, golf clubs, and whiskey hidden in his house if such a thing were really wrong.

"I don't get it, Mike."

"I'm an MP, I can get away with it. It's the sweetest little racket in the world. I have people buy this stuff in the PX; I let them through the gate when I'm on duty; I buy the stuff from them at a slightly higher price than they paid; I sell it to the Japs for a small fortune."

"But it's illegal."

"Illegal as all hell if you get caught. MP's don't get caught, though, they catch other people. That way I have less competition."

"Damn my salty hide!"

"Pretty neat?"

"Damn my salty hide!" There was nothing else Johnny could say without losing an old friend.

"It's getting late. Let's get back to the base."

"Damn my salty hide!"

After watching Mike go through the gate onto the station, Johnny turned back toward the town of Iwa Kuni. He retraced his steps through the town and down the dusty path near the bridge. He knocked on the door of Mike's house. "Suzie?"

"Hi Johnny. Do you forget something?" She was in a bathrobe. Her silky hair twisted over her left shoulder and came down in front.

Johnny did not remove his shoes. He stepped into the house and slid the door shut behind him. "Yes, I forget something." He reached for her and undid the front of her robe. He pushed the robe from her shoulders and it fell to the floor. She was small; it was easy to hold her still with one arm while he opened his trousers with the other.

At first she looked terrified. Then she smiled. She slid to the floor and pulled him down on top of her. "It is not polite to wear shoes in Japanese house."

Johnny put his lips to her neck and felt her nails in his back. What he whispered against her soft breasts was audible only to himself.

Soon there would be nothing but sky, no land and no sea.

"What'd you do on liberty last night, Johnny?" Gunny Baxter was just trying to be friendly.

"Learned what people see in the Marine Corps."

"What?"

"Learned how good it feels to be a pure bastard."

The gunny did not understand; to him the Corps was God, Mother, Country, National Anthem, Great Protector, Loving Provider, Truth, Virtue, Wisdom, and The American Way of Life - nothing more.

The plane taxied into position, droaned loudly, rolled along the runway, and rose into the air. Soon it was many miles from the town of Iwa Kuni.

Chapter 13

Here We Come

Johnny stood in front of the mirror in the men's room. Back in the old days, a couple of weeks ago, he used to swear when he discovered a spot on his uniform or a dirty sock in his shaving kit, some clod's idea of a joke. Now he just mumbled "pretty typical," and waited for the next undersized calamity.

His garrison cap fell into the washbowl next. He was rather happy about it; after all, it could have been the commode. He placed it back on his head and walked out to the waiting room.

"Lance Corporal John R. Shellburn, report to the information desk," the loud-speaker said.

Pretty typical, he thought. What now?

"Here's your orders, soldier," said the smart-ass Air Force sergeant at the window.

"Marine," Johnny corrected.

"You won't be much of anything unless you hang on to those orders." The sergeant turned his back and went to work on something else.

How great it would be not to be much of anything again! No silly uniforms to get spots on, he dreamed, and no orders to worry about losing!

A staff sergeant came walking toward him, a Marine staff sergeant. "How's it going, Corporal."

"Pretty typical, Sarg. You?"

"Fine. I understand our flight leaves in thirty minutes."

"Good. All these airman-type doggies are driving me nuts."

"It'll be good to get out of this rice-eatin' hole for awhile."

"Well if Stateside prices are still high, and if Stateside women still dress like men, I think I'll be real happy only leaving this rice-eatin' hole for awhile."

"You'll know soon enough."

"How long does it take for one of those civilian jobs to fly over the Pacific?"

"About thirty hours or so."

"San Francisco, here we come!"

"Then Washington."

"Yep, then Washington. You ever pull liberty in DC, Sarg?"

"Oh, God!" the sergeant said, rolling his eyes, "Did I!"

"I hear it's quite the town."

"It is The Town, period."

"It sounds almost as good as Yokohama."

"Lad, let me set you straight. There are more women in Washington then you can shake your stick at. Government secretaries and such all over town - barracks full of them."

"I'll believe it when we get there so I can see it."

The loud-speaker said, "Flight 73 for San Francisco, via Wake Island, leaving in fifteen minutes."

"That's us," the staff sergeant said. "Got all your gear checked in?"

"Right, Sarg."

"Come with me." The sergeant pulled a bottle out of his shaving kit and headed for the men's room.

In the men's room Johnny helped him transfer the contents of the fifth into a great number of shaving lotion bottles.

"Nothing like plenty of in-flight refueling with VO flying fuel." The sergeant chuckled to himself as Johnny poured the whiskey through the funnel.

"Hey, that sure looks good." It was the Air Force sergeant from the information desk. "Mind if I have a swig?"

"Get lost, wing wiper!" Johnny kept pouring.

"Hey, Corporal, who do you think — "

"Shut up, Sarg," said the Marine staff sergeant. "Just keep pouring, Johnny." It was the first time the staff sergeant had called him by name. It was typical of something, something vague - but still typical.

There was no loudspeaker in the men's room and they lost track of the time. Some Marine stuck his head in the door and yelled, "Anybody here for Flight 73?"

"Right here," said the staff sergeant as he gathered up the bottles and dumped them into his bulky shaving kit.

"Well get goin'. Hell, they ain't gonna wait!"

"Here we come!"

Johnny followed the sergeant through the terminal and out to the plane. They charged up the gangway.

"Got your ticket?"

"Yep, Sarg, got my ticket; got my orders; got a coffee stain on my uniform."

"What?"

"Nothing."

The stewardess smiled like a well-trained robot.

The sergeant got in his seat and tried to flirt with a young mother across the aisle.

Johnny fastened his safety belt. "Got your safety belt fastened, Corporal?"

"Belt fastened, orders in hand, and spot on uniform - situation normal."

"What?"

"Nothing."

"What happened to your hat? It looks like you dropped it in the commode."

"I wish I had; I would have flushed it down." Johnny looked out the window at the runway lights. "You know Sarg, this is all pretty typical of something - I don't know what."

"What are you talking about?"

"Nothing, Sarg. Not a goddamned thing!" It was lucky the engines were revving up; it gave Johnny an excuse to yell.

Chapter 14

Over America

Across the street from the Marine Memorial Hotel was a coffee shop. Johnny Shellburn ordered a coffee, went around the corner to heave in the gutter and returned to drink the contents of the hot cup. He hoped he'd never see another staff sergeant so generous with his whiskey.

He thought maybe a good dose of fresh air would clear his head; so he walked on down the hill toward Market Street. A cable car came up toward him. He sincerely wished it wouldn't make so much racket so early in the morning.

He was really in no mood for walking. If he was still in Japan, where prices were reasonable, he'd take his fresh air in the back seat of a taxi cab with the windows rolled down.

But he was not in Japan and it was time he started remembering it. He was in America. Soon he'd be above America, in a plane for Washington D.C. That much he knew. He did not know, of course, that between San Francisco and Washington there was to be a good deal more than flight time; soon enough he learned.

The stewardess was one of those homely types that airlines are not supposed to hire.

"By God," said his companion, the staff sergeant, "I've seen her before."

There was a cold dignity in the lean corporal's blue eyes. He was thinking, That's your misfortune, not mine. Perhaps Japan has spoiled me.

Thus when the plane ascended, and he should have admired the brown California fields, he thought of Yoko, her grace, her soft beauty. For a second he forgot that she was gone from his life.

"Now I remember!"

This flying from one place to another with half-witted staff nco's would have to cease. A person couldn't think.

"She was stewardess on a flight to Chicago once. We made a two-hour rest stop or, refueling stop, or some damned thing, and this buddy of mine took her to a hotel and got a piece off her."

"I'd have to be pretty hard-up before I'd pick that one."

"Yeah. Me, too," said the staff sergeant.

While the staff sergeant was trying to figure out how long the stop over in Kansas City would be, the corporal was watching the slender wing divide the frosty whisps outside. All of America was sprawled out below.

It's funny, he thought, that you never see people from a plane. It's as if the towns are all deserted. Make a liar out of me! There's a little man on a tractor. He looks like an ant, but who ever heard of an ant driving a tractor?

What's the difference between people and ants? Is there any? Take this staff sergeant, put him down there on a field or beside a road, and what have you got? A man? Nonsense.

Yet ants could not have built a plane. For that matter neither could the staff sergeant. In fact he'd probably make a worse job of it than any given ant. Who built this plane? I am not concerned with those people. I'm concerned with the ants I meet every day.

Shall I treat the staff sergeant ants as men just because they are the size of men? Never. People are mine to make use of just as I'd make use of an ant. What possible use is an ant?

"Want a shot?" The staff sergeant offered him a shaving lotion bottle filled with whiskey.

"No thanks." He shuttered. "I have a hangover from our last flight."

Soon he was thinking of that last flight. It was a hot morning when the plane zeroed in on Wake Island and landed. He got out and looked around him. Wake Island! he thought. He hadn't known it would be so small. How much greater that made the epic of those who fought there! And now it was over nothing small they flew - now it was over America.

Below them were villages, a cluster of them. Then clouds came between the land and the sky, and Johnny tired of looking out the window.

The homely stewardess gave them coffee and tea.

The staff sergeant smiled at her and spiked his coffee with whiskey.

The corporal held his teacup in the Japanese manner and sipped loudly. The airliner moaned and circled over the airport of Kansas City. After a short refueling stop, they were in the air again.

There was something about this monotonous droning across the nation that was hypnotic. You lost your sense of time. You slept awhile and then you woke up without knowing how long you slept. You had eons to draw up the loose ends of your experiences and try to weave a logical pattern of some kind. It was like the endless days on a ship in the Pacific.

The corporal remembered a morning when the sea was as grey and cold as wet concrete. He was on his way to Japan at the time. He sat beneath a warm air vent and stared blankly at the other troops. His throat was sore. Going to sick bay was out of the question; the line was as long as the ship. Then an announcement came up over the ship's loud-speaker: "There will be a checker tournament for the dependents in the officers' mess at 0700." He remembered thinking, If I had my way I'd shoot every civilian dependent in the world. Bastards!

Those were the grey days, he thought. But they did come to an end. Remember that hilly shore? Those trees? Those houses? And there I was, standing on the deck with two thousand other jarheads yelling my fool head off. That day we passed many fishing vessels in Toyko Bay - junks as ancient as the Orient, except for their motors.

Liberty call went that night in Yokohama. I walked in a place called the Olympus and found me a true love and found me a good buddy, all in one trip. Yoko sat with me and Jack Robles tried to start trouble. Next thing I knew he was buying me a drink. Yoko, why did we have to fight over such a silly thing? Jack Robles, you old son, what are you doing now? Things really started off with beauty, didn't they? And now the paint starts wearing off. Yoko turns out to be a prissy little whore and you get tired of trying to talk philosophy with a sentimental drunkard.

So here you are, Corporal, on TAD orders for Washington DC. The fair-haired lad of the First Wing, that's what they'll call you when you go back, Mr. Big. Will that piss you off? Nonsense. Any one of those silly bastards would give his right arm to get back to the States - all except you, Corporal. That, of course, is why you're here.

Look below you! Hundreds of brand new homes, all alike, all with television. Television, the electronical narcotical. Think zero and watch, you stupid, home-bred dependents! You'll find out, ants.

The plane began to lose altitude as it approached DC. The night curtain fell just as they were landing. The staff sergeant pointed out a round light that was the clock on the tower of the Smithsonian Institute. The homely stewardess had enjoyed their company and the staff sergeant stopped to talk with her. The corporal walked on into the gigantic terminal with the wall of windows. He saw a nice-looking girl in the coffee shop; so, after checking out his bags, he went in there for a cup of hot, black coffee.

He sat at a table; she sat at the counter. He smiled at her; she got up and walked out. Hell, he thought, who gives a damn about you - round-eyed bitch.

Hey now! He nearly spilled his coffee. The girl who was sitting at the next table was Japanese. Now, he thought, if I can't handle this, I've lost my touch. I'll really impress her. I'll say hello in Japanese. Then we'll settle down and discuss our mutual home across the sea.

"Kombanwa," said the corporal with a bow.

"I'm sorry, mister, but you must have the wrong person. I don't speak Chinese; I was born in Brooklyn."

The corporal grew angry. He picked up his bag and walked to the door of the coffee shop. He paused on the threshold. He turned. "ANTS!" he shouted. "ANTS!" he cursed. "ANTS!" he bellowed like some Old Testament prophet in Babylon.

Chapter 15

A Christmas Story

The gin fizz glistened cheerily in the varicolored glow of the Enlisted Club's Christmas decorations. Pat smiled and counted on his fingers, "September, October, November, December. If the next four months pass like this, we'll be back here in Japan from maneuvers in no time!"

"But Pat," said Henry Hamilton, "who wants to be in Japan tonight?"

"Me, I do. And I want to get drunk."

"On JC's birthday you want to get drunk?" Henry's intentions were more serious than his flippant tone, but he knew how to communicate more effectively than most moralizers - lightly - painlessly.

"Yes. I wanna get stinkin', stoned, bombed and blasted. Happy Birthday, JC, wherever you are!"

"If you learn to tolerate the people around you, then you wouldn't find it necessary to act like them so often."

"Act like who?"

"Bob Kidd. Johnny Shellburn."

"Go to the devil, Hamilton."

Henry smiled sadly, got up and went to the devil, or to the barracks, or some place, leaving Pat Hoolahan to drink alone.

"Happy Birthday, JC! Happy Birthday!"

Pat's voice was loud and hoarse. "Happy Birthday to you. Happy Birthday to you. Happy birthday to you, Dear Jesus. Happy Birthday to you."

There was laughter in the barracks.

"Merry Christmash!"

"Merry Christmash yourself, Christian."

"Merry Christmash, Jack."

"Merry Christmash, Mouse."

"Guess what?"

"What?"

"It's Christmash!"

They joined in drunken laughter then, arm-in-arm, they weaved down to the other end of the barracks.

Pat bumped into the fire extinguisher. "Help me get the pin outta the fire distinguisher, Jack. I wanna distinguish a fire."

"What? There's no fire."

"I know," Pat hung his head in shame, "but I'm homesick for snow at Christmashtime. I wanna fill the barracks with snow. Help me get the pin outta the fire distinguisher." Pat looked doleful as he begged, not attempting to take the pin out himself - a simple operation.

"No snow." Robles decreed.

"Yes!"

"No snow."

"Yes."

"No snow."

"Yes!" Pat jumped and yelled like a small boy.

"No snow."

Pat took the extinguisher off the wall and searched elsewhere for a partner in delinquency.

He came upon Johnny Shellburn, just back from the States.

"Well if it isn't the fair-haired lad. Help me get the pin outta the fire distinguisher."

There were no volunteers among the many hands.

He walked up to Sergeant Wooly: his last hope. The fat little buck sergeant was asleep on his bunk. He looked strange without his glasses on.

"Sergeant. Please, Sergeant, wake up. Help me get this pin outta the fire distinguisher!"

"What's the matter with you, Hoolahan? Get away."

"Wooly has no balls! Wooly has no balls! No balls, Wooly, unless you help me."

"Go away, Hoolahan."

Pat had a new crusade now. He went over to a nearby GI can, dropped the fire extinguisher in it and then returned. "Wooly, you have no balls." He hit the sergeant on the arm. "See? No balls. Why don't you fight back? Huh, Sarg? Why don't you fight back? 'Fraid of me, eh?" He clobbered Wooly a good one, this time on top of the head. "Huh? No balls, eh? Wooly has no balls at all, everybody. No balls at a—"

Wooly had gotten up and was holding Pat by the back of the collar; he was guiding Pat over to his own bunk and kicking him in the rear end between steps.

Pat was silent. Once the ordeal was over and Pat was in his rack, tucked in by Sergeant Wooly, he said, "Merry Christmash, Sarg, and Happy New Year, too."

"I'll Happy New Year you if you get out of your rack and start anymore trouble."

"Yes, Sergeant Wooly. You're a good man, Sergeant Wooly. You got a bucket full of balls."

Pat pulled the covers up over his head and shut his eyes. Suddenly he felt like vomiting. He jumped out of his bunk and tripped up against the GI can where he'd put the fire extinguisher. He threw up in great gusts. Afterwards, he crept back to his bunk. Somebody turned the barracks lights out. It was ten o'clock.

After about ten minutes of silence, Pat started crying. "I'm sorry, Hamilton. I'm sorry." His sobbing ceased and he let out with a real wail. "I'M SORRY, HENRY! I'M SORRY!"

Hamilton, heard him from the next cubicle. "Sorry for what?"

"I'M SORRY I GOT DRUNK ON JC'S BIRTHDAY!" His voice was a high-pitched, terrified scream. "I'm sorry, Henry! I'm sorry! Sorry!"

"That's okay, Mouse. Quiet down."

"I'm sorry!"

"Okay, you're sorry. Be quiet." Henry's voice was deep and harsh.

Pat was quiet.

"What's going on?" asked Phillips, the Duty NCO.

"Nothing. Hoolahan was just having nightmares or DT's or something."

Bob Kidd came walking up in the darkness. "Pardon me, Sergeant Phillips. Let me use your flashlight a minute."

Phillips handed his flashlight to Kidd. The beam danced on the barracks windows, aimlessly, for a moment. Then Kidd directed it on Pat Hoolahan's bunk. Troops began to gather around in the darkness to see what Kidd was going to do.

The light showed Hoolahan with the covers over his head.

Kidd said, "Patrick Hoolahan? Do you hear me?" Bob disguised his voice; it sounded deep and hallow.

"Huh?"

Hastily, Kidd pulled a blanket off the end of a nearby bunk and draped it around himself.

"Patrick Hoolahan? Do you know who this is?"

"No."

"This is JC, Pat. I heard you were drinking on my birthday." Pat's panicked scream cracked open and penetrated the still barracks from end to end. "I'M SORRY, JC! I'M SORRY!"

Sergeant Phillips, who knew he should put a stop to this, became helpless with silent laughter.

"I'm sorry, JC!" The covers began to slide down as Hoolahan peeped out. "I'm sorry, JC!" The shadow-like figure of Kidd loomed over Pat, the light beam shining from it into Pat's eyes. Pat screamed without words.

The barracks echoed back not a scream, but laughter - insane laughter of men who'd been bored, drunk and homesick too long, sadistic laughter of men who had no purpose in life anymore.

Pat screamed again.

Henry Hamilton chuckled. Jack Robles laughed in great inward gulps of air, laughing too hard to breathe properly. Sergeant Wooly laughed uproariously, as only fat men can. Johnny Shellburn twisted and slapped himself and pounded on the edge of his bunk in an uncontrolled fit of hilarity. His sides hurt, but he kept laughing.

Pat screamed again. He sounded like a man in torture. Only Bob Kidd didn't laugh. He stood there in the darkness, peering down at squirming, screaming Pat Hoolahan. "This is JC, Pat, and I sentence you to five thousand years in purgatory for drinking on my birthday."

"No! No! No!"

Kidd turned out the flashlight and thrust it into Sergeant Phillips' hand. The sergeant was doubled up against the wall laughing. Kidd scanned the barracks, coldly. He walked down the aisle and disappeared out the door into the night.

The laughter and screaming continued for several minutes. Finally, all became quiet.

The next morning Pat awoke late. He was reminded that it was Christmas by the decorations in the barracks: great strands of toilet paper and fluffs of shaving lotion over everything.

He remembered only one thing of the preceding night: someone woke him long after midnight to impart that one roll of toilet paper would stretch clear from one end of the barracks to the other, lengthwise, and halfway back again. He got up and went to the head. On the way he passed a number of friends. They all looked at him strangely, uncertainly. Only Bob Kidd met his glance with a confident return. It was as if all the others had committed a terrible crime the night before and only Bob Kidd was without guilt.

Pat remembered sitting in the Enlisted Club with Henry Hamilton, nothing more. Well, there was not much importance to be placed in the expressions on people's faces anyway, he knew that, so he let it pass from his mind and sink into the depths of his subconscious, where no incident is ever forgotten.

Chapter 16

Yokohama Sunset

Johnny scanned the alley with his eyes. A girl stood in the shadow of the nearby doorway. He took a final, fierce drag and tossed his cigarette away. He stepped into the shadows and their eyes met.

"You want I show you a good time?" she asked.

"How much?"

"You speak how much." Then she added, smiling, "How much do you think I am worth?"

"One thousand yen for a short time."

"Fifteen hundred yen more better."

He pulled out his wallet and opened it. "I have only fifteen hundred, see? I need some of it for taxi and train fare to get back to the base. I'll give you twelve hundred if you pay for the room."

"Not need to pay for room. I have house. Come on." She took his hand and led him down the alley.

As she undressed, Johnny saw that he'd made a very good bargain for twelve hundred yen.

"It is cold, no? We make it warm now." She turned back the heavy quilt and climbed in beside him.

Johnny kissed her firm breasts and began playing his lips about her body skillfully. She did the same with him. She was not in a hurry; Johnny was glad. When they finished, she put her head beside him on the pillow and whispered, "You want to go again?"

"Honto." Sure.

"Me too."

This time Johnny stayed on his back. She sat up and worked the lower part of her body rhythmically. She smiled down at him and kept asking him questions, like a barber making conversation while giving a haircut.

"When you come to Japan?"

"Six months ago, but I went back to the States for a couple of months."

"How long you are going to stay here?"

"Next week my outfit goes to the Philippines and Taiwan on maneuvers. We'll be back in three months; then I'll be in Japan until September.

"You are Marine?"

"Yes." He growled it and grabbed her, pulling her close.

She did not try to ask more questions; the breathing came too hard.

When they were through, Johnny sat up, checked his watch and lit a cigarette. "You want to know something?"

"What?" she asked.

"When I was back in the States, I was homesick for Japan." Suddenly he remembered. "I forgot to pay you."

"You keep." She was getting dressed now.

"What?" Johnny thought his ears were getting bad.

"You keep money."

"But -"

She grabbed his arm and led him to the porch. "Here are your shoes."

"I don't get it. Japanese working girls don't go for nothing."

"I am not working girl. You thought I was, so I let you think so." Suddenly, her English became faultless. "I am a student at the university."

"But –"

"Please, my parents will be home soon. Please go now." She pushed him gently onto the street and then shut the door between them.

"Well, damn my salty hide!" He stared at the house in wonder. It was a pretty high-class place for a whore. "Well damn my salty hide twice!" He checked his watch; it was time to start back.

In front of the train station he thought, This is my last liberty in Japan for three months and I still have twelve hundred yen to throw away.

He spotted an old beggar asleep against a wall. When no one was looking he bent down and slipped six hundred yen into the old man's open hand. Then, since he still had ten minutes to catch the last train, he stood across the street and waited to see if the old guy would wake up.

By and by, a Japanese rag picker came walking down the street. He stopped to take a second look at the sleeping beggar. Money! He looked first up the street, then down. The coast was clear. He grabbed the money and ran like the wind.

Johnny laughed like a god.

Before catching the train, Johnny crossed the street again. This time he put six hundred yen securely in the old man's shirt pocket.

I'll miss Japan, he thought as he sat in the train. Anything can happen on this damn rock, absolutely anything.

Chapter 17

Dune and Headland

Pat Hoolahan noticed that the Philippines jungle resembled green fire in the morning sun. Among the flames, explosions cracked to fullness under the heat of his glance. Fountains of volcanic verdure rocketed up, halting against the deep sky. An emerald holocaust was spread along the ridge and out across the valley. It was a vast, damp conflagration. It was a forested jungle at morning's full heat. It was a scene of intense panic and serene reality.

The jeep was pulled up at the road's side. Pat was the driver and Johnny Shellburn was the only passenger.

"Will you look at that, Johnny? Will you look at all those shades of green!"

Johnny closed his book of Kipling's poems and surveyed the land from the side of the road clear down to the sea.

"Damned beautiful."

"It'd be a great day to go fishing."

When they arrived at the radar site, Pat felt a little guilty about stopping to admire the country. The gunny and the others were hard at work erecting the antenna. Pat wheeled the jeep up behind the water wagon and he and Johnny jumped out.

"What'd the old man say?" asked the gunny.

"He said to keep working till noon chow. Then he'll send up Gunny Baxter and the relief crew."

"Fine. Hoolahan, you and Shellburn start unloading that last truck."

"Will do, Gunny Masters."

"Pat," Johnny said when they got out of the gunny's hearing, "when the hell are you going to learn?"

"Learn what?"

"To quit jumping like a damn puppet every time some nco tells you to do something. 'Will do, Gunny Masters,'" he mimicked.

"Just knock it off, Shellburn. Okay?"

"Okay? Slave away if you want." Johnny walked over to the shady side of the loaded truck and sat down. He opened his book of Kipling.

"Hey! Aren't you gonna help me unload?"

"Take a break, man. There's no hurry."

"But the gunny ..."

"The gunny sucks wind just like the rest of the Marine Corp. Sit down and relax. Here, listen a minute."

Johnny read from the book:

> For-called, our navies melt away;
> On dune and headland sinks the fire.
> Lo, all our pomp of yesterday;
> is one with Nineveh and Tyre!
> Judge of the Nations, spare us yet,
> Lest we forget - lest we forget!

"So, what's it supposed to mean?"

"Kipling wrote this back in the Old Empire days of England. It was a prediction of what might, and did, come of the British Empire. The same thing's going to happen to America."

"How do you figure?" Hoolahan sat down in the shade.

"Well, hell. Look around you! Look over there at Gunny Masters. Tell me he isn't an exact replica of some old British nco in India."

Pat looked. The gunny was wearing a Jungle Jim helmet, had a handle bar mustache, a red rag around his neck, and no shirt. His face was ruddy from the sun. He was frowning and walking toward the truck. "By God, you're right!"

"Hey, you two. I thought I told you to unload this truck."

"We were just taking a short break, Gunny."

"You'll be taking a short break in the neck if you don't get that damn truck unloaded by chow time."

"Yeah." Shellburn climbed up onto the truck; Pat followed.

"I want to have a little talk with you, Shellburn. Report to me when you're through here," the gunny said.

That afternoon Pat and Johnny sat in their quarters. Pat cleaned the dried mud from his boots and Johnny thumbed lazily through his Kipling book, talking.

"So, the gunny says, 'Shellburn, you've been getting a bit too salty lately. When a senior nco says for you to do something, you're to say 'yes,' not 'yeah'."

"I said, 'Gunny, let me tell you something: One of these days this whole fuckin' Corp of yours is gonna fall right down on your head. When I see the inefficient way you so-called leaders are running things, I feel like joining the Russians.'"

"Christ! One of these days you'll open your mouth all the way into the brig, you silly fool."

"You think I sweat the brig? Hell, I'll go to the brig any day! There's not a goddamned thing these people can do to me that I sweat."

"What finally happened?"

"Oh, the gunny walked off muttering something about getting my liberty card taken away if I didn't start acting like a Marine. Those lifers are all alike. They think you're a slob if you're man enough to say what you think."

There were footsteps coming along the wooden walk outside the hut. It was the gunny, standing in the door now. "Say, I know you men are supposed to get the afternoon off; but we're short one man. I need a volunteer."

Hoolahan looked at Johnny. Johnny opened his book and pretended to be deeply engrossed.

"Be right there, Gunny Masters."

"Thanks, Hoolahan."

Pat stepped into the afternoon heat swearing lightly.

"Okay, people, listen up. The first thing we gotta do is move the antenna across the road; we put it in the wrong place this morning. After that, we'll put up two squad tents and knock off for the day."

"Jesus Christ," Pat heard someone say, "how do they ever get by in the war time putting the sonovabichin' radar antennas in the wrong place. If there's ever another war, I'm gonna get transferred to the god-damn infantry where it's safe."

Soon they were loosening turnbuckles and easing the big antenna to the ground. Then Gunny Baxter arrived.

"Hey! Who told you people to move the antenna?"

"Gunny Masters."

"Masters? Did you tell them to move this antenna?"

"Yes I did."

"Didn't you hear? It's supposed to stay right here."

"Says who?"

"The CO."

"He's the one who told me to move it."

"The word was changed."

"Okay" shouted Masters, "Put the damn thing back up."

The Sergeant Major's jeep came rolling down the road. The Sergeant Major leaned out and yelled, "What in hell are you people doing? That antenna goes across the road. Didn't you get the word?"

"The word's been changed, Sergeant Major."

"Well I'm changing it back again. Put the bastard on the other side of the road!"

"Okay, people, you heard the man."

They began easing the antenna to the ground again. Once they had it down, it took fifteen men to lift it across the road. They were driving in stakes for the turnbuckles when the CO's jeep pulled up.

"You people get the word on the antenna?"

"What word is that, sir?"

"Strip it down and repack it. We found out we won't need it."

"Pardon me, sir," said Sergeant Majors, "but I just got word from Group Headquarters that we would be using it after all."

"When did you hear this?"

"Just before I came out here, sir. A call came in the office."

"Corporal," said the CO to Hoolahan, "take this jeep and drive up to Group Headquarters and find out from Master Sergeant Peniston what the hell we're to do with our antenna."

Pat thought he could offer a suggestion or two, but all he said was, "Yes, sir."

The buck sergeant at the desk was reading *Battle Cry*.

"Pardon me, Sarg. Where is Master Sergeant Peniston?"

"How should I know? It ain't my job to follow him around."

"Where could I find somebody who does know?"

"It ain't my job to know who does know?"

"What is your job, Sarg?"

"To answer the telephone. Nothing else. Just answer the telephone." He returned to *Battle Cry*.

Pat walked down the hall until he came to a door with "Group Sergeant Major" on it; he knocked.

"Come in."

"Master Sergeant Peniston?"

"That's who you're talking to, lad. What can I do for you?"

"The CO of MACS sent me down to find out what to do with our antenna."

"What antenna?"

"The radar antenna."

"Oh, you mean that big screen up on a tower?"

"It's called an antenna, Sergeant Major."

"How the hell should I know what it's called? I'm an administrator, not a goddamned scope dope."

"What are we to do with it, Sergeant Major?"

"Just hang on. I'll find out." He picked up the field phone. "Give me the Group CO."

Ten minutes passed.

"Hello. Colonel? Sergeant Major. Yeah. Yeah. Well we have a man up here from MACS. Yeah. Wants to know what to do with the antenna. Radar antenna. Yes. It's called an antenna, sir. That's right. Yeah. Okay. Yes, sir, will do. Right." He hung up.

"What's he want done with it, Sergeant Major?"

"Says to put her up."

"Thank you, Sergeant Major. Did he say which side of the road he wants it on?"

"Just put her up. Don't worry. If he don't like where it is, he'll have you move it."

"I know, Sergeant Major. Thank you."

There were no feelings of guilt about stopping this time. Nobody was working up at the site now anyway. They were waiting. It was late in the day and the green fire was growing dull. Down on the airstrip a jet fighter taxied into position. There was a mighty roar and as it darted down the runway and ascended over the dark jungle. The sound it made was reassuring. The Mouse started up the jeep and drove it toward the site. It was growing late.

Chapter 18

The Racketeer

Jack Robles had known Johnny Shellburn since July. It was now February and never once had he seen his easy-going Marine Corp buddy push the panic button, not until now.

"Quick, Jack, let's get out of here!" Then he said with a note of resignation, "Never mind, it's too late."

"Hi Johnny." said another Marine, coming toward their table from across the dance floor.

Johnny stood up and shook hands with the stranger. "Jack Robles, I'd like you to meet my old boot camp buddy, Mike Cervata."

"How do you do, Mike? Say! You two look almost like twins!"

"That's what we're told. Mike here is from Iwa Kuni, Japan."

"Not anymore. I've been transferred down here."

"The hell you say!"

"I requested it."

"You mean you'd rather be down in this Philippine sweathole than in Japan?"

"No, but I have some business to tend to down here."

Johnny grew pale.

"What are you so jumpy about?" asked Robles after Mike left.

"Remember when I went down to Iwa Kuni last summer?"

"Yeah."

"I put the make on Mike's girl. It was for a reason, though; it was all because that sonovabich is a no-good crook."

"Look, Johnny. Why don't you calm down and try to tell me what the hell you're talking about?"

"I'm calm," Johnny laughed nervously. "I'm the calmest sonovabich on the whole base." His voice cracked on the last word.

"Let's each order another San Miguel and relax."

When Jack went for the beer, Johnny looked for Mike but he was no longer in the Cubi Point Enlisted Club.

"Now, what's all this about you making that stud's girl?" Jack replied.

"It's a long story, Jack. Are you sure you want to hear it?"

"Christ sakes, man! Why do you think I bought you this beer?"

"Okay, let's see now." Johnny leaned back in his chair and looked at the ceiling. "It all started way back when Mike and I were in the same boot platoon in San Diego. You mentioned how much we look alike. Well our DI noticed it too. As you know, that's all it takes. A little coincidence sets you off from the others, and the DI watches you like a hawk from then on. He saw right away that we were both pretty good at our manual and such things, so he began to expect perfection from both of us. We knew what would happen if we started slacking off, so we both worked and sweated like horses. All of the time we were shooting each other questions on military subjects and pulling one another through inspections. We got to be a real hell of a spittin'-polish two-man team! You should've seen us!

"After boot, Mike was put in the MP's and I went to the Wing. I didn't see him again until I went to Iwa Kuni; I met him in the club. It turns out he's working the black market with PX goods out in town. All the Marine Corp is to him anymore is a big racket. So I get pissed off and go out in town and put the make on this little Japanese chick he's been shacking up with. I don't know if he knows about it or not, but I know Mike Cervata is vengeful as hell. If he does, then the only reason he's down here is to get even with me. Jesus Christ, I hope I'm wrong!" Johnny took a long swallow of his beer.

"Why sweat it? You're as big as he is."

"You don't understand. He won't just walk up and punch me in the nose. Mike Cervata is a racketeer. Whatever he wants done, he'll get somebody else to do it. And whatever it is, you can bet it'll be sneaky. You wait."

This boy will go insane within a week, Jack thought. The next night, he walked in to Christoper's Coffee Shop in the liberty town of Olongapo. Jack's concern for Johnny's sanity began to wane. Within two minutes, it turned to positive envy. Johnny had something to take his mind off Mike Cervata. Her name was Inez Romero. Her beauty was hard. She had a good build and a wide, sensual mouth. Her voice was a proud song.

"When I see a man I want to go to bed with, I tell him. Johnny, I want you to take me to bed."

"Seeing that the conversation's gotten this far without my help," Jack said, "I think I'll be going."

It's a positive fact, thought Jack while hailing a jeepney in front of Christopher's, that Johnny has a way with women.

Jack got pretty drunk before turning in that night, so he was not quite sure he saw what he thought he saw while passing Christopher's on the way back to the base. It was a scene he remembered clearly the next morning, but the whole idea of it didn't jibe with what had gone on previously. He thought he'd go talk to Mike Cervata and find out the story.

"They tell me up at PWO that you have a Master-at-Arms down here at the chow hall named Mike Cervata. Is that right?"

The big Navy first class glared at Jack. "What's it to you?"

Christ! Jack thought. Do they have these junior Napoleons in every branch of the service? "I'd like to speak to him if it's okay with you?"

"Yeah. Go right ahead."

"Where is he?"

The swabie laughed like he'd just eaten a lemon peel and thought it was funny. "I got no idea. He's over the hill."

"No shit!"

"He went to Manila on his day off yesterday and never came back." The big swabie looked perplexed when Robles walked away laughing.

"Well, Johnny, the gods are on your side."

Johnny sat on his bunk in a half-stupor. He gave Robles an indifferent look; his eyelids drooped.

"Good old poetic justice!"

"What are you talking about?"

"Mike Cervata just got his!" Jack said.

"What in the hell are you shouting about?"

"Mike Cervata is over the hill."

"If they catch him, he'll get out of it." Johnny replied.

"That's a cheerful outlook. How do you figure?"

"The bastard's a goddamned genius. He can figure an angle on any-thing. You should have stuck around last night."

"At Christopher's?"

Johnny nodded. "You remember how hot that dame, Inez Romero, was for me? That bastardly Cervata walked in the door, snapped his fingers, and she left with him. Just like that. He literally snapped his fingers!"

Robles decided to remain silent on what he'd seen.

"Say, Jack?"

"Yeah."

"Is it true they have a deal out in town where if you know the right people you can get somebody bumped off for twenty-five pesos?"

"That's what I'm told."

"I wonder who the right people are."

For one reason or another, Jack never expected to have the plea-sure of a long talk with Mike Cervata. Thus his surprise to find Mike in Christopher's a couple of days later.

"Hell. How come you aren't in the brig?"

"I don't think I'd like it there."

"But I thought for sure that first class who runs the chow hall would put the screws on you for being AWOL."

"Oh, he tried."

"Goddamnedseagullshitinsonovabich! I've been in the Orient longer than any man in my outfit, Cervata. And until I met you, I thought I knew every way to beat the game. I'm ready to be your student. What are your enrollment fees?"

"Buy me one thirty-centavo coffee and I'll tell you all I know."

"Deal! Waitress? Two coffees."

"First, I have no system or set of rules; but handle each new situa-tion as it occurs. I do, however, keep two important jewels of human knowledge in mind. The first of these is that if you want to prevent somebody from doing something, use fear. If you want to cause them to do something, use reward. The rules are so simple that most people forget them. Don't.

"The deal about my being over the hill is a good example of the first one. I was in Manila on my day off and I was detained. When I finally got back, I checked into the situation at the chow hall. The first class in charge did not turn in my name as being AWOL. He wanted, rather, to have something to hold over my head, a dangerous thing to try with Mike Cervata. Not reporting a man who is absent from duty is known as turning in a false muster. The penalty is heavy. When he refused to believe my story about being kidnapped by the huks, I said, 'Well if I'm in the wrong, I want to go to the brig for it. Let's take this whole thing up to the Old Man.' He suddenly decided to 'let it go this time,' knowing I'd take him and his false muster over the side with me. Fear."

"In Johnny Shellburn's case I wanted to inspire fear to prevent him from messing around with any future girls of mine. I needed help, so I bribed that nice looking whore, Inez Romero, to play true love with him till I came on the scene."

"Yes," Jack said, "I saw you paying her off with a stack of pesos when I was coming in off liberty the other night. I couldn't figure it out."

"Reward." Mike said.

"Is it that simple?"

"In words, yes." Mike replied.

"Thank you very much, Professor Cervata. This has been a most educational cup of coffee."

"One more thing," Mike remembered.

"Yes." Jack paused in the door.

"It would not do for Johnny Shellburn to find out the affair with Inez was faked."

"No, that wouldn't be so good from your standpoint." Jack suddenly realized he now had something on Mike. He thought what a pitiful creature this was behind the blackmail and the bribes.

"I don't advise you to inform him. You see, I do know the right people."

"The right people for what?" Jack questioned.

"The ones who'll bump a man off for twenty-five pesos. Isn't that what you and Johnny were talking about the other day when I was in Manila, over the hill?"

Jack Robles was ready to be godseagullshitindamned but there was no room for the words to pass the lump in his throat. As he walked away from Christopher's, he kept very quiet.

Chapter 19

Farewell Song

Like a great ape in Marine Corp utilities, Jack Robles toiled with a giant boulder. He hoisted it over his head, like Superman, and sent it bouncing and twisting down the hill into one of the white huts.

"Who in hell's throwing rocks at my house?" yelled one of the men inside.

"I am, Jack Robles, with twenty-one more hours in the Far East."

Killer Willy Cecil stepped out and looked up.

"Come on up here, Willy! Help me celebrate!"

Willy trudged up the slope.

"I'm the shortest one in the Philippines, Willy. Just twenty more hours and fifty-seven minutes and I'm homeward bound! Yahoo! Short!"

Willy - long, tall Willy with the silly grin - stood catching his breath and looked at salty Jack Robles, madman of the MAG. "So you think you'll make it back this time, Private Robles."

"You better Hong Kong believe it! My time of departure has just about goddamn well arrived!"

"How long have you been over here, Jack?"

"More than two years."

"How many times have you been in the brig?" Willy knew the answer; he was playing school teacher.

"Thrice. That's Roman for three."

"What was it you got run up for last?"

"Stealing the CO's jeep."

"And the time before that?"

"Beating up the mess sergeant."

"And the first time?"

"Hell, I ain't no history expert. I got a jeep up here on the road. Let's go for a ride."

"I guess somebody's gotta go along and keep you outta trouble."

Jack aimed the jeep down the road toward Subic Bay and they took off.

"Christ! Go slow, man. MP's patrol this road."

"Fuck the MP's! I'm too short to sweat it!"

The lights were soft and the dance floor was crowded in the Subic Bay Chiefs' Club. The music was low and dreamy.

"Make way! Make way!"

A working party of two U.S. Marines in utilities moved among the dancers carrying a large garbage can. They dumped its contents in the center of the floor. Before anyone knew what happened, the tall pfc. and the grinning hawk-nosed private were gone.

Captain Sims sat in his room at the BOQ reading *The Stars and Stripes*. A rock shattered the window and the captain ran outside. Two Marines - a tall one and a short one - were standing there.

"Did you see who threw that rock?"

"Yes, sir! He went running off that way, sir."

The captain ran until his breath was short, but he never found the phantom rock thrower despite the help of the two enlisted men.

Lieutenant Shultz, the OD, got ready to go and check the area in his jeep. The jeep was gone. Somebody had stolen it!

Rear Admiral Plank, the base CO, drove up to his garage and pushed the electronic button to make the garage door open. There was a jeep parked inside!

The Officer's Club manager called the Provost Marshall to report the disappearance of two cases of beer from the storage room.

Jack Robles and Willy Cecil stumbled into the hut Willy occupied carrying two cases of beer.

"Call out all hands and the mascot!" Jack Robles had an announcement of great importance.

Scores of Marines in all states of dress gathered into the hut. Jack

Robles stood atop the two cases of beer. "Gentlemen, it is with great regret that I announce that I stand before you for the final time tonight."

There was wild cheering.

Jack checked his watch. "In exactly seventeen hours and twelve minutes, I and a small number of my comrades will be off to the land of the big PX. Before I go, I should like to present a gift to the enlisted men of my beloved outfit. I should like to present each man in the unit with a case of Stateside beer."

There was wilder cheering than before.

"Unfortunately, this is impossible since, through the courtesy of our leaders, I have only two cases. However, I am determined to present these two cases to the two men who prove by their intense courage that they are worthy of this honor. I am hereby declaring a scavenger hunt. The first two men who bring me any of the following items will get the beer." Jack read off the list.

The conference was made up of all the top brass, both of the base and the squadron. Never before had so many military experts been so baffled.

"Gentlemen," said Admiral Plank, "never in my entire military career have I even been aware that such vandalism and thievery could be possible in any outfit stationed on any base. Colonel, are you aware that sixteen men from your squadron are now in the station brig? Are you aware that during the last eighteen hours there have been more senseless things going on than any sane man would believe? Listen to some of these charges. At midnight last night, two Marines from your unit were caught in the act of stealing the cross from the station chapel. Fifteen minutes later, six Marines from your unit were apprehended while trying to saw down the BOQ flag pole with a hack saw. At two a.m. this morning, five of your men were identified as having been involved in removing the curtains from the station theater. At six a.m. two more of your Marines were arrested for drunk and disorderly conduct and it was later found that they had in their possession two cases of beer; beer that was stolen from the Officers' Club early last night. Also stolen were two volumes of philosophy with 'Property of Station Library Reference Section

- Not To Be Checked Out' stamped on each of them three times! Not to mention a great number of crimes for which we have no solution."

The colonel wondered why the admiral had to use such poor taste, chewing him out in front of his own junior officers this way. In the military, after all, the CO of an outfit has to maintain his respect. Oh well, that's the Navy for you!

"I have no idea why all this happened, sir. I have no ideas on the subject whatsoever." He walked over to the conference room window and looked out at the shady lane. A base taxi was slowly driving in the direction of the docks. There was a man from his outfit inside, Private Jack Robles, heading back for the States. The colonel felt a great thankfulness to see Robles going. It meant at least one man in his outfit had managed to stay out of trouble amidst all the madness. It was too bad he was losing Robles. But still, somehow, it was good to see him leave.

When the colonel got back from the conference he found a typewritten note on his desk. It read:

FAREWELL SONG

Farewell my friends that stand ashore;
your company has been a bore.
But while I'm gone do nothing strange;
with firm resolve avoid all change.
Just keep on thinking I'm a nut;
and don't desert your little rut.
Let no wild dreams obstruct your way;
and work eight hours every day.
When I return, I hope to find;
that each of you has lost his mind.

"Now who could have written that?" muttered the colonel as he made a mental note to send a word of warning to the CO of Private Jack Robles' next duty station.

Chapter 20

Soledad

"Shave, please." Mike relaxed

The barber's wife watered down the walk with a wooden pail while she chatted with Ramon Francisco, the cop.

As the barber spread warm lather on Mike's face, a rooster crowed on the next block. Mike shut his eyes to listen to all Manila awaken. There was the horn of a distant jeepney. There was the clop and rattle of a horse and buggy. A door slammed. A baby cried somewhere and somebody was singing "Summer Love."

He listened to the melody drift and glide. The singing grew louder. It was a woman's voice and it was good. Gradually he realized the songstress was nearing the barber shop. Soon her voice filled the room. He opened his eyes to see a short, stout woman. She smiled at him and her face was full and round.

"You are Spanish?"

"American," Mike said.

"You look just only Spanish," she insisted.

"My father is Spanish. Where did you learn to sing so beautifully?"

"I don't know." She blushed then struck back. "You are too young to shave. No?"

"No. His beard is heavy," the barber interjected for him.

"I bet you are just only nineteen."

"Twenty-five," Mike corrected. "Please sing again."

She began "Unchained Melody." She was a heavy woman with a kind face. It's softness and darkness vouched for her Maylayan ancestry. Her eyebrows were pointed, catlike, and betrayed a hint of the Spanish. Mike guessed she was about his age.

Her voice settled him in deep sleep. There was only her voice and the gentle touch of the razor. It was good to sleep; all night he'd been walking the streets of Manila.

He walked by the art exhibit across from the Manila Hotel. He walked along the New Luneta, by the bay; mosquitoes buzzed around his head. He walked along Dewey Boulevard admiring the plush night-clubs. A taxi driver-pimp pulled up and gave his pitch and Mike pleaded poverty. An American with no money? The driver was dumbfounded as he drove away.

Mike Cervata had a philosophy about money. In his pocket, and no larger than a cigarette case, was a Japanese camera worth eighty pesos on the black market. He could live many days on eighty pesos and then he'd find something new to promote. Whenever Mike needed money he became rich. It was all a matter of promotion. But if one could promote the things money could buy, Mike felt, why bother to promote money? He would wait until he was hungry before selling his camera; a free meal might turn up.

He walked through Ermita and Intramuros to the sector called Quiapo. There was still some change in his pocket, so he went to a nice little restaurant, The Light in Shanghi, and ordered coffee. It was two a.m. - his feet needed a rest.

Quiapo was his favorite part of Manila. It is the center of town, if Manila can be said to have a center, and it's cluttered with movies and stores and a big stone church.

In Quiapo you can sit in an open restaurant at almost any hour other than two a.m. and watch multitudes of interesting people go by. Aside from merchant seamen, picturesque old Spaniards, smooth China-men, and an occasional Hindu or Moslem - emphasis was on the female sex of the college age group. That there are well over a dozen universities in Manila helps explain this happy circumstance.

He drank his coffee slowly. His feet were indeed tired. He wondered where he'd end up selling his camera.

"Wake up!"

Mike's eyes opened and focused. Ah yes! The barber shop.

"You ask me to sing and you just only go to sleep. Wake up!" Her voice was too loud.

"I'm sorry. All last night I was awake, and your voice was so soft and so beautiful..."

"Waste your words of seduction on the American girls! We Filapinas are not such easy women as that." Her nostrils flared.

The barber laughed.

"Be silent, Carlos. It is not for laughing."

Carlos laughed harder.

"Carlos," Mike said, "women are all alike."

"Opo" Carlos replied in Tagalog. "Yes, I think maybe so. But Filapinas, they do not stay angry long."

"No," said the woman, "in ten minutes we forget - or kill!"

"I hope the smile means you have forgiven. It would be wrong to kill a perfect stranger, even a Yankee stranger. Permit me to introduce myself. I am Mike Cervata."

"I am Soledad Garcia and I forgive you."

"Seems you are well prepared not to forgive, also." He glanced at the knife tucked behind the waist of her skirt.

"I keep this just only for the next time I see my husband."

"You know, Carlos, such wives as these made a man like me swear to remain single."

"The shave is finished!" Carlos eyed his work with pride. "Sixty centavos."

"Sixty centavos exactly. Had I but one centavo more, I would present it as a tip."

"You have no more money? An American without money?"

"It's okay. I am often without money."

"How will you eat?"

"If worse comes to worse, I will go to the jungles in the country and eat papayas and mangos."

Soledad blinked. "I have never seen anyone like you before, Miguel."

"Perhaps that is no compliment," said Mike.

"Oh no, Miguel, it is a very great compliment. You do not like to be called just only Miguel. I am sorry."

"Miguel is fine. It is the real name my parents gave me." Mike looked in the mirror. "It is a good shave, Carlos. I'll come again tomorrow when I have more money."

"And where will you get more money if you are poor?" Soledad demanded.

"I am not poor. We Americans are never poor when we are out of money, just broke."

"What is the difference?"

"None." Mike stepped onto the walk. The barber's wife was still talking with the cop, Ramon Francisco. "Excuse me, please. I wonder if I may speak to you, sir, for a moment?"

"Sure."

"Perhaps you can tell me, Officer, where one can sell a small camera, illegally, for a high price?"

The cop had a large, rectangular face with a thick mustache and a bold jaw. He smiled coldly. Mike read his face: The audacity of the Yankee! Asking a cop for a black-market lead, he is either very brave or very familiar with Manila. "Well, it is possible that Maria Castillo will purchase your camera."

"I? My camera? Surely, Officer I would not do such an unlawful thing as sell a camera on the black market. Not without bribing the law with about five pesos of my evil gains."

"The law will not be so cheap as that. Perhaps ten...?"

"Ten it will be."

"I hope, then, I have the pleasure of seeing you soon."

"Tomorrow morning I will return here to spend on a shave, sixty centavos of a certain inheritance I expect to receive."

"Until tomorrow." Ramon tipped his hat and returned to his unending search for graft, corruption and crime.

"Soledad, perhaps you will be kind enough to help me," Mike said, stepping back into the shop.

"I am at your service."

"I wish to find the friend of a friend, Maria Castillo."

"Come, I will take you there. How long have you been here?"

"Two weeks." Mike replied.

"Just only two weeks and already you know too much!"

Mike threw his head back and laughed.

"Oh, Miguel, everyone is looking at us! They think I am a bad woman to be walking with an American. Look!"

Mike saw eyes turning away. He heard women giggling and whispering. No respectable woman walks with a Yankee in Manila.

"Oh God! All the world looks and makes fun."

"Maybe you better walk a block or two ahead."

"No! I do not care what they think."

"Okay. You're the boss."

A taxi driver smiled and winked; an urchin stuck out his tongue.

It was in a house near the Paco Cemetery that Soledad introduced him to Maria Castillo, a young Filipina with a trim figure and saucer-like eyes.

She looked at the camera. "How much do you want for it?"

"It is a precision instrument and very valuable. One hundred pesos."

"It is Japanese; therefore I will give you only sixty. We do not like the Japanese here."

"Perhaps the Japanese were not very nice to you in the war, but the war is over and they make good cameras. I must have ninety-five pesos or I will keep the camera."

"Seventy-five."

"Sold."

The bargain sealed, Mike put the money in his wallet. He and Soledad left the house. "I'm starved, Soly; let's go have breakfast."

"Come with me. I am known well at a certain restaurant. The meat is cooked well and the papaya is fresh. It is just one block from here."

At Soledad's favorite restaurant they had ham, rice omelets, papaya and juice. The full heat of the morning began to fill the air. A large, black electric fan turned lazily in one corner of the room.

"What are you thinking about, Soly? You are so quiet."

"I was just only remembering something. My friend, Juan Peralta, is in the PG."

"In the what?"

"The Philippine General, the hospital. I promised my other friend, Dimas, the son of Carlos the barber, I promised to Dimas I will meet him this morning and we will go visit our friend, Juan Peralta. I was thinking perhaps you would like to come with us. Yes?"

"Sure. Why is your friend in the hospital?"

"He got cut in a knife fight last week. It happens that there are too many fights in Paco. It is a sinful place, and dangerous."

"All the world is a sinful place, Soly, and dangerous."

"You have been to all the world?"

"No, but I have been to enough places to know."

"Do you always just only go alone?"

"Never." Mike replied.

"You are very strange. But I like you and I hope you will be my friend."

"Forever!" Mike exclaimed.

"Armando!" Soledad drew her knife.

Mike turned to see a tall, thin Filipino in a white suit run from the restaurant. "Who was that?"

"That was Armando Garcia, my husband. He was starting to come in here and I saw him. Before, I tell him that the next time I see him I will kill him."

"Why?"

"Because he is no good. He is just always running around with other women."

"Is that what happened to Juan Peralta, he fought with his wife?"

"No, silly. Juan, he fights with a punk who insulted me. Juan, Dimas, and I are very close. One sticks up for the other."

"I see."

"It is time for us to go back to the place of Carlos the barber. Dimas will be waiting."

Mike paid the bill while Soledad hailed a jeepney, a cross between a jeep and a jitney.

At the place of Carlos the barber Dimas was waiting. Mike noticed that he was of average height but his black hair, piled over his head and combed in a duck tail, made him appear some inches taller. His head was constantly bowed in examination of his shiny shoes, but his hair stayed in place. Mike thought that he must use glue or something.

"Miguel, this is Dimas, the son of Carlos the barber."

"Hello, Dimas."

Dimas looked up from his shoes to smile and shake hands.

"Now we must get a taxi to the hospital."

They stood on the curb waiting for a cab to pass.

"Here is one," said Dimas. He stepped into the street and waved. The taxi dashed right on by. "Many taxi drivers are afraid to stop in Paco."

"Here, let me flag this next one. Perhaps he will not fear an American." The next cab stopped. As they climbed in, Dimas told Mike that Paco was a very sinful place.

"Yes, I know - and dangerous."

Mike began to understand just how dangerous Paco could be when he met Juan Peralta who was being kept alive by a small motor and a system of tubes and bottles. Juan's breathing was hard, so he was not able to say more than a few words at a time. He was reading a Tagalog comic book.

One by one, Soledad pointed out, for Mike's benefit, each of Juan's seven wounds, one of which started at the collar bone and ran across the chest and around to the middle of the back. As Soly pointed to the slash that severed the tendon in Juan's right leg, Mike noticed a tattoo of a crucifix with three ribbons intertwined around it. Lettered upon the ribbons were the names Juan, Dimas and Soledad.

The little motor sounded like a sewing machine. Mike thought of hearing that sound all through the day and night and of knowing that your life depended on it.

Soledad went out of the room long enough to purchase two cigarettes somewhere. When she came back, Juan Peralta was asleep. She folded his comic book and slid it under his pillow. Quietly they left the room. As they walked away, the noise of the tiny motor got progressively fainter.

"Well," Mike said, looking at the late afternoon sky, "I was up all night and it's time I got some sleep. Could I meet you people in Paco tonight?"

"All right, Miguel." Soledad grinned. Her round face expressed mischief. "I think maybe you don't feel so good after the hospital. No?"

"No, I feel fine. You will permit me to be excused," he said with grave courtesy.

"Yes. What time will we see you?" asked Dimas.

"About eight, okay?"

"Fine. Keep out of trouble," Soly said.

Mike hailed a jeepney for the New Luneta.

Upon arriving at the Rizal Monument, he jumped out and walked over to his favorite tree in the park. He stretched out under a low branch and went to sleep.

A cool breeze woke him up that evening. He rolled over and stumbled to his feet. He yawned, rubbed his eyes, and headed for the Manila Hotel. He entered the hotel grounds through the USO entrance.

"Hi Mike" said the clerk, a little man with a grin which comprised many small teeth and a wrinkled nose.

"Hi Dino. I'd like to get at my suitcase for a minute."

"Sure deal." Filipinos have varying degrees of accents in English; Dino had none at all, and prided his mastery of Yankee slang. "Big doin's here tonight. Bunch of Ausies up on that SEATO maneuver. Going to have a big dance; should be some nice dames around."

Mike recognized the invitation. "Not tonight, Dino. I promised to meet some friends over in Paco."

"That Paco is a good place to stay away from." He handed Mike the suitcase. "Rough neighborhood."

"I know. It's sinful and dangerous!" He took a pair of trousers, a pair of socks, a shirt, a towel and shaving kit from the suitcase. "I'll be back in a minute."

"Sure enough, kid."

He went around behind the USO area and into the main hotel. He walked down the hall to the men's room. Standing at the basin he stripped down, washed and dried himself and then dressed in his fresh clothes. After brushing his teeth and combing his hair, be bundled up the dirty clothes and returned to the USO lounge.

"So you're having over a bunch of the boys from Down Under?" He put the dirty clothes in a laundry bag and put the bag and suitcase, along with the shaving kit and towel, back in Dino's custody.

"Yeah. Sure you can't make it? Free food and all that."

"Well, we'll see."

"Take it easy, man." Dino's nose wrinkled and he exposed his small white teeth.

"Sure will." Mike whistled "Waltzing Matilda" as he strolled out of the gate. "Psssst. Jeepney! You go to Quiapo? Good."

In keeping with his routine for Manila, he had dinner at the Light in Shanghi. The street was crowded now and he enjoyed the slow-pitching mob.

"Hey, Joe. You give me ten centavos. Okay?" It was a dirty little rascal about eight years old.

"Get out of here!" shouted a waitress.

The boy backed toward the street. Mike flipped him a ten centavo dime. He caught it and ran.

"You should not give them anything," she scolded Mike, "or ten thousand of them will just only keep coming here."

"Sorry ma'm." he wondered what word, phrase, or grammatical feature of Tagalog is translated as "just only". "I'll have a chicken dinner."

"Anything to drink?"

"Yes. Bring me a San Miguel."

When she returned: "What time is it, ma'm?"

"Seven fifteen."

"Salamat," he thanked her.

The chicken was especially good because Mike had forgotten to eat lunch that day. He topped the dinner with half of a papaya and another San Miguel. By eight he was in Paco.

He was surprised to find the place of Carlos the barber closed. "Wonder what's up?" There was a crowd of rough characters about a block away. They were silent; every one of them was looking toward Mike. Mike decided to sit on the curb and wait for Soly and Dimas to show up. The crowd started coming toward him. "Well, old boy, what are you getting into now?" He decided to stay calm and ignore them.

"Hey, Joe."

He looked up as the crowd gathered around him. He stood up. "Something I can do for you gentlemen?"

A spokesman stepped forward. His face was grave. "My name is Fred."

"How do you do? My name is Mike."

"You are the American."

"Yes." Mike said.

"The one who has been seeing Soledad Garcia?"

"Yes." Mike repeated.

"Please forgive me," said the spokesman, "and please understand that I do not wish to be rude. I say this for your safety and for the benefit of all. Get out of Paco!"

Mike guessed there were about forty of them, all punks with glum expressions and too much hair. He was not about to start arguing.

Fred continued, "I am sorry to say we had some trouble here. Had you just only arrived a moment sooner you would be dead now."

"What kind of trouble?"

"A shooting. Now please leave."

"Just one question: Who—"

"Did Soly introduce you to Juan Peralta?"

"Yes." Mike said.

"You are just now looking at the knife used on Juan Peralta." He held a blade in front of Mike's nose. "Go!"

"Psssst. Jeepney!"

The jeepney went up Dart Street and then up Gral Luna toward United Nations Park. Mike got off at the Paco Cemetery. He knocked on Maria Castillo's door. "Yes, who is it?"

"Mike Cervata, the one who sold you the camera. May I speak with you?"

She opened the door.

"There was a shooting at Carlos the barber's place. I believe Soly was involved. Do you know anything about it?"

"Oh my God!"

"What's wrong?"

"Armando Garcia, him and Soly had a fight. No?"

"Yes. Why?"

"Today, just only after you and Soly leave, he comes here." She started sobbing.

"Well, what of it?" Mike felt his body tense.

"I sell him a gun!" She fell to her knees, crossed herself and began praying.

Mike turned and walked back to the street. He looked at the dark cemetery and felt a chill in the hot, still air.

The rooster, one block away, crowed loudly; there was the horn of a distant jeepney and the sound of a horse and buggy; a door slammed; a baby cried; somebody's radio sang. The tune was "Summer Love".

The place of Carlos the barber was still closed. Mike sat in the gutter; the morning sun shined in his face. He heard footsteps and looked up to see Ramon Francisco, the cop.

"Hello."

"Hello, Ramon. I believe I owe you some money. Here."

"Thank you. If ever again you wish the aid of the law, I am at your service."

"Where is Carlos the barber today?"

"This morning everyone is at the hospital. You did not hear about the shooting last night?"

"Yes." His eyes dropped. "I guess it was partly my fault."

"I do not think so. How were you to know that Armando Garcia would become jealous and try to kill you?"

"Kill me?"

"Yes."

"He did not shoot Soledad?"

"No. Why do you ask a question like that?"

"Pardon me, Ramon, perhaps I'm confused. I understand there was a shooting last night, right?"

"Yes."

"When I got here last night, the shooting was over. Now who got shot?"

"Nobody got shot."

"But everyone says there was a shooting. Maria Castillo sells a gun to Armando. Today Carlos, or somebody, is in the hospital. What happened?"

"Carlos the barber, the wife of Carlos the barber, the son of Carlos, Soledad Garcia, and Maria Castillo are all in the hospital."

"Christ! What happened?"

"Nothing. They go just only to visit Armando Garcia."

"Armando? I thought he did the shooting."

"That is right."

"So what happened to Armando Garcia to make him end up in the hospital?"

"He shoots at Carlos the barber."

"I don't think I understand."

"It is very simple. Armando Garcia prepares to kill you, the Americano, because he sees you and Soly together in a restaurant. He then thinks you are the lover of his wife."

"I see."

"So do you know how he prepares to kill you?"

"He buys a gun from Maria Castillo."

"Right. And do you know what else he does?"

"What else?"

"He comes here to the place of Carlos the barber and says, 'Where is Solodad?' Carlos tells him, 'At the Philippine General Hospital.' Armando then learns that Soly, Dimas, and you, the Americano, are expected to return to the place of Carlos soon. So what does he do?"

"What?"

"He takes out the gun and says, 'Reach for the sky!'"

"Armando has been watching American movies."

"Carlos and his wife, they reach. Then he hears the voice of Soledad Garcia singing 'Summer Love'. He steps out to the street and prepares to fire the gun at you."

"So what does he do when I am not there?"

"Nothing, because Carlos, who thinks maybe Armando plans to shoot his son, Dimas, runs out to the street and yells. Armando turns to shoot at Carlos, but he misses. And do you know just only why he misses?"

"Just only why?"

"Because he is hit over the head with a bucket by Carlos' wife."

"The wooden bucket?"

"Yes. And then, just in time, I arrive."

"In time for what?"

"For to bandage up the head of Armando Garcia."

"I see. And is that all of the story?"

"All except the happy ending. Soledad, the wife of Armando, forgives Armando for running around with other women because she is happy to learn that Armando is jealous because of you, and the wife of Carlos the barber forgives Armando for shooting at her husband, Carlos the barber, because she is happy to learn she broke open the head of Armando Garcia, the husband of Soledad, the friend of Dimas, the son of—"

"Never mind, Ramon. I think I've got a rough idea of the whole mess now. Don't confuse me again. One more thing?"

"What is that?"

"Well, last night when I came here there was a big crowd. The leader was a character named Fred."

"Oh yes! The Citizen's Committee!"

"The what?"

"Yesterday after the shooting everyone gets together and decides Paco is becoming a very sinful place and—"

"And dangerous."

"Yes. How did you know?"

"Never mind. Please go on."

"Well, the people of Paco decide what is just only needed is a Paco Citizen's Committee to clean up the vice and corruption."

"And they elected that punk named Fred to lead it?"

"No. Fred is just only vice-chairman. They elected Armando Garcia to head the Citizen's Committee."

"Armando? Now wait a minute."

"What is wrong? Armando is the only one in Paco who nobody is angry with. They have all forgiven him. The Citizen's Committee is now having the first meeting. That is why everyone is just only at the hospital. Where are you going?"

"I don't know. I just want to get out of Paco before the Citizen's Committee goes into action!"

Chapter 21

The Dragon

At dock in Kaosiung, Taiwan, he stood along a spar and peered with narrow eyes out over house tops. There, beyond a warehouse, a sharp and spine-backed-designed roof looked like dragon wings. It reminded him of tales he heard in childhood, and those forgotten till that day, about the mainland - lost since then. Beyond that, all the other roofs were grey and neatly laid in rows and interspersed with trees.

So this is what it all becomes at last, he thought, and thought, not knowing exactly what obscured concept the words contained.

A Chinese worker was shouting, urging a beast of burden along the nearby street.

"I wonder," a voice behind him joked, "about what the local IQ is here."

Corporal Shellburn turned to face the man and spoke: "It's probably pretty low, perhaps not much higher than yours."

Shellburn walked on down the deck, clenching and unclenching his fists. Certainly these men know better than that, he thought. Why do they pretend they think that all foreigners are stupid?

Two days ago, aboard ship, they'd received an orientation lecture on Taiwan. They'd been told that the people would be filthy, venereal disease ridden and dishonest. "Tell it to the Marines," Johnny muttered afterwards.

The whistle sounded; the troops went below to start unloading the ship.

Johnny Shellburn stood along the railing watching the sun's final light. Nervous for some unknown reason, chewing on a cigar, he walked around to the port side.

The dock hummed. Chinese laborers argued loudly. Marines loaded trucks up with tents and boxes, provisions for the maneuvers.

Johnny wandered. On the stern, wooden boxes stacked neatly stood filled with garbage. Six other men loitered there - Marines, men from his unit. Under them in the bay was a boat manned by an old Chinaman. The old man was grey, bent and bearded. His job was taking garbage boxes from the vessels. The Marines lowered the first crate down on ropes.

The old man bent down now to unloosen knots in the ropes.

Johnny watched them lift the next crate to the rail; he realized what was going to happen too late. Purposely, they let the box fall. It landed right on the old man's back; his pained groan was drowned out by the laughter of the six Marines. For a moment Johnny wondered what to do. He decided to bite into his cigar and swear; after that he went below deck. He walked along the corridor until he found Willy Cecil sitting under a ladder shining his shoes.

"Hi, Johnny."

"Goddamned idiotic bastards! The Corp is full of 'em!"

"You sound pissed at the world. What's up?"

"Oh, the usual thing. I just watched six of my fellow Americans convert another Nationalist Chink to Communism. Walters, Brown, Hoolahan and some other jerks dropped a garbage box on some old man and then laughed their fucking asses off about it."

"Shellburn, you're gonna blow a gasket worrying about the poor Japs, Flips and Chinks one of these days."

"Hell, I'm worried about the Americans. Those same six idiots are going back to the States one of these days, getting married and settling down to each raise three more idiots. What kinds of sadist bastards are the rest of these clean-cut slobs in our country? Give any six of them the chance and they'd do the same thing."

"Give any six Chinks the chance and they'd do it to an American."

"Never mind, Willy. you missed the point. Shine your fucking shoes and forget about it. I don't have to live with the Chinks." Johnny walked on down the corridor wondering what he should have done. Would it have done any good to talk to them? Nonsense. Should he put them on report? He was no rat. What could a man do? All a man can do is take a good, long look at life and decide to get mad.

"NOW HEAR THIS. NOW HEAR THIS," came a voice. "COR- PORAL SHELLBURN, REPORT TO THE TROOP OFFICE."

"Jesus Christ, what now?" He stormed toward the Troop Office at the other end of the ship.

"Lance Corporal Shellburn reporting as ordered, sir."

"Take this six-man detail down to the docks," said the captain, "and get that first row of loaded trucks dispatched for Pingtung."

"Yes, sir." And wouldn't you know who the six studs would be! "Come on Walters, Brown, Hoolahan, the rest of you, let's get this job over with."

Johnny found the worst jobs he could for the six men and then found a comfortable place to sit and take down the numbers of the trucks as, one by one, they rolled out for the Nationalist Air Base at Pingtung.

The publicity people had this maneuver plugged as a giant, team-work effort of the U.S. Marines and the Chinese Air Force, but Johnny figured it differently - it would be another masterpiece of ill feeling between the misfits of America and the hired henchmen of Taiwan's hen-pecked little dictator. I'll end up joining the goddamned Russians one of these days, he thought. The idea had lost its horror for him some time ago. Fortunately, or perhaps unfortunately, it'd also lost it's attraction. People are bastards, he thought. Why takes sides?

The last truck rolled out at midnight and they returned to the ship to spend a last night on board before joining the rest of the slobs in setting up camp at Pingtung.

The next morning, Shellburn and his six friends were piled on the first truck. It rolled down the dock and onto the streets of Kaosiung. Little Chinese kids stood on the corners to cheer for the American he-roes, shouting "Okay" and "Ding How" and giving them the thumbs up sign of the Flying Tigers. The unholy six got a big charge out of return-ing the greeting and then, in unison, turning their thumbs down. The mouths of the little kids would fall open in astonished disappointment.

Near the fighter strip at Pingtung, where the eager Chink pilots tore off to patrol the boundary between Formosa and the Red Empire, the Marine Aircraft Group made a dusty camp. The area became a city of tents with outdoor showers and latrines in open view of the women who toiled in the paddies bordering the base. As if the private lives of several hundred uniformed barbarians was not reason enough to tempt the respect of the Taiwanese peasants, a unit of Marine Pathfinders was added to the operation. The Pathfinders is perhaps the proudest and finest group of fighting men in the entire Marine Corps, but put those paratrooping raiders within fifty miles of Shellburn's MAG - the one unit in the Corps with an exaggerated sense of humor - and the occasional dogfighting over the Formosa Straits begins to look like a Chinese lovers' quarrel.

The first trouble occurred on the second day. The Pathfinders were out at five in the morning, running through the camp and counting cadence.

"HUP - TWO - THREE - FOUR. HUP - TWO - THREE - FOUR. FASTER!" Keeping in perfect formation, they ran down the dark passage between two rows of tents.

"HUP - TWO - THREE - FOUR. HUP - TWO - WHAT THE HELL!"

All at once the proud Pathfinders were a great ball of confused humanity. Half of them were rolling in the dirt swearing and the others were stumbling through a bewildering forest of bodies, arms and legs. After five minutes of soul-searching profanity, they found the cause of their trouble. Some MAG bastard strung a trip line across the way. It was a declaration of war!

Johnny wondered who was making all the noise so early in the morning. He yawned, rolled over and went back to sleep muttering half aloud about those goddamned, gung-ho Pathfinders. He slipped into a lovely dream: Walters, Brown, Hoolahan and company, together with the Pathfinders and about half the officers in the MAG, were marching into the sea. As they passed him, one by one, he wrote down their serial numbers. Suddenly he, too, was struggling in the water. The water was warm and smelled like canvas. He tried to swim but he was tangled in his mosquito net. Somebody was yelling, "Who pulled down the fucking tent?" He woke up. Sonofabitch!

He crawled out from under the fallen canvas. Every tent in the area had been pulled down. Why those goddamned crunchy bastards! This, he thought, is a goddamned declaration of war!

He helped get the tent back up, got dressed, swore at the world and headed for morning chow. He ran into Willy Cecil on the way.

"How're you on this fine morning, Johnny?"

"Shit."

"Man, you sure are cheerful lately."

"Fuck you."

"Aw, don't talk naughty."

"That's the only way a man can talk and tell the truth at the same time." Johnny clamped down on a cigar. He had stopped smoking cigarettes because he'd gotten into the habit of chewing off the filters.

"They're gonna open up an Enlisted Club over in those bamboo huts."

"I bet I'm the first one to get drunk in it. When does it open?"

"Tonight. The Chinks are going to put on some kind of a variety show for us first."

"Christ!" Johnny spit. "Why can't the Chinks and the Pathfinders and the MAG and Walters, Brown, and Hoolahan and the Reds and the Americans and the Japs and the Flips and Mike Cervata and me all leave each other alone for awhile? I get so bastardly tired of getting fucked with all the time, and of being expected to fuck with everyone else."

"Don't make such a big issue outta stuff. Can't you just calm down and go along with the program?" Willy sincerely didn't understand.

Johnny wished Stick Wickers or Jack Robles were still around. It was so damned silly to try to talk with somebody and just get a blank stare in return. Christ! He promised himself that when he got out he was gonna start a derecruiting campaign. I'm going to put a poster on every wall in America that says, CIVILIAN LIFE BUILDS MEN! But he knew, even as he thought it, that the civilians were just as screwed up as the military. An idea came to him.

"Willy, I hear you can buy a slave girl on this island for seventy-five dollars - lock, stock and barrel."

"Yeah, I've heard that."

"When I get my discharge, I'm coming back here, buying myself a harem, going to the Philippines, buying an island all to myself, and having a big orgy for the rest of my life. To hell with the human race!"

"Mind if I come along?"

"Sure," Johnny said through his teeth, "the more the merrier."

Willy wondered dimly why Johnny was laughing. Oh well, Shellburn was a little nuts. Everybody knew that.

The chow was usually bad. Even when it wasn't, everybody griped about it anyway. But, on that second morning in Taiwan, it hit an all-time low: bread, toast, shit-on-the-shingle, and French toast. The only thing to drink was water and they were stingy with that. Why is it, Johnny wondered, that the chow is always bad when I'm in a foul mood? Then the answer came: the chow was always bad and he was always in a foul mood. He felt secure suddenly - there were two things in the world he could depend on. He wondered if his stomach was being eaten up by bad chow and hate juices. They bolted chow and went to muster.

After muster they were kept in formation. The Sergeant Major wanted to say a few words and he looked madder than Johnny felt. Somebody must have pulled his tent down, too.

"Listen up. You people seem to be under a misunderstanding as to our mission on this operation. We are here to play like we're fighting a war with the Chinese Communists, not each other and the local Chinks."

The Sergeant Major could be a clever bastard at times. "I don't know how this childishness got started between this outfit and the Path-finders, but it had better cease or you people will not get liberty the whole time you're down here. As for the present, the opening of the Enlisted Club will be postponed until you men start acting a little more like United States Marines.

"Tonight, the Nationalist Chinese USO, or some damned thing, is putting on a variety show for our benefit. If you people conduct your-selves properly, you'll get liberty starting tomorrow night. If not, you'll rot on this base until you're all so horny you'll be looking for stray cows to screw."

"Section leaders, dismiss your sections."

"Shellburn," said Johnny's section leader, "take Brown and Hoolahan with you and go put the Sergeant Major's tent back up and then report to your respective working areas."

"Aye aye, sir."

He made Hoolahan hold the tent stakes as he drove them in. After missing with one stoke and hitting Hoolahan's hand, he felt better about everything. In order to be completely impartial he later dropped the hammer on Brown's toe. After the tent was up, he dismissed them and headed across the field for the Administration tent.

It was a hot, dirty morning. The distant mountains were smeared by the high, dust-filled winds. Johnny stooped at the water tank and wiped his face with wet hands. The water dried quickly and the sun was hot on the back of his neck. He turned in the tent entrance and walked over to his field desk. Bob Kidd was sitting there picking his teeth with a broken pencil.

"What can I do for you, Chaplain?"

"I'm supposed to have a new Page Seven made up. Somebody lost my Record Book."

"I'm glad you dropped in, Bob. You in a hurry?"

"Nope. Say, when did they make you into a Basic Training Clerk?"

"Oh, ever since I won that speech contest the goddamned Exec thinks I'm a boy genius for Basic Training or something." Johnny sat on a crate with his head against the Mail Orderly's desk. "I've got a problem to talk to the Atheist Chaplain about."

"The Atheist Chaplain's all ears."

"Well, it's not so much a personal problem or anything. It's just this damned losing routine, Bob. It's getting me down."

"I'm afraid that's an evil that comes in the same package with the rest of the military."

"Shit. I wish to hell I could be sure it's just the military, but I think it's the whole fucking world."

"Well, with the population explosion and all..."

"Skip the puns, please. I figure this way, Bob: either I'm fucked up or the rest of the human race is."

"Whose side are you on?"

"I wish I knew."

"Well, the trouble with you is you're a romanticist. You don't like to see things as they really are. Naturally, life keeps jumping up and slapping you in the face. One of these days it'll knock you right over."

"So what do I do about it?"

"Side with reality. Decide to like everything."

"In other words, give up and go along with the program."

"Fall in love with truth."

"There're two ways to say everything."

"At least."

"Well, thank you, Chaplain, but how do you go about getting with the program?"

"You can start by typing up my Page Seven. You'll have to go from there yourself."

Kidd got out of his chair and Johnny sat down, blew the dust off the typewriter and got to work. After he finished, he handed the sheet to Kidd.

"Well, so far, what do you think of reality, Corporal Shellburn?"

"It tastes like shit."

Kidd laughed and strolled out into the rising wind.

Johnny pulled a paperback book out of his hip pocket, put his feet up on the field desk and opened it to the title page - *The Count of Monte Cristo*.

Just before noon chow the Training NCO, Staff Sergeant Ulman, came in and jumped all over Johnny for reading during working hours. "And why aren't the tent flaps rolled up?"

"It's too windy out, Sarg. Say, I've been wanting to talk to you about something. The people in the S-1 office need another typewriter, and they said they'd take care of all the typing for the Basic Training if we'd let them have ours. How about it?"

Ulman's beady green eyes glanced from Shellburn to the typewriter and back again. "Sorry. I went to a lot of trouble to get us a typewriter and we're hanging on to it."

"But Sarg, you know how lousy my typing is."

"We're keeping the typewriter; now roll up the tent flaps."

"Well fuck you!" Johnny said it mildly, in a conversational manner, light and cheerful; but the staff sergeant's beady eyes got round and mad; he thought it was Shellburn's reply to his order.

"Look, goddamn you, don't get salty with me! Roll up those tent flaps!"

Johnny leaned against the pole in the center of the tent. "You gonna push it?" He'd always rather argue than explain.

"NOW GODDAMN IT..." He was yelling at the top of his lungs; Johnny listened quietly for several minutes.

"You through yet?"

"You want me to have you put in the brig?"

"Go ahead, I don't mind. There's not a goddamned thing this Corps can do to me any more. I just don't give a shit."

The sergeant blinked his green eyes rapidly. He was dumbfounded. Finally, he stormed out of the tent flexing his jaw muscles in silent anger.

Johnny sat back down at his desk and thought of how he'd someday bring vengeance on the sergeant and his loved ones. Well, it was time for noon chow. He picked up his mess gear and headed for the chow hall.

"How was chow, Johnny?"

"You have to ask?"

Henry Hamilton flashed his toothy grin. Henry was squadron Mail Orderly, and he sat there now sorting the incoming afternoon mail.

"Henry, mind if I ask you something real personal?"

"Fire away."

"Well, being colored and all, I imagine you run into a lot of shit?"

"Once in awhile."

"How do you keep from getting so pissed off that you want to mow everybody down with a machine gun? Man, I got no problems. I'm white. I'm a Lance Corporal with a clean record. The Executive Officer thinks I'm a fair-haired lad. I've got an easy job with a department head who's a little bit afraid of me. I enjoy reading and I've got plenty of time on my hands. Yet so help me, Henry, I could kill every stinking bastard in the world right now."

"I'll tell you. it probably won't do any good, but I'll tell you. Least-wise it won't hurt. I believe in Divine Justice. I believe every human act contains its own reward or punishment. So every time I see some idiot do something I don't like, I know that he'll get his for that."

"So when you see a man get away with murder, you feel sorry for him."

"No. I don't feel sorry and I don't envy. I just feel content. Whatsoever a man soweth that shall he also reap."

"What about the unthinking slob who goes through life stepping on other people's toes? What happens to him? He gets away with it."

"Who gets away with it? The Mr. X of your example? Or Sergeant Phillips of real life? Who? The typical con man everybody talks about? Or Mike Cervata? Who? Three gangsters in somebody's book? Or Walters, Brown and Hoolahan? If it seems like a man gets away with something, look again. He doesn't."

"But I can't wait for The Judgement Day."

"I'm not asking you to wait. Reward and punishment comes in this life, swiftly, almost together with the deed."

"You don't convince me." Johnny leaned back. Why did Hamilton have to be so blasted religious? His ideas were good, but he could never produce a rational argument to defend them. Johnny wanted, profoundly, to believe in Divine Justice - but he couldn't. He clamped a fresh cigar between his teeth. He lit it and walked over to the tent entrance.

The winds were strong now. They were sweeping in many directions. A dusty, whirling puff came spinning into the S-1 tent across the way. Johnny laughed as clerks scrambled after important papers caught up in the air. Some of the sheets soared up and up, in wide circles, until they vanished into the hazy heavens. Johnny laughed again; it was good to see somebody else with problems.

Staff Sergeant Ulman walked up to him. "Shellburn, Bob Kidd's Page Seven blew away. Type up another one."

After typing up the new Page Seven, he spent the rest of the afternoon typing letters to his friends just to keep busy.

The winds died down at nightfall, moving slowly away toward the mountains. Johnny stood watching a great, twisting column of dust roll off in the distance. It reminded him of a dragon's body.

"Hey, Johnny." It was Killer Willy Cecil coming back from the shower in his usual Lincolnesque strides. "I know where we can get some plum wine. Interested?"

"Interested? Hell yes!"

"Wait till I drop this gear off at my tent."

They walked from Willy's tent over to a patch of trees several yards from the camp. Willy whistled and a little Chinaman came out and handed them two bottles in exchange for some military scrip. They stuck the bottles in their utility jackets and headed back across the field. Back in the area, everyone was passing the word. "Muster."

"Christ. What now?"

"Probably for that variety show."

They milled into the mustering area and fell in formation. The Sergeant Major had a few words to say.

"Listen up. Now I warned you people this morning. I'm warning you again because I want to be sure it's perfectly clear. If there is any horsing around at that variety show tonight, no liberty for at least three days. That doesn't mean you can't cheer and clap; it means I don't want to hear any wise remarks or see anybody throwing anything. Is that clear to everybody?"

The Sergeant Major looked tired. He always looked tired, like some sleepy gangster played by Edward G. Robinson.

"If you act decent, I'll see what I can do about having the club opened up after the show is over. Just remember that we're guests in this country. Even if the whole island is a pile of shit, it's our job to be nice and put up with it. Does anyone have any questions about what I just said? Fine."

As the troops filed into the bamboo hut, Willy and Johnny ducked around the side and sat down against the outside wall in the shadows. They uncorked the bottles.

"Yeah, Willy, I think I'm gonna start going along with the program."

"This is a hell of a way to start."

"No. This is part of it." Johnny guzzled a long swallow. "It's not by refusing to fuck off that you go along with it, it's by fucking off only in the accepted ways. It's okay to browbeat the native population and cause another war, but it's evil to talk back to Staff Sergeant Ulman. It's okay to ditch a people-to-people variety show, but it's evil to say bad things about the Corps."

"Fuck the Corps."

"Yeah, fuck the Corps." Johnny took another drink.

"What made you decide to change?"

"Reality."

"What?"

"The great dragon of reality that rises up when you're thinking about One World, United and Democratic, and spits Pat Hoolahan in your face. Or a garbage crate on an old man's back." Johnny drank again. "You can't fight the dragon, Willy. It's every place at once, winding through all the world and spreading hate among men."

"Is that so?"

"Yes. Oh, don't be disillusioned, my boy. I didn't believe in the dragons once, but that was before I came to the East. The dragon is everywhere, but I didn't know that until I got here. I'd only gotten glimpses of it before. Lately I've been wrestling with it."

"Sometimes I wonder if even you know what you're talking about."

"Just between us, I have my doubts." He winked. He didn't really have any doubts about the great dragon of reality, but it made Willy feel better and also made him more cooperative when Johnny suggested they go over to the trees for some more plum wine. They came back this time with two bottles each.

Johnny uncorked the first one. "I wrote a letter to Jack Robles today. I told him I'd found it."

"Found what?"

"The great Universal Truth. You know, he commissioned me to continue the search when he left. He said, 'Johnny, it's around here somewhere. Keep looking for it and write me a letter when you find it.' Today, Killer, I wrote that letter. I said, 'Jack, I've found it; it's the smell of vomit on board ship when the sea is rough. It's the smell of a fart the guy in front of you lets out when you're at attention in formation. It's the cry of an old man when he's made the victim of a cruel joke. It's the sound of the Pathfinders counting cadence when you're trying to sleep. It's the voice of the Sergeant Major chewing you out. It's the feeling you get when a fly lands on your nose during chow. It's the steady drip when you come down with the clap. The Universal Truth, Jack, is the great dragon of reality.'"

"Fuck the dragon."

"Yeah, fuck the dragon."

They both drank.

Through the thin wall, they could hear a Chinese girl singing "Kiss

Me Another Kiss" in very poor English. The troops were clapping and whistling. "She must be pretty good looking. She sure as hell can't sing."

"If they have an intermission, Killer, let's go inside and see the last half. Some of these Chinese chicks are great."

The intermission came at the end of "Kiss Me Another Kiss". It was a lot of work killing the rest of the wine before time to go back in the hut, but they both managed.

The inside of the hut was like pictures Johnny had seen of the inside of a Red Chinese prison: hard floor, no chairs, and large bamboo pillars holding up the roof. He and Willy sat down next to Bob Kidd.

"I'm glad to see you, Bob. I decided to take your advice. From now on, I side with reality."

"Good."

The Chinese MC came out to announce the next act. "Your next entertainment will be a five cowboy act. Let's give them a big clap!"

Five Chinese cowboys came out and sang a Western song in Mandarin dialect. It was awful. The troops applauded. Afterwards, the girl who sang "Kiss Me Another Kiss," and she was beautiful, came out and sang "Kiss Me Another Kiss" again. It was the only American song she knew. As she turned to walk away from the mike, the troops applauded her nice rear end. She thought they were applauding the song, so she did it two more times.

Johnny abandoned himself to the spirit of the mob, clapping and whistling louder than anyone else.

The Chinese MC wanted to get on with the show, so he came up to the mike and said, "Thank you for the tremendous claps, but — "

Johnny stood up and shouted, "THAT'S OKAY, WE'LL BE THANKING YOU FOLKS IN A COUPLE OF WEEKS!"

The room got so silent he could hear Bob Kidd whispering, "That is not what I meant by siding with reality."

The troops looked at him coldly, but the coldest stare of all was the Sergeant Major's. It reminded Johnny of a dragon's face.

Chapter 22

Taiwan Tammy

The truck loaded with U.S. Marines in civilian clothes rolled out the main gate at Pingtung. Liberty at last! Johnny Shellburn felt a surge of long-repressed joy rise up within him.

A hell-for-leather Chinese pilot brought his jet fighter down from the orange night sky, buzzed the truck and skimmed the paddies for a recklessly perfect landing on the distant runway. They fly like crazymen, Johnny thought, the idle warriors of the sky - itching to shoot down a Red MIG.

"Boy!" Willy Cecil looked in the direction of the runway with open admiration. "You have to give it to those cats in the guts department!"

Suddenly Johnny liked lanky Willy and the unknown Chinese pilot more than any other two people on earth.

The truck rolled into the town of Pingtung, circled the statue of Chiang Kai-shek, and halted. The Marines roared cheerfully as they piled out to seek adventure in the night.

In the throng of pimps, barkers, and peddlers, Johnny and Willy discovered a petticab driver who led them through the circle flocking the truck to his bicycle-wheeled vehicle across the street. They hopped in to have a ride through the town with no particular destination.

"DING HOW!" shouted the kids who ran along beside them and stood on the street corners they passed.

"DING HOW!" Johnny hollered, returning the thumbs up sign of friendship. "Look at that little guy," Willy laughed. "Not a tooth in his head."

The little boy, who looked like an illustration out of *Mad Magazine*, grinned back at them.

Ding how, Johnny thought, Ding how. Okay. Fine. Number one. He looked down the intensely Chinese street with its twisted-cornered roofs, and the corners of his eyes wrinkled in pleasure. Ding how!

The petticab driver stopped because, no doubt, he was paid by the management to do so, at a bar called the Evergreen Club. They paid him his fare and went inside.

The bar was dark and cluttered with the usual array of bottles and cheap decorations. It occurred to Johnny that, for the American serviceman, USO's and consulates in foreign ports were unnecessary - the bars would always make him feel at home. Well, he thought, here I am again. His mood of happiness began to escape. He ordered a beer from the bright little bar maid, picked a couple of songs on the juke box, and talked to Willy about the opening of baseball season. Ye gods, he thought, it's springtime already! Where did the year go?

Some other Marines came in and sat at the far end of the bar counter. He heard them shouting and making bold passes at the bar maid. Her name was Tammy; they called her Taiwan Tammy and told her she was beautiful beyond all of their dreams. She wouldn't even smile.

Johnny finished his beer and decided to go back to the base.

There he is, thought Tammy, the blue-eyed one who never speaks to me. She smiled at Johnny as she had every night since he first came to the Evergreen Club a week ago. Johnny sat down at one of the tables across the room without returning her smile; it was a set routine by now. Why didn't he laugh loudly? Why didn't he tease her and ask her to dance with him? What was he thinking of as he sat all evening over a half-finished glass of beer? Her curiosity overpowered her pride. She walked across the room and stood by his table.

"May I sit with you?"

"You work here; sit where you wish."

She moved gracefully into the chair across from him. "Why do you never speak?" Her English was precise, her words well chosen.

"An empty wagon makes the most noise," Johnny replied. His eyes were cold and hostile.

Who are you, she wondered silently, who quotes Western proverbs?

Once in a while Tammy would get up to carry drinks to a table, but always, she'd return to sit across from the one who seemed lost in thought, unaware of her existence.

Over an hour passed before she tried again. "What are you thinking about?"

"Tammy," he smiled faintly as he spoke, "I'm trying very hard not to think." He finished his beer and left.

The next night Willy challenged Johnny to a petticab race from Chiang's statue to the Evergreen Club. "Loser buys a bottle of plum wine. Okay?"

"Okay, but why the Evergreen Club?"

"Some reason you don't want to go there?" Willy grinned as if he knew something about Johnny that Johnny didn't know.

"No, no reason."

"Fine. Pick your driver."

Johnny picked a tall Taiwanese with sufficiently muscular legs and a cab that seemed it would hold together. He offered the man two cigarettes if he peddled faster than Willy's driver. At a shout, the rickshaw-bicycle-Roman-chariot-Ben-Hur racers were off. Johnny felt a cool wind make tears in his eyes.

"HA!" Willy's cab slid ahead.

Johnny swore. "THREE CIGARETTES!" he yelled to his driver.

The driver threw his weight forward and peddled harder. Little by little, they began to pull up alongside Willy.

"HEY! FASTER!" Willy stood up and urged his driver on.

"FOUR CIGARETTES!" Johnny yelled.

"AW, COME ON," Willy bellowed. "YOUR HEART AIN'T IN IT!"

"DON'T LET HIM BEAT YOU WITH THAT TALL, HEAVY BABOON ON HIS BACK!"

They came to the bridge. It was an arched affair that passed over a railroad cut. They both jumped out and helped push the cabs up the grade to the top of the arch. Johnny got there first, but Willy was close behind and the rest of the race was a downhill dash where his weight would be an advantage.

"NOW! GO!" But Willy was at their side, shouting insults.

"YOUR GRANDMOTHER WAS A GUNNY SERGEANT."

"FIVE CIGARETTES!"

Willy's driver seemed to grow tired and relax for a moment; Johnny wheeled ahead, pulling up in front of the Evergreen with Willy about five yards behind. He laughed and shouted back at Willy, "TEACH YOU TO TALK ABOUT MY GRANNY!"

"Aw, go to hell!" Willy grinned. With rare sportsmanship, he gave his driver a three-cigarette bobby prize. "Well, let's go in and get the goddamned plum wine."

Johnny's next race was with sobriety. The sooner he could get drunk the better. He didn't know why. He didn't care why. He drank.

As he brought the bottle down, he saw Tammy's eyes upon him. Willy got up and wandered off without a word; Tammy came and took his place.

"How are you tonight, quiet one?"

"Tired and about to get drunk and go back to the base and sleep."

"I'm going with you." she said.

"What?"

"I'm going to ride back in the petticab with you, to the main gate. I'll pay."

"What's your racket, Tammy?"

"I don't understand."

"What're you after. Everybody in this world's after something when they start doing people favors for no reason. You can't fool me. I know about this human race. It stinks."

"Maybe you should not be so general."

"And where the hell did you learn to speak English like that? You speak it very well. I don't like it."

"Thank you."

"Don't be sarcastic."

"Sorry."

"Skip it." He drained the bottle. "Where's Willy? I guess he ran out on me, eh? Well, I'm going. You coming?"

"Yes." she replied.

She clutched his arm as he walked out and climbed into a petticab. He helped the driver push the cab, with Tammy in it, up the arch. At the top he jumped inside and drew her close to him with his arm.

They moved along a silent road, through the wide and empty rice paddies. Only the bicycle chain of the petticab made important noises.

The main gate was a dim light across a distant field.

"You wanted to know where I learned English."

"Yes."

"From an American Marine like you."

"I don't believe it." But he did and was happy that somewhere in the confusion of recent years one member of the human race had done something constructive. All Johnny had seen lately was vandalism in its various incarnations. "Marines don't help people, especially Chinese. They hate everybody in the world and each other as well." He had seen them beating up coolies and pulling down one anothers' tents.

"Why do you say what you do not believe yourself?"

"I don't know why anybody says or does anything."

"Why don't you trust me? I love you."

Johnny stayed silent.

They passed a clump of trees and she kissed him and whispered, "Let's stop here and make love."

"Sorry, no."

"You still don't trust me."

"No."

By and by the petticab came to the main gate.

Johnny jumped out. "Goodnight, Tammy."

"Goodnight, Johnny. Please come and see me tomorrow night."

"Yeah." He showed his liberty card to the MP and walked over to the truck stop. There was Willy Cecil. "Hey! What have you got to do with all this?"

"With what?"

"Wipe that silly look off your face. You know damn well what. Who put Tammy up to this true love bit?"

"I'm sorry, Johnny. Hell, I was just tryin' to restore your trust in the human race."

"Well you almost did it. In fact you would have if I could only really believe *you're* human, you skinny ape."

Willy laughed.

Johnny wondered if there was a better man than Willy anywhere in the world.

A Nationalist Chinese fighter slammed along the airstrip and soared above the paddies and circled upward beneath the stars over China.

Chapter 23

Chinese Fire Drill

The big operation on Formosa was a complex experience until Corporal Klemn Carpenter arrived, then it became pure confusion. He mustered into the outfit with the new draft and then wandered off to chat with the local farmers on this year's crops and the drought. It took two hours to find him; the Sergeant Major didn't run him up with morning colors because Klemn had not yet signed the document stating he'd read the Squadron Orders, which - among other things - forbid going off the base to inspect local crops during working hours. When the Sergeant Major finally latched onto him, he put a check-in sheet in his hand and said, "Here, Corporal Carpenter, go around and warn everybody we've got another eight ball in the outfit."

"Shucks, Sergeant Major, you can jes' call me Corporal Klemn ifen you want."

"Thanks, I'll remember your generosity."

Lance Corporal Johnny Shellburn, who was trying real hard to be a squared-away Basic Training Clerk lately, was Corporal Klemn's first victim. Johnny looked up from his desk to see the red-faced, stocky corporal squinting through his Coke-bottle glasses and looking kind of silly - like he didn't know quite what to do. He snapped to attention and then decided maybe to be a little less formal, so he tipped his utility cap like he thought it was a ten gallon hat and said, "Howdy!" Johnny didn't return the greeting, so Corporal Klemn resumed the position of attention.

"You don't have to come to attention for me, Corporal, I'm one rank lower than you are."

"The hell you beller!"

"You checking into the outfit?"

"Yep. Just got here today. How did you know that?"

"I'm sure I would have remembered if I'd ever seen you around here before."

"Well I'll be a Polk County dude! You must have one of them photographical recollections."

"Would you mind writing your name, rank, serial number, MOS, marksmanship score, gas mask size, and swimming qualification down on this slip of paper, please?"

"Say that again. I didn't catch the last part."

"Never mind. Just give me your check-in sheet." Johnny signed it. "Here. I'll get the information out of your Record Book someday."

"Thank you kindly."

"That's okay, Rebel."

"Hell you beller! I ain't no Rebel."

"You sure don't talk like a Yankee."

"I ain't no Yankee neither, dangitall. I'm jes' a peaceable cuss whut sticks to his own hills," he said cantankerously, doing an about face and stepping into the dry blaze of midafternoon.

Klemn stood there at attention before the Sergeant Major's desk. "Here's my check-in sheet, Sergeant Major."

The Sergeant Major leaned forward and looked closely at the new man. "Let's see, Corporal, where're we gonna put you? Who'd really be able to use a man of your many abilities? What's your MOS?"

"That's double S, Sergeant Major."

"What?"

"Moss is spelt with two S's."

"I'm not talking about moss or fungus, Corporal. What is your Military Occupational Specialty?"

"Huh?"

"What's your job, Corporal?"

"Corporal Klemn to you, Sarg."

"What did you do in your last outfit, Corporal Klemn?"

"Oh, I know what you mean. What was my work?"

"There you go!" The Sergeant Major heaved a sigh of relief, sat back down, removed the check-in sheet from his clenched fist, and covered his face with his hands. "You got a cigarette, Corporal?"

"No. But here, Sarg, have a chew." He handed him a plug of tobacco. "Now you was sayin' about my work?"

"Yes."

"Never did any."

"WHAT?" he screamed. The check-in sheet was crumpled in his fist again.

"Never did any work. Less ifen you call bein' Squadron Mascot work."

The Sergeant Major balled up the check-in sheet and threw it into the air with a whoop of laughter. "No! Now I understand. A joke. Ha ha! Whose idea was it? Pretty good!"

"Don't reckon I foller you, Sarg."

"You can come off it now, Corporal Carpenter - or whatever your real name is. You fooled me. Fine. No hard feelings. What'd you do? Have a bet with somebody?"

"Yeah, I had a bet once upon a time. Ole Pappy Fletcher bet me I wouldn't go join up with no Marine Corps."

"You mean this isn't a joke?" The Sergeant Major sobered up and let his eyelids droop back to a position of bored dignity.

"I reckon you're still a bit beyond me. Is it you want me to tell a joke or somethin'?"

"No, Corporal, just tell me why you don't have an MOS." He unballed the check-in sheet and smoothed it out in front of him.

"I dunno, Sarg. I guess maybe I got in the wrong line when they was issued."

"Yes, that must be what happened. Go over to the Squadron Office and tell them to send your record book over here, AND DON'T YOU COME BACK TILL I SEND FOR YOU!"

"Sure enough, Sarg."

"AND QUIT CALLING ME SARG!"

"Sorry, Sarg Major."

"GET OUT!"

Johnny had just recovered from his first meeting with Corporal Klemn, decided not to try to figure it out, and had gotten back to work on a couple of lesson outlines he was typing up when Klemn came charging back into the Basic Training tent madder than a wet rooster in a canary cage.

"I tell you, and I'm speakin with a straight tongue jes' sure as God made little green apples, that there Sergeant Major feller swore at me somethin' awful jes' now. Chased me plum outta his office!"

"Just calm down, Corporal. It'll take folks around here awhile to get used to you."

"Yawl don't cotten to strangers right quick in these parts do you?"

"No, I guess we're kind of unsociable that way."

"I reckon this ain't nowise like my last outfit. Why back there, the old man himself called me into his office once and said, 'Klemn, you're a goddamn jewel.' That's jes' what he said. I ain't lyin'."

"I believe you."

"No sir. I see right now where I'm gonna have to prove myself to these here people."

"Reckon so." Johnny caught himself slipping into Klemn's Southern Iowa twang.

"Makes a feller plum dissatisfied with the whole human race sometimes. Like the time that varmit tried to make off with old Pappy Fletcher's tractor. That started pertnear the biggest ruckus since Aunt Bessie shot a hole in Uncle Elmire's chicken coop. You ever hear about that?"

"Reckon not."

Klemn told Johnny the whole story, which lasted several minutes and took in the private lives of everyone in the Middle West. That, in turn, reminded him of another example to illustrate his point about humanity. "Of course you heard what happened over in Clementsville?

"You didn't?

"No kiddin'!

"You don't get around much, do you? Over in Clementsville they built this railroad right diagonal across the town. Well then, the folks on one side of the railroad track started up a war with the folks on the other side. For one to two years since I joined up and left, them folks's been chuckin' rocks at one another, shootin' each other's chickens, and jes' raisin' the devil. And you know what? There ain't one bit a difference amongst them people 'cept that railroad track. Kinda discourages the preacher. He figures the folks across the track'll start a new church any day now."

The Sergeant Major appeared in the tent entrance. "I'm going to put you in Motor Transport, Corporal Carpenter. You do have a Government Driver's Licence, I hope."

"Sure do."

"Good." The Sergeant Major's voice was calm again.

"Issued by the Government of Iowa State jes' 'fore I joined the Corps."

The Sergeant Major made a visible effort to control himself. "I'm afraid that won't do, Corporal."

"Hell you beller? Ifen it's good enough for the whole state of Iowa, I don't see why it ain't no good for this little ole base."

"CORPORAL! Pardon me. I mean, Corporal. Is there anything you know how to do?"

"I can sing:

> Oh I had a little chicken what wouldn't lay a egg;
> Poured hot water up and down his leg;
> The little chicken hollered and the little chicken
> screamed.
> Little chicken laid a hard-boiled egg."

"Corporal Carpenter, I have an idea. From now on, you are the Permanent Roving Fire Watch. All you have to do is walk around the area and, if there is ever a fire, come and tell me."

"When do I start, Sarg Major?"

"Right now. Start roving." The Sergeant Major turned back and headed in the direction of his office, looking down at his feet and kicking the dust as he walked; Corporal Klemn Carpenter started roving.

"FIRE! FIRE! FIRE!"

"Corporal, the only reason I made you Fire Watch is because we never have fires around here. Besides that, you've only been on the job ten minutes. Now suppose you explain yourself for barging into my office like this."

"That hay field out back a the tents is afire! I swear it!"

"Corporal, if that hay field was on fire there'd be fire engines from the—" At the sound of the sirens, the Sergeant Major grabbed his hat and tore off for Klemn's hay field.

"See, Sarg Major! I weren't lyin'. It's afire."

"Muster all hands! Get a bucket brigade started!" The flames were sweeping across the field in the direction of an aviation fuel line. "On the double!"

A fire engine arrived. It was manned by Chinese Airmen. They looked blankly at the Sergeant Major for instructions.

"Around in back! There's a fuel line back there. We'll have to get it first."

The Chinese Airmen didn't speak English.

"Around in back! IN BACK! THE FUEL LINE!"

They didn't respond.

Corporal Klemn Carpenter rushed back onto the scene with a bucket brigade, took in the situation, and jumped up into the cab of the fire truck.

"Move over, Charlie!" he said to the driver. He hit the gas and went barreling straight into the flames toward the fuel line.

The fire was out. It was evening and the sky was dark with clouds. Corporal Klemn, the Sergeant Major, and Johnny Shellburn stood on the edge of the black field. Klemn was wiping the soot off his glasses.

"I'm real proud of you, Corporal Carpenter. That was very brave the way you drove right through those flames."

"Aw shucks, Sarg Major. I didn't do that on purpose."

"No?"

"Course not. There was smoke on my glasses. I couldn't see where I was goin'!"

"Why didn't you take them off?" Johnny asked.

"When I got 'em off, like now, I'm pure blind!"

A Chinese colonel walked by. The Sergeant Major and Johnny saluted him. He stopped and stared at Klemn. He walked up and stood in front of the Corporal, pointed to his rank emblem, and shouted, "Colonel!"

Klemn put his glasses back on and looked at the colonel a little bewildered. The glasses magnified his blue eyes so they looked like they were pressed up against the bottoms of Mason jars. Klemn grinned kind of silly.

The colonel's face grew red. He frowned, pointed to his rank emblems again and started jumping up and down. "Colonel! Colonel!"

Klemn scratched his head. "You Chinks sure do strange things."

"Colonel! Colonel!"

"Jes' hold on, Colonel. I'll play your silly little game." Klemn pointed to his corporal stripes and started jumping up and down. "Corporal! Corporal!"

The Sergeant Major and Johnny left them there, jumping and shouting. Johnny looked at the sky and said, "I sure hope it doesn't rain. I don't think our tents will stand up under too much bad weather."

"Reckon not," the Sergeant Major said in a distinct Corporal Klemn accent.

"Well, ifen it does - it'll be right good on the crops."

"The hell you beller?"

Chapter 24

Felicidad

Something new had been added to Christopher's Coffee Shop in Olongapo since Johnny's unit had been away to Taiwan. Her name was Happiness; in Filipino they say: Felicidad.

Her neck strained forward and her chin remained level with the earth as she talked to him. It seemed as if she were arching her neck. Her black eyes were narrow and bright. She gave Johnny the impression of unbounded pride. Her lips were thin and her mouth was given to an ironic smile. There was gold in her skin and a mechanical cut to her eyebrows. Her hair was richly black. Her face reacted swiftly to each of his words. Her speech was rapid and meaningful; her sentences sounded like they were going somewhere important.

"Do you know Ericson?" she asked.

"Leif Erikson? The viking?"

"No." Her laughter as the pure sound of joy.

"Leif Erikson was a great man."

"So is Adam Ericson."

"Your boyfriend?"

"Yes."

Johnny was silent for a moment. "Tonight I feel like the Christopher Columbus of Christopher's Coffee Shop. I come here and make a great discovery only to find some guy named Ericson discovered it first."

She smiled.

A quick-witted woman, he thought. No explanations necessary.

"For that, I'll buy you a cup of tea," she exclaimed.

"Thank you, Felicidad."

Men turned from their drinks at the bar to follow her walk. As she put the tea down on his table, her eyes challenged and examined him and her interest was flattering. She sat down and considered him as a judge would consider new evidence on behalf of a condemned person.

"If anything should go wrong between Adam and I, I will try very hard never to fall in love with anybody again."

"You read questions in my eyes?"

"Yes. Many. But that is the only one to be answered."

"People are not often successful when they try at love - one way or the other."

"I know. That is why I am not at the university this year."

"You are a student?"

"I was. Now I am a woman who works in a coffee shop."

"Because you fell in love?"

"Yes. Because I fell in love."

"What university did you attend?"

"University of the Philippines in Manila."

"I know the place; it is the best school in Manila."

"I know. I never concern myself with anything but the best."

"Life is too short for us to do otherwise."

"You're right." It was an admission; she'd never thought of that way before. Once again, he won her interest. Her eyes studied him.

He sensed his moment. "Thank you for the tea, Felicidad. I must be going." Half of life, he thought as he stepped onto the street, is knowing when to get up and leave. The other half is knowing when to return. That's what life is, a line of moments.

He found a jeepney and took a ride to the Bar Revenge where he had two glasses of rum before heading back. He wanted to hit the sack early, inspection was tomorrow. After that he'd worry about the social end of life in the town of Olongapo, and the beautiful girl in Christopher's Coffee Shop, and his moment of return.

He stepped through the door, walked to the bar and ordered a beer. Slowly he turned around and surveyed the room. Adam Ericson - it had to be him - was sitting at a table with Felicidad. He looked concerned and a little hurt. He had hair which was neither dark nor light. That was all Johnny could remember afterwards.

Ericson was talking carefully and it looked like hard work. Felicidad was listening, but letting her attention wander. Her eyes met with

Johnny's. There was silent communication between them for a long time while Ericson talked, unknowing.

Suddenly, cutting him off in the middle of a statement, she got up and walked toward the bar - toward Johnny. Johnny felt victory and hard triumph over Adam Ericson. He felt no pity and very little fear as she sat next to him and smiled cheerfully.

"You and your boyfriend don't seem to be getting along so well." He ordered a beer for Felicidad and glanced out of the corner of his eyes toward Adam Ericson's table; he was gone.

"No, we had a fight. Suddenly, I think I hate him more than I've ever hated anyone!" Her hand shook as she picked up her glass of beer. "Yes, I hate him."

"Be careful. Love and hate, like heat and cold, can be confused."

She didn't speak, but drank the beer.

"Why don't you take the rest of the night off. We'll go out and get drunker than skunks - both of us."

"Good idea." She told the boss she wasn't feeling well and went to get her purse. "Where first?"

"The Bar Revenge."

"The name is symbolic."

"Aren't they all." As they stepped outside the breath of the night felt sultry.

"Pssssst. Jeepney!"

They jumped inside the jeepney and rode up the bumpy, unpaved Magsaysay Drive toward the Bar Revenge. Spanish music floated out of the Tijuana Bar as they passed and a crowd of Motor Transport boys poured in. The night was a carnival. It would be set off in the unreality section of his memory.

The bar was hot, noisy and full of smoke. In the darkness of one corner, a pyramid of beer glasses stood upon a table. He saw Willy Cecil, Abe Diamond and Klemn Carpenter sitting there stacking more glasses on the pyramid. "Hi, Johnny."

"Say, Willy. How's it go?" He took Felicidad's arm and led her away, to the other side of the dance floor. "I'm not going to share you with anybody tonight."

"Good," she said as they sat down.

"A bottle of Manila Rum and two glasses."

"Coming up."

The music was a fast-paced Latin tango. There was the music, voices, and the sound of glasses and bottles rattling - that was all. It sounded like a revolutionary army marching on some Latin American capital. Viva! The waiter brought the rum.

Johnny poured and lifted his glass. "To the revolution!"

"The revolution," she murmured. They drank.

Somebody knocked a glass off the bar and Johnny heard it shatter.

"I come with low words, high knowledge, and a revolution." he drank. "The world is turning upon itself tonight. And so it comes to pass that before anything new can be created (qualitatively speaking) there must be a struggle within the old order. Long live the revolt!" There was the clash of arms and bottles. "The great rebellion is at hand!"

She poured more rum in their empty glasses.

"To a lasting friendship between two nations," he toasted.

"To a lasting friendship." she replied.

Somebody banged the pyramid of glasses on the table across the room and they came crashing down, breaking around on the dance floor. Willy Cecil, Abe Diamond and Klemn Carpenter were thrown out.

"The first purge of the new regime," Johnny shouted. "Long live the new regime!"

"What makes you such a revolutionary tonight?"

"It's the only way to be. If you don't like things, change them - fast. The new regime will change everything. Drink to the new regime!"

She laughed her pure, clear laughter, threw her head back, and drank. Johnny drank too.

"Who is the new regime?"

"I am the new regime."

"Who was the old regime?"

"Eric Adamson, or whatever his name was - he is now an unperson by the way - Adam, that's it, Adam Ericson was the old order."

"You are very honest with me."

"If I was honest, all this talk of revolution could have been left out. Only indirectly am I honest."

"Let's drink some more."

"Yes. Let's drink some more." He felt life slowing down and slipping away. Oh god, he thought, give me intensity! Make life fast and hard! Even the music seemed slower than before.

"How much more rum to go?"

"About half a bottle."

"My only objection to getting drunk is it takes too long."

"Yes." She drank.

By the time the bottle was empty, Johnny was feeling different - not better, but different. He stood up and it was then that he realized just what a big bottle of rum it'd been. He took Felicidad by the hand and steered for the door. When he found his way through the moving targets, he noticed the Bar Revenge was now on the wrong side of the street. In fact, the whole town was turned exactly around.

"Well, we did it. We got drunk."

"So what?"

"So let's go get drunker."

"Let's go. On with the revolution."

The rest of the night consisted of bar signs flashing, drinks pouring, a fight with a sailor that got broken up, an argument with Felicidad that flashed on over nothing and cooled off into nothing again, and - around one-thirty - a ride to the main gate in the back seat of a jeepney with their two bodies pressed hotly against one another, her crying and him afraid and lonely in an empty universe of night. She kissed his ear when the jeepney halted by the bridge and sobbed, "Adam, I -"

"See you tomorrow, girl. Go home and get some coffee." He jumped out and walked across the bridge in loose, drunken steps. He pulled out his liberty and ID cards for the gate sentry. The sentry waved him through. As he fumbled, putting them back in his wallet, he thought for a moment that somebody else's name was on them. He checked again. No Johnny thought, they do not say: Adam Ericson.

Johnny woke up to the sound of the jungle. The sun was rising and, somewhere in the distance, the Duty NCO was going from hut to hut, turning on the lights and shouting, "REVEILLIE!"

Willy Cecil rolled out of the next rack and stood up like a feeble giant, mumbling to himself, cursing drink, the passing of time, mornings in general, and this morning especially.

The Duty NCO reached in and threw on the lights. "REVEILLIE."

The other men in the hut started getting up. Johnny unwrapped his arms from his pillow and covered his eyes with his hands.

Willy slammed the door on his wall locker and sat down to put on his boots. "Some chick you were with last night, Johnny."

"Felicidad? Yeah. She's quite a woman."

"How is she in bed?"

"I don't know."

"I'll bet you don't." Willy laughed.

"I wish I was half the lover you think I am." It made him mad that Willy should think he'd made it with her. He didn't know why. He wanted to, Lord knows. Maybe that was it. He wanted to and he didn't - and yet, as Willy indicated, he could have. Something went wrong, he guessed. The right opportunity probably presented itself and he probably didn't see it soon enough. All of life is like that, he thought. You evaluate moments as they fly at you - and if you don't evaluate each of them properly, you're sunk. "One of these days Willy, I'm going to come up with a theory on dealing with women."

"Patent it and you'll make a fortune."

"Let's wash up and get to chow."

"Wait up. I'll be right along."

Willy laced up his remaining boot, grabbed his shaving gear, and he and Johnny trotted down to the head.

"What the world really needs, of course, is a theory on dealing with rot-gut rum the morning after."

"You can say that again." The cold water felt good on Johnny's face. As he dried his face with a towel, he noticed the person shaving two basins down was looking at him out of the corner of his eye. I'll bet that's Adam Ericson, he thought.

He thought wrong. Adam Ericson was in the truck on the way to the chow hall. At least this guy looked more like him than the other one did. If he could only remember more about him.

In line at chow, he saw the real Adam Ericson looking at him with that same hurt expression on his face.

Johnny and Willy returned to the hut after chow and squared things away before they went to work.

He saw Adam Ericson on the way to work. That wasn't him in the chow hall after all. He came walking down the road that led to the offices with a vindictive look for Johnny.

Since the big inspection was over and the Basic Training Office was ship shape for another three months, Johnny was loaned to Captain Sims to be a Security Section runner. He was given a forty-five pistol and some envelopes to deliver across the base.

As he drove along the jeep, he passed Adam Ericson four times. He turned in the envelopes to the runway Communications Center. The man who signed for them looked suspiciously familiar. Johnny glanced at the signature; no, this man's name was Elmer Wasnewski.

On the way back, he stopped by the PX to get some cigars. The man behind the cigar counter looked like Adam Ericson, but he was Filipino. That evening Felicidad looked dissipated. There were lines around her eyes and the corners of her mouth. She looked at him dully, indifferently.

"You look like you've been drinking."

"Yes." She didn't smile.

"I'll have a cup of tea."

As she walked by the bar, the usual eyes followed her. Johnny felt like walking up to each man there and saying quietly, "Don't waste your time." In a few minutes, he thought, Adam will be here; this time she'll leave me and go to him.

She placed the tea before him and he paid her; she sat down. "How are you tonight?"

"Don't ask. You're not interested."

"You're right." There was no expression in her voice.

"How are you?"

"Recovering."

"Good." Where did I go wrong, he wondered. I guess maybe I moved too fast. That's my main trouble. I'm a revolutionary; I can't wait; I always try to make things happen. That's why I've been running second all of my life - first in the eyes of others, but second in my own. I'm a revolutionary capable of changing everything but that single fact.

"Why do you try to go through life so fast?"

"I was just wondering the same thing. I think it's because I measure life by a different scale than others. Most people want to live long; I want to live intensely. I don't care if I die early in life, jut so long as I can live fully first."

She looked at him. The lines around her eyes vanished and, for the moment, he had her interest again. "Give me your address in the States. When you go back, I want to keep in touch with you."

"Fine." He wrote his home address on a card and gave it to her.

"Thank you." Her eyes were still judging him.

He sensed his moment; it was time to go.

Adam Ericson was standing outside Christopher's Coffee Shop. He'd been looking in the front window. He looked at Johnny, his eyes full of hatred. Johnny jumped in a jeepney for the Olongapo Public Square. Ericson jumped in the next jeepney to follow him; it was time for a showdown.

Johnny got out at the square and waited for Ericson. Ericson's jeepney came along soon, but it was empty. He walked around the square. The Olongapo Public Market was empty except for a couple of fruit stands which remained open, the Public Restaurant, a tiny sari-sari store, a few aimless wanderers, and a cop. The cop eyed the Americano suspiciously.

The Americano had a look of trouble in his eyes, but there was no trouble to be found. He'd come here to try and settle things; but nothing is ever settled. The thought made him smile. The cop walked away and on the Americano's face was happiness - in Filipino they say: Felicidad.

Chapter 25

Lost Our Dough

Willy Cecil's walk was the walk of a man striving, literally, to shrug off responsibility. He crossed the bridge from the base to the town of Olongapo in his usual loose steps. He habitually shrugged his shoulders while he moved forward. On his face was a sheepish grin which hinted perhaps that, subconciously, he realized the significance of his mannerisms.

"Hey, Joe. You want to buy pesos?"

Willy stopped and reached a long arm way up in the air to scratch the top of his head. He then rotated his finger in his left ear. He eyed the peso vendor for several moments.

"I'll give you thirty-four for ten."

Willy considered. He had ten dollars of military scrip in his pocket along with four pesos and twenty-three centavos. I will be out of funny money pretty soon, he thought. Thirty-four's not a bad price lately. Well, might as well.

He dug out the ten dollars and made the illegal exchange. He put the pesos in his wallet without counting them and shrugged on.

"Hey, Killer!" Johnny Shelburn called to him from across the road. Johnny was sitting on the running board of a parked jeepney reading a book. He had a black turtle-neck sweater on under his white shirt; the temperature was tropical. Oh well, Johnny Shellburn was nuts. Marine Corps life had gotten the best of him long ago.

"How's things?"

"Pretty fair."

"What you readin'?"

"*The Upanishads*. Kind of a Hindu bible."

"Aw shucks! You on another Orientalism kick?"

"Afraid so."

"Johnny, you ain't happy unless you're doin' some kind of weird thing all of the time. Why can't you be like everybody else?"

"Good God! What a thing to say!"

"Sorry." Willy didn't know what he was supposed to be sorry for, but he sensed it was the right thing to say. "Where'd you get that book?"

"Stole it from Mike Cervata. I think he got it at the Hindu Temple in Manila."

"I thought Hindus were only in Africa."

"India, Willy. They have a few in the Philippines, too. Where you headed?"

Willy shrugged.

"Me too. We better hurry or we'll be late." Johnny stuck his book in his hip pocket and joined Willy to walk into town.

As they passed Christopher's Coffee Shop, Bob Kidd stuck his head out of the door and yelled, "If it ain't the two meanest Marines in the MAG! Where ya off to?"

"Where? We're off to see the Wizard of Oz, naturally. Come join us."

"I'll do that."

They wandered down Magsaysay Drive, swung a right at the Bar Revenge, and struck out for Olongapo's main drag of bars and night clubs. On the doorstep of one of the houses they passed a young Filipino was playing "The Sloop John B," on a guitar. They joined him for a couple of choruses as the western light, now high on the nearby mountain, retreated and left a vacuum for the night to fill.

Willy looked at Johnny Shellburn and Bob kidd singing and thought how great it would be if they'd both quit talking so much, as they always did, and just sing. Neither one of them could sing worth a damn, but any change would be an improvement. The song ended.

"Welp," said Willy, "Should we head on?"

"Okay." Johnny said goodbye to the Filipino in Tagalog.

Bob Kidd said to Willy, "What's this word, 'welp'?"

Willy shrugged.

Bob advanced an idea. "I think it's a combination of a very resigned 'well' and a panic-stricken 'help!'."

"I dunno. Maybe."

They walked on down into the well-illuminated carnival depths of Olongapo. Girls stood in the doors of the night clubs tempting them.

Shellburn said to Kidd, "At last, Bob, I've developed a philosophy of life. I call it Hindic Humanism. It's a cross between Marxism and Vedanta."

"Groucho Marx or Communism?" Willy asked. It was the first time in his life he had attempted to enter a philosophical conversation; he was ignored.

He decided to quit listening to them and just watch their facial expressions. When Johnny talked, he grew excited. As he looked at you, his eyes were parallel and reflected the pale blue of some hazy, distant sky in back of you. Bob Kidd just listened and asked questions, anymore, keeping his face almost expressionless. When Johnny asked him point blank, he gave his opinion in a loud voice and with a lot of arm waving - but, judging by his eyes, he didn't care whether he was heard or not. It's pretty funny, Willy thought, that neither one of them have a thing to say; they both just like the sound of their own voices.

Willy's attention wandered to his surroundings, Olongapo - the miniature Sodom and Gomorrah of the north end of the South Seas - where you could buy anything from murder to narcotics and rent women by the hour, day, or month. Look at those damn-fool moths, he directed himself, banging against that neon sign. Big bastards! Must have a wing span of four inches each. I wonder why they don't wise up.

Johnny's excited voice broke up his thoughts. "That's just it, Bob, you gotta be detached as hell. You can't give a damn about life; otherwise it's got you by the balls. You have to view everything in its proper prespective."

"I don't know who said this, but it's very true: 'He who goes through life avoiding pain only succeeds in avoiding pleasure.'"

"Maybe it's worth it."

"Do you really think that?"

"Of course."

"Do you really think that?" Bob Kidd repeated.

"Yes. Well I feel — "

"Save your feelings for your girl friends. Do you think that?"

"Man," Willy moaned, "Put on a new record. I'll see you guys. I'm gonna go get loaded."

They were too busy talking to hear what he said.

Willy walked into the closest bar. Klemn Carpenter was sitting there pouring tabasco sauce in a glass of whiskey on the rocks.

"What are you doing?"

"Makin' fire water, Willy. Have yourself a seat."

Ole Klemn was Willy's type of people. He didn't know why he bothered with Shellburn anymore. He sat down and ordered a rum and Coke.

"I'll catch it this time around." Klemn pulled out a wad of pesos.

"Hey, let me see those a minute." Willy took the pesos, glanced at them, and laughed. "Klemn, you got fished."

"What?"

"You got taken in by some crooked peso vendor. This is Japanese occupation money." Poor, unsuspecting Klemn.

"The hell you beller? What's Japanese occupation money?"

"It's the money the Japanese issued down here when they took over during World War II. It's about as valuable as Confederate money in Chicago."

"You ain't kiddin' ole Klemn? Is you?"

"See for yourself." He gave the money back to poor, ole Klemn-from-the-hills.

"Well, I'll be hog tied and pig bound."

"Don't sweat it. I'll loan you some real pesos. I got thirty-four for ten..."

"That's just what I got."

"And I can afford to spare a-" Willy swore in a loud, angry whisper. Klemn took a look at the pesos Willy was loaning him and started laughing.

"Welp, I got enough left over from last night to pay for the drinks. Then I guess I might as well head back for the base."

"Yep. Might as well." Klemn couldn't stop chortling.

They took a jeepney on what was left of yesterday's pesos. The night was a hot gloom, and the lights on the bars flashed with tropical rhythms and jungle colors as the jeepney bounced down the rugged streets of Olongapo. A pretty Filipina waved at Willy and he shrugged.

"You know what we did, Klemn?"

"What'd we do, Willy?"

"We lost our dough in Olongapo."

"Well, don't take is so bad. Jes' think - if the Japs ever take over again, we'll be sixty-eight pesos ahead."

"Hey, I never thought about it like that! Well, well, welp - I guess things always look worse than they really are!"

Chapter 26

The Hero

Strange roads lead to high glory. Pat Hoolahan followed the strangest glory road of all.

The Sergeant Major needed a truck driver in a hurry. He telephoned the Motor Transport Officer. The Motor Transport Officer appointed the Motor Transport NCO-in-Charge to appoint a truck driver for the Sergeant Major's detail. The Sergeant Major had been appointed to appoint a truck driver by the Squadron Commanding Officer. The Squadron CO got his orders from the Group CO. The Group CO got the word from Rear Admiral Flank, the Base CO.

To simplify, the Base CO told the Group CO to tell the Squadron CO to tell the Sergeant Major to tell the Motor Transport Officer to tell the Motor transport NCO-in-Charge to appoint a truck driver.

Pat Hoolahan got picked.

"Pfc Hoolahan, report to the Sergeant Major. He needs a truck driver for some working party or such."

"Pfc Hoolahan, report to the Commanding Officer. You're going to be on some kind of gravel run out in the jungle."

"Pfc Hoolahan, in fifteen minutes you will report, in uniform of the day, to the Group CO. He needs you for a special assignment."

"Pfc Hoolahan, Rear Admiral Plank wishes to send you on a very important mission. Report to him as soon as possible."

"Congratulations, Pfc Hoolahan, you have been selected to represent your nation as an ambassador of good will. Report to my office at 0800 hours, tomorrow morning, in working uniform."

The next morning Pfc Hoolahan reported as ordered. The Admiral led him out in back of the office. There, beneath a large tree, sat a Marine Corps truck from Pat's motor pool. The Admiral pointed to it as if it were something to be proud of. "You will drive this truck, Pfc, to the main gate. There you will be met by a Filipino driver. You will turn the truck over to him and you will ride shotgun out to Barrio City, a small village in the interior."

"Pardon me, sir. Just what is the nature of this assignment?"

"People-to-people, Hoolahan, people-to-people. The people of America are loaning a truck to the people of Barrio City, so they may build up their roads before the rain season sets in." The Admiral reached into his pocket. "Now here's some money for chow and such things as you'll be off the base all day. You will continue with this assignment until the middle of next week. That will be all, Pfc; carry out your orders."

"Yes, Admiral." He leaped into the truck cab and revved up the engine. The main gate was only a short distance down the road. When he got there a squat Filipino jumped on the running board and climbed in to take over the wheel. "I am Juan Renaldo at your service." He had big teeth and a wide face.

"I am Pat Hoolahan, Juan." There was still a note of bewilderment in Pat's voice. He felt he didn't yet understand what was going on and he wasn't sure he wanted to find out.

"We go now to Barrio City for breakfast at the house of the mayor."

"Of course," Pat agreed with a headshake. "Barrio City."

Soon they were rolling down a straight road that cut through the Philippine jungles in an ever-narrowing line. Soon there was nothing left but two tire ruts with thick forest on either side. Great trees arched overhead and gave the impression of an outdoor cathedral. "Just only behind this mountain we come to the place of Barrio City."

They splashed through a stream and came up out of the jungle. They followed the road, now dry and rocky, around the side of the small mountain and down into a jungle clearing. The clearing was Barrio City.

"Up ahead is the house of the mayor where we will have breakfast."

They came to a slow stop at the end of a long row of mat houses. The house of the mayor was unlike any home Pat had seen in a long time. It was made of concrete, painted yellow, and decorated with modernistic wrought-iron designs. A maid opened the door and a blast of cool air rushed out.

The living room was Spanish. Over the fireplace there was a big silver saddle. A voice called them to the patio.

"Pat Hoolahan, this is the mayor."

"How do you do, sir?"

"Fine." The mayor was about Pat's height, thin and dark. "Please sit down. Breakfast is ready."

A photographer from Informational Services took pictures of Pat and the mayor at breakfast, Pat and the mayor shaking hands, Pat and Juan Renaldo shaking hands, Pat with a string of white flowers around his neck, Pat standing next to the truck, Pat sitting in the truck, and Pat standing alone.

"What it is that we are doing," said the mayor after breakfast and publicity, "is filling in the roads of the city with gravel." A group of laborers climbed into the back of the truck. "Your job is just only to ride along and see that everything goes smoothly."

And then, below all the ambassadorship-formanship see-that-every-thing-goes-smoothly baloney, Pat figured out what he was really there for - to see that nobody stole the truck. He laughed out loud under the pretense of friendliness. "Sure thing. I guess we better get started."

Renaldo climbed in and Pat jumped up on the running board, as his half of the seat in the cab was being used by the photographer. When they got to the jungle gravel pit just out of town, the photographer took pictures of Pat holding a shovel. Meanwhile, the laborers began filling the truck. After the pictures, Pat wanted to help with the work but he was only in the way, so somebody handed him a jug of coconut wine and he went over and sat under a tree. The photographer put the cover back on his camera lens. They went back to Barrio City with the gravel. The truck began creeping along the road between the rows of houses.

The laborers shoveled the gravel off while another group followed, spreading it over the road. Pat stood by the road and watched.

Soon he was a guest in the home of an elderly couple. They insisted he drink their rum and try about twenty different Filipino dishes. They told him of the debt of gratitude they owed him for the liberation from the Japanese.

"Well, I didn't have much to do with that. I was just a little guy then."

By the end of the day, he'd lost track of the number of people who'd thanked him for liberating them, the number of glasses of rum and San Miguel he'd been offered, the number of Filipino dishes he'd tried, and the number of pictures the photographer had snapped.

"I don't know if I can take a week and a half of this, sir," he told Admiral Plank when he reported in with the truck that evening.

"Just remember, Pfc, you're winning friends for America."

Two days later, articles on Pat Hoolahan filled the papers. The articles told of how Pfc Hoolahan gave of his own time to bend his back in toil for the people of Barrio City. There were everywhere, those articles, in the base bulletin, the local Filipino papers and even in *The Stars and Stripes*. Pat started walking around with the bill of his utility cab pulled down over his eyes. When in civilian clothes he even started wearing dark sun glasses. The light was just too goddamned bright for him.

As each day passed, more publicity came blurting out. More and more people were congratulating him - for what, nobody seemed to know. Only Lance Corporal Shellburn wasn't fooled. He walked up and said in a low tone, "Don't worry, Mouse. When nations need heros, they make them." If Pat hated anybody for more than ten minutes, it had been Shellburn for the last couple of months. However, on this occasion he had to agree, he was a press agent's hero. The weight of glory grew heavy as each of his actions became magnified.

As the end of the final day of his assignment, Admiral Plank shook his hand and said, "Well done, Pat." Pat caught the base bus for the PX Snack Bar. It had been an unusually rummy day and he needed a cup of coffee.

"Hey," whispered Mike Cervata, "Who's that famous-looking man coming in the door?"

Abe Diamond looked. "Isn't that Pat Hoolahan, the well-known truck driver for Rear Admiral Plank?"

"I don't know. Let's ask."

"Okay."

"Pardon me, sir, but are you by any chance that well-known, people-to-people truck driver we've all read about and admired?"

Pat flushed. "Damnit. Will you guys please come off it. That stuff gets old."

"Bring your coffee over to our table, Pat. Or do you have a private one reserved?"

"No bull, knock it off. It's not funny anymore." Pat sat down and poured cream in his coffee.

"Tell us how it feels to be Admiral Plank's boy, Pat."

"Pretty silly if you really want to know."

"I hear they're having a fiesta in Barrio City this weekend."

"Yeah, I've gotta get dressed up and go back and crown the queen of the beauty contest tonight." Pat looked at the floor as he spoke.

"Hey! That's great! Mind if Abe and I come along? How about it, Abe? Shall we go watch that famous truck driver crown the queen?"

"We shall."

"I wish you guys'd knock it off."

"Knock it off! I'm serious. Let's go get cleaned up right now."

"Okay. If you really want to go, I can't stop you. I think you're both acting kind of stupid, though."

"Well it's not every day a man gets to see a well-known truck driver crown a queen."

"That's true," Pat admitted.

When Pat crowned the queen, flash bulbs and fireworks broke the darkness and the fiesta started. The queen stood up and Pat was supposed to kiss her. She was taller than he was and he had to stand on his toes. Somebody threw a streamer and somebody else handed him a San Miguel. He held the beer in his left hand while he shook hands with Admiral Plank, the MAG CO, the mayor, the mayor's brother, the mayor's uncle, and the queen's aunt who was also the mayor's wife. The photographer made him go through the process a second time without the beer. After that he was handed another San Miguel and released. Juan Renaldo, Mike Cervata, and Abe Diamond joined him.

"Let's go find some girls," said Pat.

His three friends agreed and Juan led the way.

Monday morning, the Base CO told the Group CO to tell the Squadron CO to tell the Sergeant Major to tell the Motor Transport

Officer to tell the Motor Transport NCO-In-Charge to appoint a truck driver to take Pat Hoolahan to the Base CO's office.

"May I congratulate you once again, Pat, on the fine job you did in representing your nation as an ambassador of good will. I hereby return you to regular duty with your squadron and wish you the best of luck throughout your military career. My car is waiting outside; my aide will drive you to your Group CO's office."

"It is with great pleasure, Pfc Hoolahan, that I take note of your activities in representing the United States Marine Corps in this People-to-People Program. Your example has been an inspiration to all of us. Keep up the good work. There is a jeep waiting outside to return you to your Squadron CO."

"Pfc Hoolahan, your squadron is proud of you. Please report back to my office this afternoon at 1600. Promotions are coming out and, well, I have a surprise for you."

"Pfc Hoolahan, I've been a Sergeant major for a number of years now and I seldom misjudge men, but, frankly, I underestimated you. Your recent change in attitude, as is evident by the newspaper articles I have before me is most welcome. I hope you keep up in this spirit. Now get down to the Motor Transport and get back to work."

"Hoolahan, I'm glad you were able to control your conduct out there long enough to fool a few people. You always have been a good worker, but I've seen you raise hell with the native populace more than once. Now we have a couple of trucks out on the deadline..."

That evening Pat met Mike Cervata and Abe Diamond in the PX Snack Bar as they had planned. Pat sat down.

"Any word on those DR's, Mike?"

"Yeah. I talked to the Sergeant of the Guard this afternoon. Not a thing to sweat."

"What happened?"

"You'll never guess," said Abe.

"They tore them up."

"But why? I don't get it."

"Politics. How could they submit Disciplinary Reports on us?"

"Yeah, Pat, we had a hero in our midst."

"Aw, knock it off."

"No kiddin'. That's what saved us. How would it look for the brass if the word got out that their boy, along with three friends, were caught on the night of the fiesta tearing apart a whore house in Barrio City?"

"That's true," Pat admitted. "Have a cigar. I'm a Lance Corporal now."

Chapter 27

Letter For La Chica

La Chica:

The man who delivers this to you is a friend of mine. I asked him not to stop by with it until I and my outfit are bound for Japan again. As you read this, I am probably somewhere between Olongapo and Yokohama. The sky is probably grey and the ocean rough. I am probably standing on the deck thinking of a nice, warm Philippine weather and of you - the girl I will always call "La Chica."

I remember how you looked at me the first night Johnny Shellburn and I walked into the Island Lounge Restaurant arguing philosophy. And, also, I remembered how Johnny Shellburn looked at you.

You had on your yellow dress that night, I remember that, and you came over to sit with me and talk, pretending to be interested in Johnny's book on Hinduism. I knew then that you were interested in me; you made it clear. So clear that I relaxed, thinking things would work out in time. I'm sorry.

I left early that night, left Johnny behind, happy and confident. When Johnny told me the next day that he had a date with you, I thought nothing of it. I don't know whether I underestimated him or overestimated you, but I'm sorry my judgement was not more perfect. Maybe I just did not think about it.

I know how it happened and I'm not blaming you. Johnny took you out, told you he wanted to go to bed with you and you were afraid to answer. He took you to a hotel, got a room, and dragged you there without further questions. That's Johnny's way. I've seen him do it time and again. He is direct and blunt, but his method works.

We change our taste, our likes and dislikes, even our loves, to conform with reality. It's part of adjusting to life. I've preached it all along, and I saw it happen to you. Since Johnny had made himself important in you life, and since I hadn't, you turned your attention more and more toward him. I saw it happening; I knew it what was happening; and yet, I did nothing to stop it. I'm sorry.

I wasn't sorry then, but I'm sorry now. For tonight I saw you hanging on Johnny's arms crying "Don't go!" And I saw Johnny pushing his way out the door and saying, "Leave me alone. I'm no good, girl." I saw this tonight. If we were not heading back for Japan in the morning, there would still be some time for me to do something, to give you the love you cried for and the love I could have given. But now the orders are stamped.

Experiences, even bad ones, are worth something. I don't know what you got out of this one, but I learned one thing that will serve me forever: the worst thing a man can do is just stand and do nothing. I'll not repeat that mistake.

Please write, La Chica.

Sincerely,
Bob Kidd

Chapter 28

July in Japan

Johnny Shellburn wrote a letter to his folks, mailed it, took a hot shower, skipped shaving, put on his dress shoes, put on his black trousers and a red shirt, threw his grey coat over his shoulder and went to the Duty NCO's room. He checked out his liberty card, walked over to the Enlisted Club, bought ten bucks worth of yen and climbed into a cab to get taxied to Yamato Station. Today he needed sex and he didn't feel like messing around.

He sat down in the Yokohama-bound train and relaxed. He had been to New York and had ridden the subways. It struck him now how much like the subways these Japanese trains were. The design was nearly identical. One difference however, was how these three-car electric trains sped over the open fields.

The sun had just risen, but the sky was overcast. The farm houses - Oriental lanterns during the nights - were well blended among the trees now. He put his jacket on and turned up the collar. He leaned his head against the window and let himself be vibrated to sleep by the rumble of the train.

It was a holiday and Abe Diamond was sleeping in. Some idiot lit a string of firecrackers in the barracks. Abe sat up and slipped his feet into his Japanese shower shoes. It was time to get up anyway.

If there was anything Abe hated more than loud noise in the morning, it was the necessity of making decision at that hour. To go to the Fourth of July picnic? To go on liberty? He put off the thought a few more minutes. A cold shower would do him good.

Someone tugged at the collar of his grey jacket. "Yokohama Station." The Japanese conductor grinned. So it was; good thing Yokohama was the end of the line. "Domoarigato," Johnny thanked, returning the grin. He rubbed his eyes as he moved along in the crowd. Outside the station he caught a taxi for Isezaki Street.

Abe was on his way back from the showers, a wet towel over his shoulder and his shaving bag in hand, when someone outside yelled, "WHAT'S NEW IN THE FAR EAST BESIDES YOU GUYS?" He knew the draft was in. A new bunch of boots, a whole bus load, would now come tramping into the barracks with their bewildered faces and green seabags. "The poor bastards!" he said aloud - and thought to himself, The lucky sons of bitches! The cycle was complete, he, Johnny Shellburn, Willy Cecil and a bunch of the others had arrived last July and, at the end of the summer, their tour would be up. "YAHOO!" Abe yelled. "SHORT!"

Johnny walked down Isezaki Street for awhile and then switched over to the alley that runs parallel with Four-and-a-Half Street on the opposite side of Isezaki. This wide alley was, he knew by former experience, the best place to pick up street creeps. He walked at a brisk pace, watching the sky for signs of rain.

He went for several blocks without coming across a likely girl. It was too late, and too early, in the day. He switched back over to Isezaki Street and started back, thinking about ducking into a bar for awhile. He passed no bars that seemed right for his mood. Finally, he passed a mamasan who was handing out little ad cards they were for the Bar Three Star.

"Doko?" asked Johnny. Where?   "You follow me," said the old mamasan.

As he walked down the street behind the mamasan, he wondered if any of the people they passed thought the mamasan was some street creep taking him to her room in a short-time house. He fell about ten paces behind her.

The Bar Three Star was a couple of blocks off Isezaki on a little, out-of-the-way side street. Inside were three girls and no customers. He sat at the bar and one of the girls got up and came around behind it.

"Beer," he put two hundred yen coins down on the counter.

"How are you today?" She poured his beer.

"Fine."

She leaned on the counter; he had a good view down her dress. "How long you been in Japan?"

"One year ago today I came."

"So, you like?"

"Number one."

They talked and then didn't talk for quite a while. She asked him to buy her a beer. He said he was almost broke but he invited her to share his and she did. She checked her watch.

"Nanji?" he asked. What time?

"Eight," she said. "Maybe you would like to take me home?"

"How far do you live?"

"Oh..." her voice trailed off into an evasive, soft laugh.

"Need to take streetcar, bus, cab - what?"

"Nani?" What?

"Oh, never mind. Sure, I'll take you home."

"Okay. I go change first." She disappeared through a beaded curtain.

Abe Diamond, wearing his dark suit, put his umbrella under his arm and went up the Duty Room for his liberty card. The boots were standing around up there, waiting to be assigned bunks. He ignored them with the proper amount of salty dignity. Willy Cecil, a Lance Corporal now, was assistant Duty NCO.

"I'd like my liberty card, Willy."

"Sure, Abe." Willy had been working on bunk assignments for the new men; he put the assignment cards down to look up Abe's liberty card; everything held priority over the boots as far as Willy was concerned. "Here you go."

"Thanks, Willy."

"Sure, Abe." The old salts always called each other by their first names; it was another way of distinguishing them from the boots. "Okay. Who's this man, Peterson?"

"Here."

"Peterson, you have the first bunk, bottom, in the second cubicle on the left. Back in the old days, it belonged to a man named Jack Robles.

Treat it with respect. Robles was a saltier man than all you guys will ever be put together."

Abe laughed. Willy was really pushing it. Abe stepped outside and looked at the sky. He opened his umbrella and walked toward the Enlisted Club to get some yen. He was going to Tokyo today.

Johnny sat there, smiling at this beer. How about that? She was a real doll, too. As the time passed, he listened to the music from the radio behind the bar. He listened to song after song; time kept passing. The beaded curtain hung there, very still; more time passed. He'd been sitting there at least half an hour. He was getting restless and he was starting to think that maybe he had been stood up.   It was a favorite joke of some of these girls - yeah, very funny - to stand a guy up for fun - yeah big joke, bitch! He let two more songs go by, finished his beer, sat the glass down with a slam, and walked out.

"Thank you," churped one of the girls, automatically.

Willy Cecil shrugged up and down the barracks like somebody important, giving advice here, chewing a man out there - feeling big. They're not like our crowd, Willy thought. These men are tame; we were wild. I remember how I came in the barracks — too long for my uniform, grinning.

Willy glanced at his wrists; he was still too long for his uniform. He grinned.

"Pardon me, Corporal, but where are the Admin Offices?"

"Out in the working area. Why?"

"Well, I thought we should report in."

"Don't sweat it. You're reporting in enough now. After the holidays your Draft NCO will turn in your orders. There's a Fourth of July picnic today - go get drunk."

The boot private looked at Willy as if he thought the old Killer was a little touched.

Oh well, Willy thought, maybe I too am nuts - just like the rest that came over with me. Welp, so what? Willy walked away singing softly, "Oh, officers don't bother me. No, officers don't bother me-e-e. They stand there in circles, their hands in their pockets, and shout on things that they know nothing about." He walked back into the Duty Room; Henry Hamilton, the Senior Duty NCO, was there.

"Take the rest of the day off, Willy."

"What?"

"Go to the damned picnic or something."

"But I'm supposed to be your assistant today."

"Willy, this is the last time I'll be standing the duty. I'm shorter than you are; my draft leaves for the States next week, you know. So I don't mind taking over all to myself this one last time. Now get."

Johnny got a cab for Yokohama Station and then bought a ticket to Ueno Station in Tokyo. He'd read somewhere that in that area was a great brothel section. It was probably gone now, but he'd take a look anyway.

He walked around for about forty-five minutes, looking at the streets and seeing them just plain, average Tokyo streets with no girls on them in the daytime. He found no signs of a brothel section, so he returned to the station and bought a subway ticket to Shimbashi.

Willy put on the standard Marine Aircraft Group picnic uniform; shower shoes, old utility trousers, and a sweat shirt. Willy's sweat shirt was covered with markings: *Lost our Dough in Olongapo; Our Motto is Yamato; Japan, Philippine Islands, and Taiwan; Born to Raise Hell; Give Me Liberty or Double the Guard; Death Before Dishonor;* and *USMC.* He decided to add one more. He got out his marking kit and wrote in black ink across the front of the shirt: *Too Short to Sweat It.* He put the shirt back on and headed, in his silly lanky strides, for the baseball diamonds by the East Gate, where they were having the picnic.

"Hiya, Willy the Killer!" It was Mouse Hoolahan. "Gonna slaughter us in slaughterball again this year?"

"Yep - if it don't rain too hard."

"Come have a beer. The picnic isn't supposed to start till eleven, but I'm on the beer detail and I have the key to the locker." He opened up the ice locker and got a beer for the Killer.

"Thanks, Pat. You men sure are in a good mood now that you've only got a week left. First, Hamilton gives me the day off, then you give me a beer."

"Well, your draft is next after ours. We old timers have to stick together."

"It sure will seem empty without you guys It already seems all wrong to go to a Fourth of July picnic without Robles, Wicker, Brown, Walters, and all those others. Christ, the only guys from the old crowd that'll be around after I go are Kidd and Cervata. Kidd goes home a month after me, and Cervata goes home a month after that. Christ," Willy got a look of panic on his face, "then there'll be nobody in the Far East but a bunch of boots!"

"Then guys like Klemn will be the old salts."

"Ha!" Willy's imagination was too limited to picture that. He looked at the group gathering around for the picnic, nothing but a bunch of new faces. "Dumb boots!"

Johnny wandered around the winding, narrow and bar-lined alleys of Shimbashi. He refused invitations to "come and have one beer - no cover charge," and threw away the bar ad cards he'd been handed.

It began raining pretty hard. The next press agent for a bar he met had an umbrella, so they proceeded together to the Bar Somethingorother.

The Bar Whatchamacallit was down a winding flight of stairs. He was greeted at the bottom by a grinning, white-coated bartender. Johnny went over and sat at a small table, almost knocking the damned thing over with his knee as he sat down. A group of bar girls were huddled over in a corner having a Japanese gossip session. The bartender spoke harsh gibberish to one of them. She moaned, got up and came over to sit with Johnny. Oh, the trials of duty! He felt like telling her to get lost. He ordered a beer, giving the waiter a thousand yen bill. The waiter returned with the beer. "One moment. I catch change."

"Diajobi," Johnny replied.

The waiter went to "catch" the change next door.

"What's your name?" asked the bitch.

Johnny thought, Oh my God! Why couldn't one of them ever come up and say, "The blintzes are in the ash can and I think the flock will fly tonight," or "The time has come to talk of shoes, ships, sealing wax, cabbages, kings, and the price of tea in Hong Kong," or even "Who in the hell are you, anyway?"

"Johnny. What's yours?" He might as well get it over with

"Lola."

Silence followed while Johnny took a long, slow drink of beer.

"You have cigarettes?" she begged.

"Just Ikoi," he told her, referring to the pack of Japanese cigarettes he'd carried in his coat since before going to the Philippines. Johnny guessed they were only about six months old.

"Good. I always buy Ekoi when I get cigarettes." There was greed in her eyes.

He tossed the pack down on the table. "Work out." He felt around in his pocket till he found a light. She took one drag and put it down.

He didn't say anything.

"You buy me drink?"

"No can do. S'koshi o-kane." Not too much ready cash, bitch. "That's okay. You buy me just one."

"That isn't okay," he explained with super-human patience. "I'm going to be in Toyko all day and I don't even have fifteen hundred yen."

She gave him a bored look of disbelief.

"Honto —" bitch. The smoke from her cigarette was drifting up into his eyes. He crushed it in the ash tray, pretending the tray was Lola's hand.

"Lookee," she whined, "no cover charge here. You can afford just one drink for Lola."

"If Lola wants to drink, Lola can get another glass and drink some of my beer."

"Okay. Then you give me a hundred yen."

"Good Lord, girl. It's you who should be paying me to drink my beer. If you don't want it, don't drink it. I'm not going to hire you to do it."

"I not make any money if you not buy me drink, janaino." ·

"The name is Johnny. Look, it's a big gomen, from the bottom of my heart but I have to eat today and I can't buy you a drink. Maybe some payday, when I get overpaid or something, I'll come back here and buy you your lousy drink. But no can do today. Dig?" Bitch!

"I don't believe you will ever come back."

No shit, Little Beaver! Oh this bitch was brilliant. "Well, that's your privilege."

"Nani?"

"Forget it."

There was a silence and then the wheels seemed to start turning in her head. Her voice got tender, soft, and sweet. "You get change back yet?"

"No. Boysan go catch. Why?"

She piped a short Japanese sentence to the bartender.

Soon the waiter arrived with a couple of hundred yen - all that was left of the thousand - and a drink for the lady which must have cost plenty! The sly little bitch looked at him proudly.

He looked down at his beer. The wheels were now turning in his head. He wondered whether to go to the bartender, who probably owned the hole, and raise hell - or bear up under the injustice with Christ-like silence. He decided on a compromise: he would be Christ-like and silent until he finished his beer and then he'd go over to the bartender and raise hell, call out the Japanese Police, the Military Police, and the Shore Patrol - have the bitch, the bartender and the waiter thrown in jail - then come back with a sledge hammer and smash the whole goddamned place to little pieces. After thinking about it some more, he decided to skip the Christ-like part of it all together.

Lola spoke: "Are you angry with me?"

Now this was real class! This was what you paid Tokyo prices for. In Yamato the same girl would have said, "You pissed off at me?" Here she said, "Are you angry with me?" He decided to be Christ-like just a little while more. "S'koshi," he said. A little bit - bitch.

"Gomenasai, I get your five hundred yen back. Okay?" She called the waiter.

The Christ-like bit was paying off. She had a conversation with the waiter during which she actually blushed and, Lola behold, there was his five hundred yen. Well, maybe she wasn't so bad after all.

She looked at him softly. "I am sorry. No?"

"I'm sorry too." He offered her another cigarette.

She refused it. "Did you really only have fifteen hundred yen?" she asked.

"Not quite that much."

"I'm sorry." She cocked her head a little to one side and wrinkled her forehead, a very sympathetic look that he knew would vanish with the next dumb thought that was generated in her numb brain. At that moment the look was gone. He guessed she was keeping the dumb thought a secret, for she said nothing.

He drank some more of his beer.

"Where you going to stay tonight?"

"Oh, I'm just going to walk around town when night comes."

"All night?"

"Yes. I can do without sleep that long. I'll drink a little coffee."

"So?"

"So." Then, for no good reason, he reached into his pocket and brought out a hundred yen. "Here. I'm sorry I am not rich enough to buy you a drink."

She took the money.

Two fresh, rich-looking customers entered the bar.

"If you want to go try your luck with them, it's okay with me."

"No can do," she said. "We have to take turns." The girls whose turn it was went over and sat next to the customers.

"This is not your lucky night, huh?"

"That's okay," she said. "If boysan say he not buy me drink when he have money, he bad. But you good boysan. You no can help."

Yeah he thought. I great boysan. I beat up old ladies and kick dogs and tie Boy Scouts in square knots. I number one boysan.

"After you finish beer you going to go out walking?"

"Yeah."

"Take it easy. No?" She got up, crossed the room and rejoined the gossip session.

Johnny finished his beer and went out walking.

It got started too fast for Willy to really figure it out. It must have been that they didn't like being told they were dumb boots; Willy and

Pat were slugging it out with all six of them. Willy was big and Pat was hot-tempered, so it wasn't quite as uneven as it might sound. Still, the going wasn't too easy.

There was one guy on Willy's back, and Willy was exchanging kicks and slugs with two others. Three of them finally got Pat on the ground, where two of them sat on him. The third one came over to help subdue Willy.

"YOU BOOT BASTARDS! TRYIN' TO GET SALTY WITH THE OLD KILLER!" Willy shouted. "Okay. Which one of you kicked over my goddamn beer?" The man on his back landed in the face of one of those in front of him. He concentrated on the toughest one, a wiry pfc, until the pfc's face was so covered with blood that it was getting in his eyes. Next, he turned his attention to a dumb looking corporal with one bad eye already. He figured on blinding the whole half dozen of them if he could.

One of them slipped on the grass, so Willy let fly with an unmerciful kick to the side of the head. One of the others tackled him when he was off balance from kicking and brought him down. The two had left Hoolahan; all six of the bastards were on him now. Shit, this was nowhere!

Willy swung and kicked blindly in every direction. He connected squarely with somebody's chin. It was Pat Hoolahan; he was out cold! Smooth maneuver, Willy.

It was six to one now, but two of them couldn't fight worth a damn and one of them'd been kicked in the groin - so things were looking up. Willy swung out with new vigor.

The old Killer was a wood-chopping machine delivering deadly blows among the enemy, but his ears were ringing and he was growing tired. He knew he would not last much longer, not even long enough to wipe out the five boot bastards still in the fight.

Suddenly, he heard a yell. It was neither a Rebel yell nor a Yankee war cry. It was jes' the outraged beller of a feller whut sticks pretty much to his own hills - a peaceable cuss, Klemn Carpenter.

Tokyo, you Paris of the Orient! Abe Diamond wandered among the crowds and the bustle of the world's largest city. He began humming

"April in Paris". He could only remember the first part. He was never too good at remembering tunes. April in Paris; Paris in springtime - he hummed it over and over.

He bought himself a couple of ten-yen Japanese biscuits and submerged into a subway station.

He came up at Shimbashi and wandered up one street and then back down another. April in Paris; Paris in springtime.

At one point he was stopped by a well-dressed Japanese gentlemen. "Would you like to see a private show? Very sexy."

"Perhaps."

"What do you want to see? Man, man? Woman, woman? Man, woman? Or one-woman magic show? How much? Only three thousand yen."

Abe Diamond broke into a fast walk that was just short of a real run. "Never mind. O-kane-nye. Get lost, Buster!"

Buster followed Abe for two more blocks, lowering his box office price with every fifth step. "One thousand five hundred. Half price!"

"Forget it, man. Forget it." He turned up Ginza Street. "Tokyo prices. Got to expect these Tokyo prices."

April in Paris; Paris in springtime. He was tired of that handful of notes by now. Over and over he hummed them as he surged with the crowds of the Orient. "La-da da Da-da; Do-dum de dum-dum." He couldn't get them out of his mind.

"Welp, guess we showed them."

"I reckon they'll know next time."

"Did Pat ever come to?"

"I don't know. Them MP fellers was cartin' us off 'fore I got a chance to notice."

"What do you think they'll do?"

"Oh, I reckon they'll bust us all down a rank for fightin' on a patriotic holiday."

"It's okay with me, just so those boots get busted too."

"Reckon they will."

"You know, Carpenter, for a peaceable cuss you sure do put out a mean fight."

"Hell, Willy, got to keep the peace somehow?"

"You know, I think I'll declare you an honorary salt in the Far East for savin' my neck like that."

"The hell you beller!"

"Have a seat, Abe."

"Hi, Johnny! Thanks."

"Remember this place?"

"Sure do. Stick Wicker took us here before he went back to the States. Hew went out for a walk and you, Yoko, and I fell asleep right at this table."

"Seems like yesterday."

"It sure does. When I woke up this morning, some bastard'd lit a string of firecrackers in the barracks. And I thought to myself, That's your Far East tour going by - poppity-bang-bang-bang."

"You realize this is the first time we've spoken to each other since last summer."

"Yeah. We got in an argument one afternoon. I remember."

"Silly."

"Yes."

"Well, the reason I came out on liberty today was to find me a woman. No luck here. The street creeps should be out in Yokohama by now; I think I'll head back there."

"Sounds like a good idea. Mind if I come along?"

"Why not?"

Chapter 29

Yankee Fever

When Johnny Shellburn stood on the curb, hypnotized by bright lanterns swinging overhead - and, for some unfathomable reason, Japanese, American, and Soviet flags on the lamp posts - he told himself he came to see people standing up for their rights. He was humming "America, the Beautiful."

Now he could hear the drum of the marchers. There, down on Ginza Street, came the first group. He thought of the Buddhist chant: Nani ginko, nani ginko.... The toneless repetition and the basic rhythm were similar, but the demonstrators were chanting something different.

The faces were passing: green, red and everything but golden faces in the tinted lantern light.

Nani ginko, nani ginko, nani ginko...

Signs in Japanese and English! YANKEE GO HOME! GO HOME. U-2! PEACE! KEEP OUT OF JAPAN! GENTLEMEN'S AGREEMENT - REMEMBER?

Nani ginko, nani ginko, nani ginko...

He got a look of admiration in his eyes and made it burn.

"Yankee Go Home!"

"Diajobi!" he answered, smiling.

Nani ginko, nani ginko, nani ginko....

If the MP's caught him, that would be the end. He told himself the MP's must not catch him. Ginza Street was, tonight, off limits. He decided to leave.

"Hey Mac! You in the service?" MP's, two of them, stood behind him.

"Yes." He didn't know how to explain it; he hadn't meant to come to the demonstration. He hadn't even been thinking about it. He'd walked through the shadows toward Ginza Street thinking of home.

"You're under arrest.

"HEY!

"HALT! HALT!"

He plunged into the crowd as into an ocean surf. Around the corner! Down the alley! They're coming! Quick, to the right! He ran along the side of a building.

He jumped against the fence, curling his fingers around the steel. The pointed toes of his shoes barely fit into the links and most of the weight hung on his fingers. He was breathing through his teeth in short, frantic gasps. He hauled himself over the edge of the building's top and fell to the roof.

Between breaths he heard nothing but the chant of the demonstrators. There was no more rattling of the fence. He'd lost them.

He laughed a little.

Nani ginko, nani ginko, nani ginko...

"Blundering dolts! Whole country full of incompetents! Defenders of the status quo! Defenders of the statue quo, your time has come!"

Nani ginko, nani ginko, nani ginko...

His breath regained, he stood up and looked at the bell-bright stars.

Nani ginko, nani ginko, nani ginko...

"But God is on your side Jimmy Brown, Henry Hamilton, Pat Hoolahan. Sons of Superstition Row! Sons of Superstition Row, your days are numbered!"

Chapter 30

The Third Marine

Captain Simms felt a dull ache across the width of his back. He lifted the stained coffee cup, marked USMC, to his mouth and saw that it was empty. He leaned across his desk and placed it beneath the tap of the coffee maker. A black, oily solution splashed and whirled into the cup.

As he sipped, he looked at the twin stacks of papers on his desk. On top of the first stack, his orders to return to the States rested. They were stamped in red: CANCELLED. He pulled out the top desk drawer and slid them in, pushing the drawer shut afterwards.

There remained one stack, affidavits he must read and report on before he could hope to be released from duty as Security Officer of MACS. With this over, a week-long investigation would be concluded.

Orders from Headquarters, he thought. And nowhere else in the United States Marine Corp, but in this sloppy outfit, could such a thing happen without warning. No wonder they were hot in Washington! And I thought that we had gotten rid of the eight balls: Shellburn, Cervata, Robles, Cecil...endless list. And here they are, stacked on my desk, every last sonofabitch of them, back to haunt me.

There was a knock on the door.

"Who is it?"

"Kidd."

No "sir", no rank, not a goddamned trace of the military — just "Kidd".

"Come in."

"I'd like to speak to you, sir."

"Speak."

"I know why Shellburn did it."

"Okay, Chaplain, what's your theory?"

Kidd looked startled. Obviously he didn't realize old Simms knew his nickname. He didn't realize a lot of things.

"It's the foreign policy, sir."

"What?" Captain Simms snorted in his coffee.

"The foreign policy of this country drove him to it. Shellburn was basically a good man. A little mixed up? Yes. A traitor? No."

"For your file of miscellaneous information, Chaplin: Corporal — former Corporal John Shellburn is not considered, officially, a traitor."

"Captain, when a man gets out of the Corp, goes to Moscow on his discharge money, turns up in an American Embassy, hands in his passport, and applies for citizenship in a nation which has sworn openly to conquer or destroy the United States of America - he is a traitor."

"Kidd, if you wish to express your opinion on this matter, you'll find a paper and pencil in the Adjutant's Office. Now get out. I have a job to do."

"Yes, sir."

Kidd walked out quietly and closed the door behind him.

Well, with that one back in the States this month and with Mike Cervata in the station brig, I may have time to whip this outfit into shape, or maybe it's an idle thought on the part of a mean little grey-templed sonofabitch with captain's bars.

This hot weather! It makes your sleeves stick to your arms. Well, it'll be gone soon enough.

He got up and switched on the fan.

He handled the first affidavit, the sworn statement of Jack B. Robles, Private, USMC now stationed in Cherry Point, South Carolina.

The special instructions had been to list any information or comments concerning John R. Shellburn relevant to the investigation concerning his recent application for Soviet citizenship, especially information concerning any access he might have had to Secret or Confidential files and or documents.

I have no statement to make. (signed) Jack B. Robles

He pronounced, without enthusiasm, the word bastard. By military law, a man had the right to refuse to testify.

He picked up the next sheet, the sworn statement of John H. Hamilton, Sergeant, USMC, now stationed in El Toro, California.

Shellburn had no access to Secret and Confidential information that I know of. He was an intelligent man with the makings of a good Marine. He was an agnostic or a atheist and that is why, I believe, he became a Communist. (signed) John B. Hamilton

Captain Simms smiled. Old Henry Hamilton is a Sergeant now! How about that!

He picked up the sworn statement of Lee W. Phillips, Sergeant USMC now stationed in Yuma, Arizona.

Corporal Shellburn was known to me and he did often disobey orders that were given by me and other nco's that were in the unit. He did act hostile and did misbehave in a unmilitary manner. He did do many unmilitary actions. I did bring this to the attention of my superiors, but they did not do nothing about it. I do not know if he did have secret files or not. (signed) Lee W. Phillips

The captain grimaced. Poor Sergeant Phillips!. Well, that's three worthless ones; I better note this part about disobeying orders. Gods! They'll rip this outfit apart when they read this in DC!

Captain Simms paused to refill his cup. He looked out the window. It was a drab day. Trees hung about the view of a green field with a chain-link fence beyond. Through the fence he could see gray Japanese houses. In back of one was a laundry line; conspicuous sheets hung in a dull heat like white flags. A platoon marched by, obstructing the view.

"Well, well... Sergeant Ulman finally got on the ball. Close order drill, that's what this outfit needs. Close order drill twice a day. Three months from now maybe we'll get some discipline and some pride, if they keep at it."

He picked up the next affidavit. It was the sworn statement of Wilfred T. Cecil, Private, USMC Reserve, Pico, California.

Johnny Shellburn was my best friend. He was okay until we got overseas. I think something went wrong afterwards. He started acting crazy after we got to Atsugi. He was a different person by the time we went Stateside again. I think he is now insane. He didn't have anything much to do with secret documents or any of that stuff. (signed) Wilfred T. Cecil

The captain shut his eyes tightly. He grinned, but there was pain behind his expression. Willy Cecil. That Willy Cecil!. The trouble that character used to get into! If there was one man who never did anything right, it was Willy Cecil. Oh, he tried, but somewhere inside his head there seemed to be a short circuit. God protect me from another Willy Cecil! Killer Willy. And I know how he got that name!

The captain's arm started itching. He rolled up his sleeves. Damnit! Heat rash. Well some of us were meant for burden-bearing.

The next statement was that of Steven A. Wicker, Corporal, USMC Reserve, Brooklyn Navy Yard, New York.

Stick Wicker. Good man. Little salty. But a good man.

I knew the subject for a short time only. There were no signs of Communism in his attitudes. The news came to me as a suprise. To my knowledge, he was never in an accessible position, security-wise. (signed) Steven A. Wicker

These things were not very helpful so far. Next.

The sworn statement of Abraham I. Diamond is not yet available. With due authorization, he is out of the country. His Reserve status has been altered to Standby. He is now in the armed forces of Israel.

It was a memo from Sergeant Major.

"Well damn my salty hide!" The captain wondered briefly where he'd picked up that expression. "So Abe Diamond is going to become a fighting man after all!"

Then came the sworn statement of Patrick M. Hoolahan, Pfc, USMC, Camp Pendleton, California.

One man and one man only is responsible for this matter - Bob Kidd. Bob Kidd was an atheist who spread Marxist propaganda. It would not suprise me if he didn't persuade Shellburn to join Russia. Shellburn was lacking in any conviction and ready for the first idea that came along. It is a shame that Shellburn must suffer because of another man's ideas. I don't know, but I suspect that Shellburn had access to secret information. (signed) Patrick M. Hoolahan

Good God! The captain made some notes. What provoked this? Kidd's been checked out and cleared. This is going to take some more probing. He made a note to have Hoolahan questioned further.

The next sworn statement was that of First Lieutenant Richard K. Valingsworth, USMC Reserve, Glenview, Illinois.

John R. Shellburn had no access to classified material of any sort whatever. (signed) Richard K. Valingsworth

Valingsworth, you're partially to blame for this mess and you know it. You can't run a Marine Corps with campus playboys for officers. That's typical, Valingsworth, get by with as little as possible. One sentence of no value whatsoever. That's more than typical.

He jerked forward and got up, placing the papers he had read face down on the desk. He walked to the window. The troops were still drilling. Good.

He went back to the desk and sat down. His backside was numb. He leaned forward to read the next sheet without picking it up. Absently, he rubbed his arm.

The sworn statement of James Brown, USMC, Camp Lejune, South Carolina, read as follows:

John Shellburn was hard to understand. I know nothing about the situation which would be helpful. (signed) James Brown

The captain felt relieved. That was the last one for the time being. He picked up the phone. "Get me the station brig, please.
"Hello?

"Send a brig guard over here with Prisoner Miguel C. Cervata. This is Captain Simms in the East Camp Security Office.

"Thank you."

He slammed the receiver down and leaned back in his chair, putting his hands over his eyes. The fan blew on the front of his neck.

There was a knock on the door.

"Who is it?"

"Kidd."

"Come in Kidd. This is Simms, but you can call me Captain Simms."

"Yes, sir."

"What have you got there?"

"A paper, sir."

"I can see that. What is it?"

Kidd extended the paper with his left hand. He was standing at attention, by God. It was a long, yellow sheet covered with words. It was signed, Robert Kidd.

"Oh, your version of the scandal."

"Yes, sir."

"Thanks."

"Will that be all, sir?"

"That will be all."

Kidd left.

"The last of the eight balls spins out the door. Well, I guess it's now my duty to read it." He laughed softly. "And until I got to this unit, I always thought it was officers who gave orders."

The chief difficulty concerning the incident of John Shellburn applying for Soviet citizenship does not lie with the individual, but with the contradictory foreign policy of the United States of America. Shellburn incidences will occur with increasing frequency in future years unless deeper steps are taken. In the first place, the United States presumably has no power motives on a world-wide scale. But so long as we have military bases overseas, it will appear to much of the world, including many Americans, that we have imperialistic motives. As a nation, we have two choices: 1) to become an imperialistic world power and be honest about it; 2) to become a pacifist nation: to withdraw our overseas military bases; to withdraw for-

eign aid; to build a fortress of missiles and airpower around the continental U.S. and, in general, to become military isolationist. If we take the first course, the ideas for which we stand will die. We will commit national suicide in spirit, if not in fact If we take the second course, there is some hope that the first economically free nation in the world history will survive long enough to be an example and an inspiration to the rest of the world. This is the only possible sane course we can pursue. Our present dual foreign policy has ceased being hypocritical - it is now downright schizophrenic. We are deadlocked between aid and attack. As a result, we do nothing. We say "Peace!" to Japan and send our warriors there. This is a roundabout way of doing nothing. Johnny Shellburn once gave a speech, clearly anti-Communist in tone, on this base. Today he is a member of the U.S.S.R. Johnny Shellburn has merely done what this nation has been doing for years - indulging in self-contradiction. (signed) Robert Kidd

"Well damn my salty hide!" The captain reread the sheet. It was interestingly unexpected. But it would have to go in the report. Well why not? He might have something there.

There was a knock on the office door.

"Who's there?"

"Sergeant Major, sir."

"Come in, Sergeant Major."

"Something's come up which may help on the Shellburn case, sir." The Sergeant Major had some papers and clippings in his hand.

"Yes?"

"I just talked to the Provost Marshall. They caught a Japanese saboteur on the flight line last night. It turned out he is a Japanese Communist who has been making raids on this base for the past two years - about one every three months."

"Yes?" The captain stood up.

"Here's a list of past raid dates, compiled from his confession. See this one? On that night he raided and sabotaged some radar gear belonging to our unit."

"So?"

"Johnny Shellburn was on guard duty that night."

"Then if Shellburn cooperated, that would mean he was Communistically sympathetic last summer."

"Exactly, sir."

"I've been working on the theory that Shellburn is emotionally unbalanced and made his decision recently. This would out a big hole in that idea."

"Yes, sir."

"Godammit, this is a confused case! Of course, there is no reason to believe Shellburn knew this happened. We have it on good authority that he was lax in his duties."

"Yes, sir."

"Who was OD that night?"

"Lieutenant Valingsworth, sir."

"I, see. Okay, Sergeant Major, that will be all for the present. Hang on to that stuff."

"Yes, sir."

"Oh, one more thing."

"Yes, sir."

"Draw up a roster of every man presently stationed here who was in any way associated with Shellburn."

"I've already done that, sir."

"Excellent." Most dependable administrator in the Wing. Too bad he's stuck with this outfit. Well, things will get better.

"Here it is. Everybody is on there except Corporal Klemn Carpenter, sir."

"Who is Corporal Klemn Carpenter?"

The Sergeant Major looked down at his brightly shined shoe toe. "One of the newer men. He checked in when we were in Formosa."

"Why isn't he included?"

"I'm afraid he wouldn't be much help, sir."

"Why not?"

"Well Captain. It's not that he's stupid, it's just... well, it's very hard to say, sir. You know how you were congratulating me the other day, talking about how squared-away this unit was getting?"

The captain nodded.

"Well, Corporal Klemn Carpenter is another Willy Cecil, sir. But worse. I wanted to keep him out of your sight if possible, sir. I know how Willy Cecil irritated you."

"Well, I guess we can't expect everything to straighten out right away. It takes time and patience, Sergeant Major, to get things in shape. Step-by-step Sergeant Major. Meanwhile, put Carpenter on the roster."

"Yes, sir. Will that be all?"

"Yes, Sergeant Major."

The captain laughed and stretched, standing on his toes. He reached over, grabbed his cup, and drained it.

He stood at the window, his hands clasped behind him. There was a Japanese woman out there taking down the white sheets.

The troops were off at the other end of the field, counting cadence: *"One - two - three - four! One - two - three - four!"*

We say "Peace!" to Japan - he thought - and we send our warriors there. Well, what does he want? Is there really a choice? Count cadence, warriors! Chant.

He sat back down at his desk. Now to distill and compile; to make laborious notes; to put forth conclusions, apologies and suggestions - that's the bad work. He scribbled for several minutes.

There was a knock.

"Who is it?"

"Brig chaser, sir. I have Prisoner Cervata here."

"Send him in. You wait outside."

"Yes, sir."

Mike Cervata leaned his shaven head around the door, smirked wisely, and walked in.

"Sit down, Mike."

Mike raised his eyebrows and remained standing.

"Well?"

"Sorry , sir." He sat down. "You're the first person who's been nice to me for a couple of weeks."

"Don't forget I put you in the brig."

Mike looked down.

Captain Simms felt like a bastard.

"And I can get you out."

Mike looked up.

"Something always comes through for you. Doesn't it, Mike?"

Cervata nodded.

"Have you heard about Shellburn?"

"No. Is he back?"

"Not quite. He's in Russia. Renounced his American citizenship."

"Damn my salty hide!"

"I said that already."

"You know, sir, you remind me of Abraham Lincoln - offering to get me out of the – "

"Shut up."

Cervata smirked again.

"What are you smirking about?"

"Tension release, sir." He smirked twice more.

"About getting you out of the brig...."

"Sir?"

"Don't be too expectant. It depends on how much of a help you can be. It also depends on whether or not I can get you transferred. I don't want you in MACS."

"You wanted to know something about Shellburn, sir."

"Exactly. How well did you know him?"

"We were the best of friends. We were in the same bootcamp platoon, even."

"Read over this stuff." The Captain handed him the report and the stack of affidavits. "Tell me what you think. If you are as brilliant on this case as you were in the black market, then you might do yourself some good."

"For a change."

"Never mind the repentance stuff. Start reading." The captain relaxed with a full cup of coffee.

Mike's eyes jumped back and forth rapidly, taking in full lines. There was a small furrow in his brow. He would put one page aside, following it with his eyes, then glance back at the next one.

When he got through Kidd's yellow sheet, he laughed out loud. "I can do much better than this."

The captain sipped his coffee without letting his eyes away from Mike Cervata's face. "On the desk is a clipping from page three of *The Stars and Stripes*. It tells about Shellburn's appearance at the embassy. As you can see, his father's trying to get in touch with him. They hope to change his mind."

"They won't."

"The Soviet Union is not granting his request for citizenship; they are permitting him to enter as an immigrant."

Mike smirked.

"Any answers, Mike?"

"Yes."

The captain put his coffee down and picked up his notebook.

"Now before I start, sir, there is one thing I want cleared up. You said you'd get me out of the brig if I helped you and if you could get me transferred. You can get me transferred, Captain?"

"I'll see to it, Mike. If I can't, well, that'll have to put up with you here. I'm going back to the States anyway."

"Johnny Shellburn's father was, as mentioned in the article, a Marine. What the article does not mention is that he participated honorably in the battle for Okinawa.

"Furthermore, Captain, Johnny Shellburn's grandfather was a Marine - a hero in France. He came back from Europe, after the First World War, with a chest full of medals and one leg.

"Since he was born, Johnny Shellburn lived in the hymn and history of the Corps. To make it worse, he and I had the best DI that ever came down the rank at inspection time."

"So?" Captain Simms saw the point, but he wanted to see if Mike Cervata saw it as clearly.

"So what happened when he found himself in a hap-hazard, half-assed air wing outfit?"

"He was demoralized."

"That's right, sir."

"It's funny Shellburn's family history wasn't included in any of the reports I got."

"Check it out, sir. Don't take my word for it. His grandfather's name was Richard; his father's name was Dennis."

"I'll do that." Yes, that just might be the thing to make those bastards read my report and see to it that this fucked-up overseas morale situation gets quick attention. "A Marine Corps family, huh?"

"That's right, sir."

"Okay Mike, you can go now. Thank you. I'll see that your sentence is suspended at once."

"Thank you, sir." Mike smirked again, got up and walked out.

The captain got up, walked over to the door and leaned out to watch the brig chaser march Cervata off. He called down the hall, "Sergeant Major?"

"Yes, sir."

"Get some termination papers made up on Cervata. I want him out of the brig. I don't care how you justify it. I'll get the Old Man to sign it."

"Yes, sir."

He was not sure, maybe it was because he was listening for it, but he thought he heard a note of suppressed amazement in the Sergeant Major's voice.

"I'm going to sick bay now to get this rash of mine treated. I'll see you tomorrow."

"Yes, sir."

"Oh, and one more thing, Sergeant Major. Try to get Cervata transferred to some other outfit."

"Yes, sir."

And so you go walking down the hall, he thought, and you step out the door. And what's the first thing you see? A barber-pole flag, flapping to beat hell in a new breeze. It doesn't give a rat's ass. You sweat for it.

You walk across the lawn toward sick bay - step by step, everybody, little by little. Someday we'll have a perfect Marine Corps - with beer machines on every base, like Chesty Puller wanted, and every Pathfinder with eighty jumps to his credit. We'll teach every man karate. And every six months, those that don't want to run the obstacle course every morning before chow can get out - we don't want their kind. We'll have marksmanship every afternoon and each man will be an expert with a knife. No nonsense.

He heard his troops. It was a loud sound they made. He walked in step to their cadence count.

END